NANN
DC

A Brother's Best Friend Romance

EMMA BLAKE

Chapter 1

Mae

If today weren't already my last day of work, I'd quit in a heartbeat. As I lay at the bottom of the staircase, the two demons I've been nannying for just laugh.

Everything hurts after this particularly nasty fall, especially my head and ass. *This is why you don't squirt people with water guns when they're on the stairs!*

"Ha ha, did you see her go flying?"

"Awesome!"

I can't piece together which of the twins is saying what, and my head swims as I try to focus. It's taking way too much effort, even I know that, and I have a feeling a trip to the ER is in order.

When I try to stand, pain tears through my ankle. I'll add this to the tally of injuries these hellspawns are responsible for.

"Marcus! Cayden! Get your little behinds over here!"

Being intimidating while you're slumped on the floor is

extremely difficult, but the twins come over, the tiniest bit of remorse hanging over them when they see me.

"You can't shoot me with those things when I'm on the stairs!" I take a breath through the throbbing ache. "Remember how I said someone could get hurt? Well, here we are."

"It was funny."

Marcus, often the instigator of the pair, grumbles, and, honestly, I'm so over this shit.

"It was not."

My head is throbbing, and the hallway lights are too bright. Then, opening the door right in front of where I've landed are Mr. and Mrs. Jones.

"What's all this? You can't play by the stairs." *No crap, Penelope.*

Mrs. Jones's nasally voice cuts through my ears like a knife, and then arms are lifting me up.

"Mom! Dad!"

The twins shout together, and I flinch at the high-pitched shriek children are so good at. As I realize Mr. Jones is helping me stand, a nauseating dizziness washes over me.

"Whoa, why's her face look like that?" Cayden, the quieter but still equally malicious twin, eyes me.

Mr. Jones finally speaks, and his voice near my ear makes the pounding in my head worse.

"What happened?"

"They shot me with the squirt gun and I fell." Wrapping my tongue around the words is like trying to learn how to blow a bubble with chewing gum, and the pain in my head picks up.

"Honestly, you two. Now we have to add a trip to the ER to our already demanding schedule. Ugh! Honey, just walk her to the car, and I'll drive her."

I can't really track what happens next. Presumably, Mr. Jones gets me into their car, and then Mrs. Jones drives it to said hospital.

"Couldn't we just have your last day go without incident? You're already leaving us without a nanny for who knows how long, and now this."

Glaring at Mrs. Penelope Jones is more than a little difficult right now, but I give it everything I have.

Yeah, because I wanted to fall down a flight of stairs and smash my head. Shit, how am I supposed to afford a medical bill on top of everything else?

Time seems to speed like a bullet train as the horrid woman finds someone to help me out of the car and into the hospital. She doesn't even bother to stay and see if I'm all right, so I wind up sitting on a gurney alone as I wait for the doc.

The nurse who checks my vitals leaves, and it's then I realize I've busted my lip open.

"Fucking worst last day." My words come out with a lisp, and I sigh. "Really? This has got to be a record or something."

I love helping kids, but this last job was something else. And sure, I don't know who I'll be nannying for this time around, but that's how it can be with high-end clients, especially if they're putting in a call at the last minute.

I just hope whoever it is will be less of a jerk and they finalize the details soon.

Between the Jones's later-than-stated nights out, to their constant excuses for their monster children, I've had it up to here with problem child setups.

After a few moments, the tiredness overwhelms me, and I lay back on the bed. That's when the doctor finally comes in, staring intently at his clipboard.

"Hi, I'm Dr. Finnigan. It sounds like you took one heck of a fall, Ms. Marrington. Wait. Mae?"

I struggle to sit up, but when I do, I come face-to-face with my brother Johnny's best friend, Reed. It's been a few years since I've actually seen him because he's been a bit MIA being a busy doctor and all, but *damn.*

Images of the thirtysomething guy I knew back then don't do justice to the handsome hunk of a man standing before me. I even like his scrubs.

Reed is somehow even more gorgeous than I remember, and I have quite a long memory when it comes to him. I mean, hell, I've been crushing on the guy since puberty.

"Reed? *You're* my doctor?"

"It would seem so." He chuckles and sets down his clipboard at the end of the bed, shining a light in my eyes.

The penlight is annoying at best, and all I want to be looking at is Reed's beautiful hazel eyes. The way the colors swirl, a little bit of blue, a little bit of green—it's mesmerizing.

"You fell?"

"I was bested by a pair of demonic twins." I flinch back from the light, my eyes watering.

"I'm sorry, what?"

"I'm a nanny and the six-year-olds I was taking care of, up until today, actually, are terrible. And I like kids. Like, a lot. But those boys? Yikes. Squirt guns indoors are not a good idea, but they're so spoiled by their parents."

It occurs to me that I'm rambling too late to stop myself, and I feel a bit like I'm drunk.

"That's right. Johnny mentioned you're a nanny. Kids usually love you. Can you follow the light with your eyes?"

"Most of the time, they do." I try to follow Reed's blinding device, but everything still feels off, and now that the adrenaline has worn off, I'm exhausted.

"So two six-year-olds got the best of you? They did good, even managed to give you a fat lip, complete with a lisp."

"Yeah, ha ha. I couldn't manage the kindergartners. You'd be doing just as well as me if you had to juggle dinner, laundry, and twins with a love of chaos."

He tries to hide his smile by looking at his notes again, and I roll my eyes. I can see the dimples in his cheeks, and everything suddenly feels hot.

This is fabulous. I sound like a boozer and must look just terrific. Why'd it have to be Reed?

"Okay." Reed steps back and addresses my ankle. "Let's see about this."

His fingers probe the side, and I yelp as pain shoots through me.

"Fudge ripple sundae!" I hiss in a breath. "Please don't do that."

Reed laughs, the sound making me feel that much more intoxicated. "Fudge what?"

Heat warms my cheeks as I realize I'm still censoring myself, like I do around kids. "Trying not to swear."

"Don't hold back on my account. I know your brother, remember?"

Oh, I remember, all right. You have no idea how often I would stare at you while you hung out with him.

After a few more moments of Reed poking and prodding my various injuries, he leans back against the counter in the hospital room.

"Well, you have a concussion and a split lip, but the good news is that I don't think your ankle is broken. Just sprained."

"Oh, goodie. I'm so glad it's just a concussion." My words are a ridiculously distorted, and I need to remind myself to avoid *S*'s.

Reed continues to bite back his laugh, and at this point, I'm so embarrassed that I'm considering moving to another state.

"You need to get some rest. I'd like to keep you here for the night for observation. Just a precaution. You'll be good to go in the morning, most likely. I'll have a nurse bring you a brace for your ankle. Keep it elevated, and I'll order some ice packs for the swelling and the head contusion."

"So, ice and sleep?"

"That's pretty much it. You can have some Tylenol for the pain as well." Reed smiles, and even after all this time, my pulse still flutters.

"Any questions for me?"

My concussed brain can only think of one, but thankfully, I still have the sense to stop myself from asking what he looks like under those scrubs.

"Nope."

"All right. I'll send someone in with the ice and Tylenol, then check on you later. Get some rest, Mae."

"Whatever you say, doc."

Reed leaves, and eventually, after I've been given some cold packs and pain meds, I drift into a fitful sleep, my thoughts filling with images of Dr. Finnigan.

I REMEMBER when he came by for a visit, picking up my brother for a trip to Vegas. Reed had just broken up with someone, and I'd heard him mention something about needing to let off some steam.

At the time, I'd just been an awkward teenager, and I couldn't stop ogling him the entire time he was at my house getting ready with Johnny.

Reed's always been cute, and it was the first time I'd

wanted to sleep with someone who wasn't just a fantasy from my favorite TV shows.

With his dark hair and light hazel eyes, Reed could've been a male model or actor, and I was obsessed as soon as we met. Johnny's best friend was a hottie, and it didn't help that he seemed so mature and put together compared to the high school guys my age.

"Don't give Mom and Dad a hard time while I'm gone, okay? I know you're thinking about sneaking out with Tori."

I gawk at my brother. What a buzzkill!

"I am not, and so what if I was? You're leaving. Go enjoy Vegas." I roll my eyes at him.

"Mae, you know I'd take you along for the fun if you were older."

Johnny's eyes soften, and I can't help but smile at him.

"I know, I know. The unplanned kid gets the shaft again." I shrug. "Go have fun."

"Thanks." Johnny looks over his shoulder, calling out for Reed. "Hey! Chat with Mae for a sec so I can finish packing."

"I'm not a baby or need supervision. You don't have to send your buddy over here to entertain me."

"On the contrary. I'm sending Reed over so you can entertain him. He needs to get out of his head. He's thinking about Leslie too much."

I stand up straighter, adjusting my shirt as Reed walks up. "Whatever."

My attempt at nonchalant could have been better, and then Reed is standing before me, towering with his six-foot-two height.

"So, Mae, right?"

"Yup. You want to go outside so we don't have to stand in the hall?"

"Sure, Lil Bit."

I lead Reed to the back porch, and we sit next to each other on the steps. The sun is just hanging on to the horizon, and the cool air sweeps across my legs, giving me goose bumps.

"Sorry about your girlfriend."

Reed looks over, smiling like it's no big deal. "Ah, it's fine. Someone better will come along."

"Oh, yeah? Like who?"

I can't believe my own words, and the heat creeping through my body as I meet Reed's eyes is like a furnace.

"I don't know, maybe someone…sweeter."

Silence hangs in the air as we stare at each other. My body is burning up, a need growing in my core that pulses stronger than anything I've ever felt.

We inch closer to each other, and it's just like the movies. Tension swells as our mouths drift closer, and Reed's hand finds my cheek.

His eyes rake down my body, pausing on the curve of my breasts behind my tight tank top. I've seen some of my brother's porn, and I imagine what it would feel like to let Reed take my virginity.

My friend Liz says it's better when the guy takes his time, and all I want in the world right now is to see what it would be like with someone like Reed, someone experienced.

With a shuddering breath, I deliberately push my chest out, hoping to draw Reed in.

"You're so beautiful, Mae."

Reed's words make my heart beat all the faster, and I stare at the tiny bit of space between us. His fingers take my chin, guiding my eyes back up to his.

"Kiss me, Mae."

Our lips crash together, and it's everything I've ever wanted. The taste, the thrill. I even love that Reed is older, more mature, and I don't give a fuck that he's my brother's best friend.

I awoke with Reed's kiss fresh on my lips, the dream clinging to me. In my hospital room reality set in and heat flushed my skin.

Chapter 2

Reed

"Yes. Yes, I can come in. Just give me a second to find someone to watch Henry. Great, thanks."

I hang up with the hospital and quickly finish my coffee. *Crap. Who can I call to watch him?*

Just as I'm about to make another call, Henry comes in from the living room to drop off his cereal bowl in the sink. I smile at him and set my phone on the kitchen counter.

"Hey, bud. I need to head into work."

Henry's face drops, and his eyes go wide. "Really? Again? But I thought you'd be home today."

"I know, but they need me to help out. There's a lot of people who need care, and one of the other doctors is out sick."

"Okay, but this happens, like, all the time. You did it last weekend, too." Henry pouts, slumping down into a chair at the kitchen island.

"I did, I know. But you know I'm a doctor, Henry. I

help people, and you realize they don't *choose* when to get sick or hurt."

I hold Henry's eyes for a moment, and he seems to come around. He sighs, and I help him down from the chair, even though he doesn't need it.

"Okay, okay. But who's going to stay with me, then?"

"That's what I'm trying to figure out." I pick my phone back up and gesture at the screen.

"Why don't you call Aunt Heather? I like being with her."

I smile. It's a great thought, and I know she enjoys spending time with Henry, too. "Good idea, kiddo. I'll call her."

As I find Heather's number in my phone, Henry goes back to the living room, where I can still hear his cartoons playing. She answers after just a few rings.

"Hello, Reed. What's up?"

"Hi, Heather. Sorry to call so last minute, but I'm needed at the hospital. Do you think you can watch Henry for a bit?"

"My favorite nephew? Of course, but are you sure you have to go in? You're covering shifts left and right."

Guilt stabs through my chest, but I can't leave the other doctors hanging.

"I'm aware, Heather. But work is important. I'll be there in ten."

"Reed, I—"

But I don't let her finish. I already know what she's going to say.

"I have to get going if I'm going to be there on time. Don't worry about Henry. See you soon."

I hang up and gather my stuff before Henry and I head out.

I'm still grateful Heather lives so close, a benefit of

having had a wife with an amazing relationship with her sister. The thought of Clara is quickly followed by a stinging sadness that I really expected to be fainter after three years.

That's the thing about grief, though. I don't think I'll ever get over losing her, especially since I should have been there to do something about it.

A car honks behind me, and I realize I didn't see the light turn green. I wave through the back window and take off.

When we reach Heather's, I help Henry out of the car with his bag of stuff, and Heather is on the front porch waiting for us.

"Hi, Henry! Head on in. I'll be there in just a second."

My son practically sprints toward her and wraps his aunt in a huge hug. He goes inside, and I sigh as Heather raises her brows at me.

"What?"

"Four weekends in a row, Reed. Four."

I bite down on my molars. "I don't have time for this, Heather. I need to get to work."

"So what else is new?" She sighs and crosses her arms over her chest. "You can't keep canceling plans with Henry like this. He's starting to expect you to disappoint him."

The comment is a gut punch, but not because Heather is rude. A part of me sees it, too.

After all, Henry used to put up a much bigger fight about it. Now, he seems…prepared, but I can't have this conversation now.

"It's just busy, and I'm needed. The patients need me."

"So does your son." Heather exhales hard and steps toward her door. "It's not fair to do this to a seven-year-old boy. He doesn't understand. All he sees is that you're choosing everything else over him."

"It's not fair when people get in accidents and wind up in the ER, either. I can't abandon them." I break eye contact with her and start back toward my car. "I'll pick him up later. Thanks for watching him."

When I look back up at Heather, there's a sorrow in her eyes I can't handle. It's too much, so I just hop in the car. Just as I'm closing the door, I hear her shout.

"I'll always be here to help with Henry. And you, if you let me."

I don't respond. I'm about to go into the emergency room, and I need my head to be clear if I'm going to successfully help people.

THE ER IS SLAMMED when I arrive, and I quickly wash up to get started with the worst cases. It's a bit of work to get out of my head at first; I know I've let Henry down *again*.

But I won't disappoint these people. They need a doctor to pull them out of what could potentially be the worst day of their life, and I won't miss my opportunity to save someone—not again.

I get the details about who needs my attention first, and I'm not surprised to see two of my regulars needing sutures.

"You two again?" I sigh. These teens are reckless on a good day, and today, they've managed to both wind up lying next to each other on hospital gurneys.

"You should have seen it! We almost landed a double grind at the same time!"

I roll my eyes as Eric speaks and then look over at his friend, David.

"Almost?"

"Landed on his truck and sent us both flying."

Their legs are torn up pretty good, and I can only imagine how much worse it would have been if they weren't wearing helmets and kneepads.

And then I'm thinking about Mae. I can't believe she wound up here as one of my patients, and after all these years, she's really grown up.

She'd have her hands full with kids like these, and I remember how much of an idiot I was when I was younger.

Mae never seemed like that. She was always trying to keep up with her brother.

An image of her when I'd visited long ago bubbles up in my mind. I pretended to forget her name, but I didn't want to admit I'd been thinking about her since Johnny first introduced us.

Girlfriend or not, Mae had been too attractive to forget, and I should *not* have been thinking of Johnny's kid sister like that.

That part hasn't changed. Mae is more beautiful than ever, and I saw her with a fat lip, so that's saying something.

Focus, Reed. You have work to do.

The sutures are pretty straightforward, and I use the opportunity to show the basic techniques up close to a med student on call. He does well, considering it's his first time seeing the needle actually go into the skin, and the guy only almost vomits once.

Next up is a straightforward head wound cleaning for an elderly gentleman who fell in a parking lot.

The EMTs that bring him in say a bystander actually helped the guy and gave them a clear rundown of what happened while applying some top-notch first aid.

Sometimes, I'm surprised by how well random

passersby can do in an emergency, and I'm grateful someone was there to help this old guy. He's ninety-three and on blood thinners, so there's no doubt this head wound bled substantially when it happened.

Another person comes in presenting with a typical case of appendicitis, but apparently, the woman waited a while before coming to the hospital, and her appendix bursts while she's here.

I rush her in for emergency surgery, and thankfully, I'm able to remove it and stabilize her before she goes septic. She'll be in for a rough recovery and a healthy dose of antibiotics, but it could have definitely been worse.

There's a natural lull in the evening, and I find one of the bunks in the on-call room to get some rest. I've trained myself to go to sleep in seconds, so I manage to sneak in about an hour of blissful unconsciousness before someone bursts through the door looking for me.

"Car accident. Woman and a child. Kid's better off, but the woman coded in the bus. Internal bleeding."

I shoot up off the bed and run to help. They'll be here in seconds, and I go straight to the surgery suite to scrub in. The team who's been here with me through the day scrubs in next to me and provides the details.

I'll be working on the woman while the kid is sent down the hall to the emergency room. He's got a few bumps and bruises and a concussion.

The woman's tire blew while she was on the highway. Apparently, she's the kid's babysitter and was taking him out for the day. Her airbag went off when she hit the median, but it flipped her car, and she took severe blunt-force trauma to her sternum. Chest sounds indicated a punctured lung and strain to the heart.

She's brought in, and I get to work checking the internal damage so I can start my repairs. While ninety-nine percent of my focus is on the current moment, I can't stop the one percent from dwelling on Clara.

It was just the same for her. A bad car accident that wasn't her fault. And she was alone with a child, too.

When she got in the wreck, I was off doing some bullshit errands. I can't even really remember what they were anymore.

The only thing I know is that I wasn't there, and I wasn't at the hospital where I could have helped her. *Saved* her.

Outside of all that, though, the OR pulses with a thick tension. The woman's internals are badly damaged, and I need to stop the bleeding first if I'm going to be able to find and repair the injury.

I get suction, which allows me moments to see what I'm looking for. I work as quickly as possible to suture the tear in her left ventricle that's leaking all the blood with each beat of her heart.

I hear it slow on the monitor behind me, her blood pressure dropping even more. Once it's closed, we pause to check her vitals.

They're not stabilizing. Her blood pressure is still dropping, so she's losing blood elsewhere.

"Damn it! Help me find it!"

The other surgeon present works with me to find the blood leak, but we're coming up blank. My heart pounds, and the frantic energy of the room picks up.

The monitor flatlines behind me, and I quickly turn to see her vitals at zero.

"Fuck! Paddles!"

We try to shock her heart back into a rhythm, but after five tries, the nurse near me just lays a hand on my arm.

"She's gone, Dr. Finnigan."

"No, we can find it. We can—"

"Doctor."

I meet eyes with Dr. Taylor across from me. Rage bursts through my chest as hard as any electricity, and I drop my tools.

"Fuck!"

Leaving the OR for the sinks, I tear off my mask and cap, throwing them in the trash. I pound my fists into the ceramic, hanging my head.

Over the intercom that connects the two rooms, I hear Dr. Taylor and the nurses call it.

"Time of death 21:15"

And then silence fills the space around me. I stand there in front of the sink for what seems like hours, staring at the gleaming silver under the fluorescent lights.

Eventually, I turn on the water and wash up, but I'm there running my hands under the water for too long. Dr. Taylor comes in, laying a hand on my shoulder.

"I'll tell the family. Go home."

I'm about to protest, but she just shakes her head and smiles softly.

"I *got* this. Go home to Henry."

Hearing his name makes a whole new burn shoot through my chest, and I just nod at her.

I'm not a stranger to losing patients. I've been practicing long enough to know it happens more frequently than any doctor likes, but that's the reality of life.

This, though, failing to save this woman from a fucking car wreck, feels like swallowing acid. Every nerve and instinct is begging me to do something to fix this.

And the rest of me knows I'm too late. Again.

Chapter 3

Mae

As I walk up to my brother and his girlfriend's house, I'm still self-conscious about how banged up I look. It's been two days now, and I'm still covered in bruises and there's a thick scab on my lip from where I split it.

I ring the bell and hear him yell behind the door.

"Coming!"

When Johnny answers the door, his face pinches in a poor attempt to hide a smile, and I roll my eyes.

"Go ahead. Get it out of your system."

Johnny bursts out laughing but then pulls me in for a hug and closes the door behind me.

"Dude, you look terrible!"

"I'm aware."

"And it was two kids that did this to you?" His eyebrow raises at me.

"How'd you know that?" I stop short in the entryway, my heart pounding.

"How do you think? Reed told me." Johnny pulls me away from the door and guides me to the kitchen table.

"Ugh. Fucker."

"Oh, come on. Reed had to tell me. Besides, he said that 'Lil Bit' handled the concussion well, all things considered."

"Such a dumb nickname. Just cuz I'm smaller and younger than you guys."

Frowning, I slump down into a chair and smile at Stevie, Johnny's wife, basically. She smiles apologetically back at me and then goes back to stirring the contents in the pan on the stove.

And yet, my heartbeat picks up as the thought of Reed talking about me rattles through my brain.

"Are you all right? I know they wouldn't have released you if you weren't, of course, but you just look so wrecked."

I sigh. I know my brother is just worried about me. After all, thanks to the age gap, he's always been more like a second dad, so I let the comment go.

"I'm fine. I'm tougher than I look. Let's get started."

Johnny cocks a grin at me and pulls out a folder from his briefcase below the table. The thing is stuffed, and as he fans out all the paperwork into specific piles, my head starts to spin.

"Jesus. There's a lot in there. Are you sure this is all for me?"

He just laughs. "Yup. I've reviewed all your statements and assets and the bills and payment info you sent over. This is all your financials."

"I'll remind you I have another bill to add to that stack." I point to my face, and my brother mirrors that pitying smile I saw on Stevie.

"Insurance covered some of it, right?" He pats my arm.

"Some, not all."

We sigh, and then Johnny refocuses on the stack of papers, smacking his palms down on the table around them.

"All right, well, first things first. I think you already know this, but after going over everything, I can tell you this, you're broke."

"Ha!" The humorless laugh cuts through me. "Yes, I'm aware. Any other insights, Mr. Fancy Financial Advisor?"

"Yes, actually. There's some spending you could probably cut down or eliminate, but all in all, you're just not making enough money to take on more debt. But I know you want to go back to school and get your teaching degree, so if you're willing to work with me on this, I think we can get you there in two years."

"Two years! That's forever!" I let my head fall to the table.

"It's better than never. And you wouldn't have to wait so long if you'd asked me for help sooner. I could have paid for some of Grandma's care."

"I know." My voice is muffled by the wood in my face, and I sit back up. "I know. She didn't want me to tell you. I just wanted to help. I was the one living with her, and you know how stubborn she could be."

"I do. And Gram was lucky to have someone like you caring for her."

"Thanks." I smile sarcastically at him, but then the weight of all my debt settles on my shoulders again.

"You're going to have to start saving." He reorganizes my bank statements and looks back up at me. "This last nannying gig is over, right?"

"Yup. Ended with the trip down the stairs. I'm starting something else on Monday."

"I hate to ask, but since I'm doing this for you and all. How's the pay?"

I exhale hard. I hate talking about money, especially with my brother, who seems to be so good with it.

"It's decent. There's a chance for an increase after the first month, but yeah. It's probably not a long-term solution. At least, *I* don't want to be doing it for the long haul. Nannying isn't what I want to be doing for the rest of my life. I want to teach."

"Hey, we'll get you there."

Johnny claps me on the shoulder, and I flinch. He's found one of my many bruises.

"Also—" he pulls out another stack of papers, which look more like college guides "—there's a bunch of good information in here about respectable school and grant programs that can help cover some of the costs. You may still need to take out a loan, but these could really cut back the amount, and they're a much better option."

"Grants?"

"Yeah, you'll fill out the information about your financial situation and what you'll be going to school for. You may be eligible for several student grants and scholarships. Those you won't have to pay back."

"All right."

Johnny helps me fill out some of the forms and walks me through his extremely detailed two-year plan. It goes over everything I need to do to save up, from cutting back on coffee dates with my friend, Vicky, to how much I need to save each week to hit the monthly minimums for his tuition forecast.

It's so much information, and as Johnny tries his best to help me through it, my mind reels at all the numbers and steps and cutbacks.

I'm not terrible at math, but there's something about

seeing my days planned out via spending that makes me despise numbers altogether.

"All right, you two. Let's take a break for some dinner." Stevie snaps Johnny and me out of our meeting, a hand on each of our shoulders, and we follow her into the dining room.

A massive spread of food is set out, and my stomach grumbles loudly.

"Wow, Stevie. This looks great."

I smile at the potatoes and vegetables she's sautéed. It all smells incredible and I sit down, ready to dig in. Between the gorgeous array on the table and the well-appointed home around me, I feel like I'm about to eat at a restaurant.

"It wasn't all me. A true team effort."

Johnny smiles at her, that obviously in-love expression he has taking up his whole face.

Not for the first time, jealousy burns in my gut as I look at them. They're so clearly a unit, and their lives are really going places.

Johnny's client list is getting bigger and bigger, and I'm struggling with a way to finally get my education. It's like I can see him on a race track, outpacing me by laps while I trudge through the mud to get to the starting line.

I want that. I want an easy relationship and live in a house we both own, where we work jobs we love and picked for ourselves, not fell into just to make ends meet.

Not for the first time, I imagine pulling dinner out of the stove while my husband feeds the baby, happily babbling in a highchair. And not for the first time, Reed is starring as my hubby.

Ugh. I feel like a teenager again, and not in a good way.

"How's the staging life, Stevie?" I ask, trying to distract myself from the envy.

"Oh, it's great. I've got some terrific Realtors I'm working with who are so detailed and open about how best to sell the house. It's awesome. And you? You're starting a new job?"

Finishing my bite of food, I nod. "Yup. Here's hoping it lands me the money I need to go back to school. The family must be pretty well-off because they're on the agency's high-end list. I guess it's sort of last minute, and the details are very hush-hush."

Johnny pipes up as he takes a gulp of his beer. "Why would that be the case?"

"Um, lots of reasons, actually. They could be famous or just really private. Or they could be on the fence about the service, so the agency wanted to find the perfect person for the job. I'd just finished my previous job, and I guess they're looking for someone who can be there basically any time, and not all nannies keep those hours."

Stevie wipes her mouth with a napkin. "Oh, wow. So you'll be there whenever they need you?"

"Pretty much."

"That's a demanding work schedule. I really hope they do pay you well for that." She tips her head at me.

"Me too."

Dinner falls into a back-and-forth of Stevie and Johnny discussing their day and me explaining what happened with the twins in full excruciating detail. We all laugh about it, but the embarrassment of allowing two kids strong-arm me is still fairly fresh.

"Did Reed say if you'll have a scar?" Johnny is a little buzzed at this point, chuckling to himself about my split lip, and I'm about ready to throw a potato in his face.

"No. I didn't think to ask. Besides, he was only in the room for, like, five seconds."

"And I bet you were so bummed. You had such a crush

on him when you were a teenager." Johnny smirks to himself and then bursts out laughing.

My stomach drops through the floor. "I did not! You're both way older than me. Gross."

I know I'm blushing fiercely, but I'm also ready to keep defending myself. Thankfully, Johnny has already forgotten it.

As dinner wraps up, I say goodbye and thank my brother for all the help. It was nice, even if he did constantly pick on me about the fall.

But what else is new, right?

I'm surrounded by Stevie and Johnny's arms as they hug me, and then I'm out the front door and very ready to crawl into my bed.

My apartment is pretty far from Johnny's, though, so I have about thirty minutes to go before I can lie down and bury my face in my pillow.

Flicking on the radio, I start mumbling to myself.

"I can't believe he brought up the crush. Ugh."

My mind whirls as I remember how close we got that one night and Reed's very disappointing exit. I'd wanted him to kiss me so badly when we were sitting on the porch, but we'd only stared at each other. Then Johnny came out like a walking cockblocker.

I fantasized about him all that night, and it wasn't the last time, either. Every time Reed came over to visit over the years, I'd dream about him at night.

But then Reed met his wife, and Johnny met Stevie, and I was left on my own, caring for Grandma Linda. It's no wonder I'm still so terrible around guys.

I've been dreaming about something that will never happen for so long, I forgot how to find happiness in the real world.

"But maybe this is your chance, Mae." I meet my eyes

in the rearview mirror as the light turns red. "Monday is going to be great. Just you wait. You'll be off to college in no time. No more evil twins, no more debt, and no more sexy doctors taking up your brain waves."

The light turns green, and I pull forward. "New house. New kid. New me."

Chapter 4

Reed

Henry sits on the couch eating cereal as I gather my stuff before going in to the hospital. We haven't talked much since I got back from that double shift.

At least I know he had a good time with Heather. When I picked him up, he didn't want to leave, hoping to challenge her to another game of Uno.

I've only had a few hours of sleep between on-call shifts at the ER, and I'm mainlining caffeine at this point. It's my second cup of particularly strong coffee, and I'd have a third if I weren't already running behind.

Taking a large gulp, I see an older car pull up in the driveway outside. Frankly, I'm surprised the thing is still running with the amount of rust and noise that surrounds it.

"Oh, good. The nanny is here."

"Dad, do I have to be with a nanny all day? Can't Aunt Heather watch me?"

I sigh. I've explained this three times already.

"No, bud. She's not always available. I'm sure you'll get along great with the nanny. And if you don't, I can always get a new one. Plus, you'll be at school for most of the day, so it's only a few hours."

Henry doesn't answer after that, going back to his cartoons, so I set down my mug, exhaling hard.

At this point, I'm not sure if it's the double shifts or parenthood that's making me so tired.

I approach the front door down the hall, grabbing my bag and bringing it along so I can get going as soon as possible.

Just as I hit the entryway, the bell rings, and I open the door wide to greet whoever this high-class agency sent me.

I expect an older woman, since I've asked for someone available all day, but that's not what I find when I swing open the door. In fact, I see Johnny's younger sister looking up at me, as confused as I am.

"Mae? Hi. Did you come here from the hospital?"

Mae is wearing jeans and a T-shirt like she did when I saw her there, but this time, I don't have the benefit of work distracting me from how good her body looks.

"No. I'm…shit. Um." She looks through her phone and then back up at me. "I'm supposed to be here for a nannying job. Do *you* need a nanny?"

My eyebrows raise as I stare at her in shock. "You're who they sent?"

"Wait." Mae closes her eyes for a second, shaking her head. "It's really you? You're the high-end, last-minute nannying job?"

"I guess I am." I sigh, holding the door for her and gesturing inside. "Come on in. I have to get going."

I grab my bag off the floor, getting a particularly nice look at her butt in those tight jeans when I do. *Gutter. Get your head out of the gutter.*

Swinging the bag over my shoulder, I switch places with Mae so she can come inside.

Her eyebrows raise. "Where are you going? I just got here."

"I'm aware, Mae. I need to head into work. You got here just in time for me to avoid being late." I call back for Henry over my shoulder. "Henry! Come say hi to the nanny. It's Johnny's sister."

Returning to Mae, I pull on my coat. "Just drop him off at school. The details are on the kitchen counter. I'll be home late. I may need to work another double. Okay? Great. Thanks for the help."

Mae just stares at me like a deer in the headlights.

"What?"

"That's it? You aren't going to introduce me? Or give me a tour or something?"

"Henry's a big kid. He'll be fine. Plus, I know you. Just text if you have questions."

She huffs out a breath, crossing her arms over her chest. "Reed, you can't just answer the door and go. It's really tough for kids to get used to a stranger, especially a nanny. And it's worse if the parent isn't around to help with introductions."

I sigh. I don't have time for this. I'm already running behind and have to attend the morbidity and mortality conference. They're mandatory, and this time, we'll be discussing the woman who died on my shift.

"You're not a stranger. You're Johnny's sister."

"But you didn't know that until, like, two minutes ago. I could have been anyone."

I chuckle, but there's little humor in it.

"You'll be fine, and so will Henry. He's quite mature for a kid his age. He's seven now, but I swear you'd think he was seventy. I'll try to be back by 6 p.m., give or take. You know, as long as I don't have to pick up that double. Just enjoy the fact it's not those twins. Okay?"

I cock a brow, gesturing to her head.

"Reed—"

"Oh, and before I forget, the emergency contacts list is on the fridge. Call me if anything happens. And don't take the highway. Also, there's a grocery list. I need you to do some meal prep after you drop Henry off at school."

I hit the remote start button for the car and jog over to the driver's side. Henry appears at the door near Mae, and I wave.

"See you later, bud! Love you!"

When I get inside and eye the clock, I realize I should have left fifteen minutes ago. I'm going to be cutting it close, but I might still make it on time.

Hopefully, they don't start the meeting right at nine. I mean, I can't be the *only* one who hits morning traffic.

The radio chimes on about a traffic jam on the highway, so I take a different route, and time seems to resume its normal pace. *I can't believe Mae is the nanny. What kind of luck is that?*

I'm glad, though. I've known Mae for a while, and every time Johnny talks about her, he's always gushing about how much the kids she works with love her.

I know Henry was nervous about the nanny being an older woman, too. So it's a double win—a young nanny I know I can trust.

The trip down the stairs aside, I'm sure I'm leaving Henry in capable hands, which is great because I really need to focus when I get to work. This really is the best-case scenario.

Still, Mae's words ring in my mind. I haven't used a nanny before, so I didn't really know what to expect. It's always been Aunt Heather to the rescue and, of course, my folks, who adore watching him during their retirement.

But they're getting older, and I can't keep putting this on Heather.

I'm sure Henry will be fine, though. It can't be any weirder than meeting a teacher. Right?

Regret creeps up my spine, and I worry I should have stayed longer to introduce Henry to Mae properly. But I have this conference, and there's no way around that.

It's not like I *wanted* to rush out.

The shock on Mae's face plays over and over again in my mind, and I remember Heather's words, too.

"I shouldn't have waited so long to get a nanny. I knew I needed the help. Why didn't I do it sooner?"

Hell, if I'd made the call when I should've, maybe I would have prevented Mae from getting that concussion. If she still wound up being my nanny.

I guess it did work out for the best, but as I pass through a green light, I promise myself to turn down that double shift if I can help it. I should be home to ask Henry how it went.

I ARRIVE at the hospital in time to park and jog straight to the M&M conference. We do these conferences every month, so I don't know why my heart keeps pounding even after I've caught my breath.

They're important, of course, but I've been to enough of them now to be prepared. The entire hospital knows they need to examine procedures and effects as a regular part of our quality assurance.

I guess it's just been a while since one of my cases was chosen. Everyone in the room knows I did everything possible to save my patient; sometimes, that's just not enough.

Finding a spot in the middle of the lecture hall seating, I pull out the patient's file I've been reviewing to correctly present what happened.

This is a teaching hospital, and while everyone does morbidity and mortality conferences, we take them especially serious here because they are, of course, teaching moments.

There are several cases on the docket today; mine is at the end as the most recent case added. It's like waiting to be examined by a psychologist in front of everyone.

The presenting doctor will detail the entire patient case from arrival to expiration, answering questions from the assembled physicians and surgeons.

We do it all the time. It isn't something to be worried over, but here I am, near panic in my chair as Dr. Anthony tries to tell me about his weekend.

I'm not listening in the slightest and just nod along where I think it's appropriate.

Doctors lose patients, I tell myself. But for whatever reason, maybe because I haven't in a while, I feel guilt crawling beneath my skin as I think of the woman who died on my shift.

These councils aren't punitive. If they really thought I did something wrong, I'd be suspended while the hospital investigated, so I already know I'm fine.

Still, my mind swirls as I wonder if I missed something —aside from the location of the other tear.

My stomach churns as the current presenter, Dr. Fletching, wraps up her talk about the second to last case. Maybe I shouldn't have had that second cup of coffee.

"All right. The last case today is Patient O'Mally. A

female, twenty-five years old, sustained multiple injuries and internal damage during a car accident last Friday."

All I can hear after that is the pounding of my heart. It's so loud that it muffles Dr. Fletching's voice.

Time slips into a fog where I'm unsure if we're still talking about the same case or how long it's been. Images of the surgery scatter through my brain, replaying the moments searching for the other bleed on repeat.

I'm nervous I'll be sick if this swirling array of memories doesn't stop, and then I remember how I wasn't there for Clara's surgery. Her doctor couldn't stop the bleeding, either.

It was a freak turn of luck. Everything is just luck. Or lack of luck.

That impending doom I felt the night I got the call swells in my veins. I should have been there for her, for *both* of them.

"Dr. Finnigan? Doctor?"

I snap my attention back to the presentation and clear my throat. "Apologies. My findings during the pre-op examination supported the presence of a tear in the ventricle. When I opened the patient up, I was able to locate the first tear, but at that point, it was clear there was another somewhere on the posterior side of the heart. I was unable to find it before the patient suffered critical blood loss. The patient could not be stabilized and expired before the second laceration was located."

The words come out of my mouth automatically. I'm not truly aware of what I'm saying. There's more discussion, and I can answer a few questions without being wholly present.

The minutes drag on as we discuss what more could have been done to save the patient and if any procedures in place delayed the woman receiving timely medical treatment.

But I can't really hear what they're saying. All I can hear is Dr. Romano's voice from three years ago telling me my wife was dead.

"So—" Dr. Fletching's voice suddenly cuts through the mental fog "—can we determine that better care could have been provided?"

I remind myself these conferences aren't punitive. People do make mistakes, so if I made one, this meeting exists to ensure it doesn't happen again.

That's all.

It doesn't matter to me right now, however. I've already convinced myself I made a mistake, and that mistake is not acting quickly enough—just like before.

Dr. Fletching addresses the crowd with her final thoughts. "So, in my opinion, we can all agree on the cause of this particular case."

My gut burns, churning harder, and I look down at the patient file in my hand. The woman's date of birth sits at the top of the paper.

August 15. She had the same birthday as my wife.

Chapter 5

Mae

Reed is out the door before I can say another word, and as far as first impressions go, I'm bothered by his parenting skills—or lack thereof. While I understand that being a doctor must be challenging, there are ways to provide stability for your kid.

Maybe he shouldn't have waited till the last minute to hire someone. Sheesh.

I look down beside me where Henry stands. He closes the door and goes back to the couch, where I see a bowl of cereal waiting for him on the coffee table.

As I walk over, I eye the house. It's beyond nice, and while there are definitely signs that people live here, it doesn't feel homey or have the piles of stuff that seem to accumulate around all children.

"Hi, Henry. I'm Mae." I look at the TV. "What are you watching?"

"It's an Avengers cartoon." He doesn't seem nervous about meeting me, but he's also not interested, it seems.

I sit down next to him, biting my lip. This is precisely why I like to have the parent around.

"Oh, I love The Avengers. I love Black Widow because, you know, girl power. But I'm definitely a Cap girl, not Team Iron Man."

Henry perks up and looks over with a smile. "I love Captain America. He's really brave. He sticks up for people, you know?"

"Yeah. That's why I love him, too. He's not afraid to stand up for what's right. Plus, he's got a very cool shield."

After shoveling in another bite of cereal, Henry wipes his mouth and squints at me.

"I thought you'd be an old lady or something."

I chuckle. "Ha! Nope. I'm actually your dad's best friend's little sister. Oof, that's a mouthful."

He laughs with me and then stands up, holding his bowl.

"So you're going to take me to school? And pick me up?"

"I am. It'll be a new routine. Is that okay with you?" I try to come across as open as I can.

"Yeah. It's better than having to wait for Dad. Um, so you know my dad?"

I furrow my brow. "Uh, sort of. He's really good friends with my brother. I've met him a few times before when they would hang out. It's been a while since your dad came by, though."

"He's always working."

A slight pang stumbles through my heart as I look at Henry. He seems so detached from his dad.

"Yeah. It must be hard to be a doctor."

"I guess." Henry reaches for the remote and turns off the TV. "I'm going to brush my teeth and get dressed for school."

I smile and nod. "Okay, I'll get your lunch bag ready. Do you have stuff that needs to go in your backpack?"

He nods his head at the kitchen counter. "There's a folder with everything over there."

"Oh." I see the plain blue folder that's neatly organized with his lunch bag and backpack sitting next to it. "Did your dad put that together?"

"No. I did. I'll be right back."

Henry takes his bowl into the kitchen and rinses it out in the sink before loading it into the dishwasher. Then he hurries upstairs, but not in that excited, clumsy way most kids do.

He just lightly jogs up the stairs and disappears around the corner.

I don't hear any banging or drawers being slammed. There's only the hum of water running in the bathroom and a door opening and closing gently.

I pack the folder into his backpack, then I open the fridge to see if there's something already prepared to send with him for lunch. Sure enough, there's a little meal prepped in a Tupperware container.

I go to the edge of the stairs and yell up. "Is this Tupperware for you? Do you need anything else?"

"Yes, that's for me. I packed it yesterday with the food Dad bought. I only need my water bottle. It's in the fridge."

Henry calls down the instructions to me like a professional, and my heart sinks even further. He's seven. He shouldn't have to be this prepared and organized.

I'm all for well-behaved kids, but his dad is right. He comes across like a full-blown adult, and I don't think that was *his* choice.

Henry has been taking care of himself for far too long. He needs some fun in his life.

I sigh as I zip up his bag, all ready to go, and Henry meets me downstairs. I hand the backpack to him, and he slips it on as he walks to the door.

"Ready."

"I see that. Thanks for being such a big help. Let's get you to school and you can see your friends."

At that, Henry lights up more, and I have hope that his days aren't all doom and gloom.

I have a booster seat from previous nannying gigs in my car, and I get Henry settled. He doesn't need much help, though.

I clear out the floor a bit more for him before hopping behind the wheel. I did most of the cleaning yesterday but forgot a few things in the back.

"Um, Mae."

I glance back through the rearview mirror as I pull out of the driveway. "Yes, Henry?"

"Why do you have a bag of bags back here? And these boxes?"

I laugh. "The bags come in handy if I have too much to carry or need an impromptu trash can. And the boxes are from my breakfast. I haven't had a chance to throw them out yet."

"Oh." I can hear the genuine consideration in Henry's voice. "So then, why do you have, like, three water bottles?"

I roll my eyes, turning onto the main road toward his school. It's a good thing Reed left directions to the school on the counter, too.

"Well, I forgot I had one in here. You know, in case I get thirsty. I forget a lot, I guess."

Traffic is busy yet smooth, and Henry quiets, but only for a moment.

"What kind of car is this?"

My head spins. It's such an odd question for a kid to be asking. "Um, it's a Toyota Camry. My parents gave it to me when they upgraded."

"Oh, cool. Dad just swapped out his car. He leases, I guess. It's way nicer than this. It's an Escalade."

I stare down at the steering wheel as I blink, then reach for my water. Is my car really being judged by a seven-year-old?

Jeez, kid. Not all of us have super loaded dads. At least mine spends time with me.

Shaking my head, my heart pinches. That was mean, even if it was just a thought. After all, it's not his fault Reed works all the time.

Silence finds us then, and I successfully drop Henry off at school. Reaching into my bag for the shopping list Reed left, I decide to get the stuff now so I don't have to waste more gas.

GETTING the load of groceries into the house and finding everything I need for this meal prepping is a pain in the ass. Reed didn't bother to show me around the kitchen or leave instructions on where all the utensils are, so I spend ten minutes just hunting for a mixing bowl.

The bit of info he did leave explains that I need to make all of Reed's and Henry's meals for the week, including cooking dinner for them each night. There is a fine line between being a nanny and a live-in housekeeper.

Reed is walking it damn dangerously.

What's more, I apparently have to do laundry and pick up a suit from the dry cleaners, too. Thankfully, I'm good at cooking, and these are simple meals for lunches that I can whip up in no time.

I still have to work my ass off to get it all done, but by the time I have to go pick up Henry from school, I've accomplished everything on Reed's ridiculous list.

In the car on the way to the school, I get a message from Johnny asking how the new gig is, and I use the voice-to-text to message back that it's actually Reed I'm nannying for.

Johnny sends back the shocked emoji face, and I send back a *Right?!* I also mention that his friend could definitely use some parenting lessons.

What does that mean?

I roll my eyes at no one, sending a reply.

Well, no offense, but your buddy is kind of a dick. He didn't even take five seconds to introduce me to Henry.

I pull up to the line of cars waiting in student pick up and throw the Camry into park.

Geez, Mae. He's a single dad who's been through a lot. Cut him some slack.

He's not wrong. I know Reed used to be married and his wife passed away suddenly about three years ago.

It's more than possible Reed is having a hard time getting used to being a widower and single dad.

All right, all right. I'll be nice. Gotta go. Henry is out of school.

With that, Henry opens the back door of my car and hops in.

"Can you get yourself buckled?"

"Yup. It's not hard."

"Of course. How silly of me. How was school?"

I proceed forward out of the pickup line and head back to Reed's house.

Henry chats away about what he did in school and his friends. I try to learn as much as I can about what he likes and which subjects he hates.

It turns out Henry is actually great with science, and there's a fair coming up that he hopes to participate in.

"That's great, Henry. You totally should. I bet your dad can help you."

He hesitates for a moment, then nods. "Yeah, maybe."

When we get inside, Henry helps me put his stuff away, and we go over his reading homework. He's a bright kid who loves to do well in school.

Dinnertime comes, and I have Henry help me cook up some spaghetti and meatballs. It's a quick and easy go-to meal that doesn't take long.

I make enough for all three of us, expecting Reed to come home around six.

He doesn't.

A little after six fifteen, Reed calls the house to say he's leaving the hospital. There was a med student who needed assistance with a procedure.

I assure Reed it's no problem and that I'll feed Henry so he doesn't have to wait. Together, we eat up the spaghetti and chat more about school.

When we're finished, Henry asks to play a card game with me, and I'm actually surprised. It's not often you find a kid who likes to play cards.

We get through a couple of rounds of War before switching it up and playing Rummy. It's one of my favorites, and Henry is a fast learner.

After playing more than a few games of Rummy, I glance over at the clock. Reed still isn't here, and it shouldn't take this long to get home from the hospital.

Another twenty minutes go by, and Reed finally walks in, dropping his stuff near the door and hanging up his coat. I expect Henry to run over and give his dad a big hug like most kids do when their folks get home, but he doesn't even look up from his hand.

"Henry, your dad's home. Don't you want to say hi?"

He doesn't get the chance to answer before Reed pipes in.

"I'll be right there, bud. I have a few more phone calls I need to make."

Reed walks back down the far hall where I know there's an office, and Henry lays down a set of three 3's. I'm still staring down the hallway, clenching my jaw, when Henry speaks up.

"It's your turn, Mae."

I turn back toward Henry with a smile. "Sorry. My turn?"

Going through my hand to see what I can play next, I grin over at Henry, trying to put us both back into a good mood.

"It's okay. It's always like this."

I frown. "He's always late?"

"Yeah, pretty much."

Setting my cards down, I cross one leg over the other as I sit across from Henry at the table.

"Well, that's no fun. Does that make you upset?"

Henry just shrugs. "I don't know. Let's just finish the game."

"Okay."

I smile, but there's sadness behind it I'm not sure I can hide. I know this has to upset Henry. Kids don't act this numb around their parents for no reason.

As we finish our game, I can see the look of disappointment Henry tries to hold back. He's still hurt, but he feels the need to keep it to himself.

That's not right. Henry expects to be chastised for being sad that his father is late again.

It's only been a day, but I've seen all I can take. I'll get this family back on track if it's the last thing I do.

Chapter 6

Reed

I sigh as I get dressed for Johnny's birthday party. The week has been so much easier with Mae around, and she's really hit it off with Henry.

Work has been as stressful as ever, and it's so nice to have someone I can trust to take care of Henry while I'm at the hospital. I realize it may not have been ideal when she first started.

Still, I have total confidence in her abilities after observing the results.

Henry has been in a good mood, the house is clean and tidy, with meals prepared every night, and Mae honestly seems to care about my son's well-being. She's always so excited to see him in the morning.

And best of all, because I've been able to get my paperwork done at the hospital, I can actually enjoy Johnny's party. According to Johnny's text, his girlfriend Stevie has apparently opened the entire house for the event.

It's even kid-friendly, so I can bring Henry and know he'll have a good time.

"Come on, bud! Let's get going!"

I call down the hall for him, and we jog down to the car together.

"There's really going to be other kids there?" Henry raises his brows at me.

"Yes. I know for sure at least two. That's what Johnny texted."

Henry nods. "Will Mae be there?"

"I assume so since she's Johnny's sister. Really liking your nanny, huh?" I ruffle his hair and smile.

"I am! She's the best!"

"That's awesome, bud. Let's go have some fun."

Henry is a bundle of excited energy as I get him buckled in the car. It's been a while since we've done anything like this, and a pang stings my heart momentarily.

That all too familiar guilt creeps along my spine. I should have been taking Henry to more fun events, but it's so hard when I'm doing everything by myself.

I shrug it off. Tonight is about relaxing and having a good time, so there's no use in wallowing.

"HA! That's amazing. You really had to advise a drug dealer?" I laugh as Johnny finishes up his story.

"He's not a drug dealer. Marijuana is legal here, remember? But yeah, he just opened a dispensary and is looking to invest."

I take another swig of my beer and sit back in the comfortable patio chair. This is so great.

Just then, Henry and two other kids, the daughter of

one of Johnny's coworkers and the son of one of Stevie's friends, dash by, playing tag in the backyard.

They've cycled through several games at this point, but they are consistently running around at top speed. I'm surprised none of them have smashed into something.

He's having the time of his life, and I couldn't be happier. People are mingling and taking in the cool yet comfortable weather, and Johnny has been regaling us all with stories of some of his most interesting clients.

"So, Johnny, how are your folks? It's been a minute since I've seen them."

Johnny finishes his beer, tossing it into the recycling can set up a few feet away. "They're great. Living it up. They'll be spending the next three months in the Cook Islands."

"Damn, that's a while." I stand up to get us more drinks. "What made them choose that spot?"

"Oh, well, they went there for their twentieth wedding anniversary, and now it's, like, their favorite place. They've wanted to go back since then. Hell, I think they'd retire there if it weren't so expensive."

"Well, good for them. I'm going to go snag us a few more beers. Be right back."

I step out from behind the patio table and start for the cooler in the garage. I turn to look over my shoulder to say hi to Stevie, then run right into someone coming out of the garage.

"Oof. Dude! Oh, hi."

I look down to see Mae holding a beer.

"Oh, hi Mae. Sorry. I wasn't looking where I was going."

She smiles and shakes her head. "It's fine. Just watch the beer. You almost made me drop my Guinness, which would have been a crime."

I laugh, playfully acting like I'm going to bump into her again, but then I notice what she's wearing.

Mae looks incredible. Her long brown hair is pulled up and off her neck, and subtle makeup draws attention to her deep brown eyes.

And then there's the dress.

Damn. My thoughts go to a decidedly *not* platonic place as I let my gaze rake over Mae's body.

She's always wearing jeans or leggings and a T-shirt when she watches Henry, which cause their own set of problems in my mind. But what she's wearing today is something else.

Mae's curves are practically poured into the black dress, which gives off a girlish vibe with its puffy sleeves and billowy skirt. The square neck reveals her ample cleavage, and the cinched waist draws attention to Mae's slim figure.

I'd managed to avoid thinking about her too much. Work is suitably distracting. At least most of the time.

But after all these years, Mae is still a total knockout.

"Reed?"

Fuck. I realize I've been staring and quickly blink, stepping aside so Mae can pass. When I do, I hear Henry yell for her, then he's barreling toward her.

"Hi, Henry!" Mae smiles down as Henry throws himself around her legs.

It's been a while since I've received the same greeting, and a twinge of regret stabs through me.

"Come here, come here! We want to show you something!" Henry takes her hand and pulls Mae away, his new friend Bethany following close behind.

Stepping into the garage to get the beers, I swallow hard. *I'm missing things. I know I am. And Jesus fuck that dress. I'm going to die.*

But I shake it off. This is Johnny's birthday party, and I want to enjoy it, not just for him but for me, too.

I rejoin Johnny at the patio table with two fresh beers, casually watching Henry and Bethany run Mae ragged around the yard. She dodges their attempts to tackle her, and I'm astonished Mae hasn't dropped her beer.

"Henry! Wait! Just let me take a drink."

Johnny and I laugh as she holds my son back by the forehead, trying desperately to take a swig of her Guinness.

"Well, they're certainly hitting it off well. I'm glad to see you're getting some help." Johnny clinks his beer against mine, and I chuckle.

"Yeah, me too. Mae's been great. It's a relief not to worry about Henry." I gulp my Sam Adams in cheers, trying to keep my eyes from landing on Mae for too long, and then nod at where they're playing. "She's been a huge help."

"Mae is great with kids. I'm sure she'll be a good teacher when she finally gets there. Maybe even a mom… or aunt."

My eyes snap to Johnny, furrowing my brow. "Aunt?"

Johnny casually smiles. "Yeah. Stevie and I are thinking about it. We want to start a family soon. We're not big on the marriage idea, but we both want kids."

I sigh, dropping my eyes to stare at the space between us and fiddling with the peeling label on my beer. "Yeah. A family."

"Reed." I feel Johnny's hand on my arm and I look up, struggling to pull my thoughts out of the past.

"I didn't mean to…the accident was not your fault. You're still a family. You and Henry."

I nod half-heartedly. It's been three years, but sometimes, it still feels like it was only yesterday.

"Yeah. I know." I don't meet Johnny's eyes. "It's just… yeah. It's fine."

"Dude." Johnny claps me on the shoulder. "You didn't plan on being a single dad. You have to stop beating yourself up about it. It was an accident. A tragic, horrible accident. You've still got Henry. Focus on that."

I know he's right. Still, following through is more challenging than that.

"I'm working on it. I swear."

Smiling at Johnny and then shrugging his hand off, I take another swig. Happy screaming and laughter erupt from the grass next to us, and I look over to see the children piling on top of Mae.

Johnny and I chuckle, encouraging the kids to "get her." It's genuinely hilarious, but something else sings through me as I see her struggle to keep her dress from creeping any higher up her legs.

"I hope you're paying her well."

I snort as I set down my beer. "Oh, I am. Trust me."

Pleasant chatter starts up around me as Johnny reminisces with his other friends and coworkers. All I can do is watch Mae roughhouse with the gang of children bent on taking her down, trying her best to accommodate the dress.

Johnny's little sister. She's always been this little thing in the back of my head, a tiny spark of something I know I shouldn't be thinking about.

And I wasn't thinking about her for the longest time, happily married and building my medical career.

Now? Well, now we're here, and that spark is growing brighter, reminding me of all the close moments I'd exchanged with her over the years.

Particularly that time on the back porch when Johnny and I were leaving to go to Vegas. I can remember the smell of her body spray and how her hair fluttered around her face in the breeze.

That brief kiss we shared.

But then Johnny came out, and we left.

As my thoughts swirl, Mae finally breaks free from the gaggle wrestling with her, and she steps away, yelling, "Time out!"

She plops down in the chair next to me, breathing hard.

"Good Lord. They're going to kill me."

I can't help but chuckle. Mae looks over and playfully glares, but then she's sighing and taking a long drink.

"Oh, that's better. You and Johnny get to catch up a bit?" She eyes Henry, who tries to sneak up on her. "No. No. I get five minutes, buddy. Please?"

Mae holds her hands up like she's begging him.

"Fine. Bethany! Let's go check out that bug!"

He runs off, and I shake my head.

"I did. Are you going to make it?"

"Your son has so much energy. But yeah, I'll be fine. I'm used to it. I still want my five minutes, though. Maybe more, hopefully, if he gets distracted."

"Hey, Stevie." I get her attention, and Johnny's girlfriend walks over to the table. "Would you put on a kids' movie in the big loft? Popcorn, maybe?"

She smiles down at Mae. "Someone need a break?"

"You have no idea." Mae hangs her head.

"Of course. Leave it to me."

Stevie goes back in the house to get it set up, and I smile proudly at Mae. "You're welcome."

"You are a fucking godsend. Thank you."

We both laugh, meeting eyes as she leans back in her chair. Tension prickles down my spine as I hold her stare just a moment too long.

Where the fuck is your head, Reed?

"Can I get you a drink?" I ask.

"Oh, yes. This is—" Mae chugs the last few mouthfuls "—empty."

"Ha. Nicely done. I'll be right back."

Going for another round, I stop to take a quick shot from the bottle of whiskey sitting on the outdoor bar near the garage door. I'm going to need some help if I'm going to make it through the night without kissing Johnny's sister.

Chapter 7

Mae

The movie was an excellent idea, and I've been able to actually enjoy the party without being tackled by Henry and his little gang. The beer flows all the steadier, and after a while, Reed calls Henry's aunt Heather to take him home.

The party empties out for the most part, and Johnny's tired friends and coworkers drag their kids home, who can't stop complaining about wanting to stay and play with me.

It's too sweet, but those hellions need their rest, and I promise to see them soon.

I'm certainly not going anywhere, however. I've had a few too many drinks to drive, and I'm not done having my fun.

Stevie is a superb drinking buddy, and we're cracking into the Pink Whitney now that the kids have left. It's some terrible fruity liquor that tastes like medicine, but it'll get the job done.

"Ugh! How can you drink this stuff?" I set the bottle back down on the bar outside, grimacing.

"It's not that bad."

Stevie takes a swig, but her face betrays how much she *doesn't* enjoy it, and I laugh.

"Ha! You big liar!"

We're a fit of giggles as we continue to work on the bottle, and soon Johnny and Reed come over to try some for themselves.

"Yup, this is disgusting." Reed frowns. "I think I'll stick with the whiskey."

I love the crinkled brow he's sporting, not to mention the complete departure from his usual attire. When Johnny indicated the dress was semiformal on his invitations, Reed definitely understood the assignment.

His black suit is crisp and tailored, but he's worn it without a tie, which gives his look this casual flair that only adds to his sex appeal.

Ugh. Why does Reed have to be so hot?

Johnny has some of our girl's drink, his eyebrows shooting to his hairline. "Whoa! It's way stronger than I would have thought. Oof."

Easy laughter rings our tight circle as we drink the night away, trading embarrassing stories.

"Oh, and she couldn't wait to take it to school. Absolutely pitched a fit about it, so our mom had to call the school and let them know Mae was going to come in with this huge fucking balloon!"

"I didn't know that part! Oh, no! Now I feel bad."

I swipe under my eyes, tearing up from all the laughing.

"Oh, don't worry. You popped it on the way into class." Johnny can barely get the words out through his laughter.

"I did." I frown, remembering how sad I was. "I was so upset."

"Over a balloon?" Reed raises his brows at me, which has heat flaring up my cheeks.

"You weren't there. You don't understand." I try to be uppity about it but fail miserably and end up bursting out laughing.

"Don't worry, Mae. You're not the only one with an embarrassing story. Remember the massager?" Johnny wags his brows at Reed.

Reed's eyes blow wide, and my curiosity is definitely piqued. "Don't you dare. You can't."

"Oh, but I can." Reed buries his face in his hands as Johnny continues. "So, I was over at Reed's place. We were, what, like, fifteen?"

"Yeah, that sounds right."

I'd forgotten that Johnny actually met Reed in high school, and the two chose to attend the same college. God, they've always been inseparable…until recently.

"So, yeah, fifteen, and we were snooping around the house like teenagers do. And Reed pulled open his mom's top dresser drawer in her closet. I think we were looking for porn or booze or something."

"Oh my God. You found her—"

Stevie finishes for me. "Vibrator!"

I can only see the tips of Reed's ears, but it's still enough to see he's turning bright pink. Stevie and I laugh hysterically, and Johnny adds the kicker.

"He brought it out to ask what it was, and I already knew at that point, so I just started laughing. And then he started pushing the buttons. I swear to God, the thing jumped around like a jackhammer."

I can barely breathe from laughing so hard.

"I explained what it was, and Reed dropped the thing

on the floor. So it started flopping around, and we had to catch it to put it back in the drawer."

When Reed finally pokes his face out from behind his hands, he sighs and shakes his head.

"Apparently, it was very expensive, and I was grounded for, like, a week after managing to put a tear in the silicone."

It's a few minutes before we can all stop laughing, and I lay a hand on Reed's shoulder.

"Well, at least that's something you won't have to worry about with Henry."

He shakes his head as he smiles. "Here's hoping he doesn't get a pocket pussy."

THE NIGHT WINDS DOWN, and I steal a pair of Stevie's pajamas so I can crash on their pullout sofa. She's already up in bed, and I hug Johnny as he goes to join her.

"This was so fun." Johnny puts a foot on the stairs. "Thank you for coming."

"Of course. Happy birthday, bro."

As I walk down the hall to double-check that the door is locked, my house or not—I'm a stickler for safety—Reed comes out of the entryway bathroom.

We're all well into tipsy territory, and Reed's nice suit looks disheveled, his jacket long gone. I can't help but snicker at him, even if he's somehow even hotter like this.

He notices and cocks a brow at me. "What?"

"I've never seen you look so…relaxed."

Reed looks down at his rumpled shirt. He's rolled up the sleeves to his elbows and undone the top few buttons.

It's so effortlessly sexy, and I struggle to remind myself

he's my boss and still Johnny's best friend. *Yup, that's very off-limits, Mae.*

"Huh, yeah. Well, it's been a while since I've enjoyed a night out. I've definitely had way more drinks than normal."

"You're not driving, are you?" I cross my arms over my chest.

"No, of course not. I'm going to crash up in the loft on those blankets Stevie set up for the kids."

"On the floor? Don't do that. You'll kill your back. Why don't you share the pullout with me? It's plenty big enough."

His eyes go a bit wide, and he shakes his head emphatically. "No way. I won't make you share a bed with me. I toss and turn. And Henry says he can hear my snoring from down the hall."

"I'm sure it'll be fine. I'm too tired to hear anyone's snoring once I fall asleep."

If I'm even able to. Having Reed that close to me is going to make unconsciousness a challenge.

I start walking down the hall toward the living room and the bed to finish setting up.

"You know, there's a loveseat up there. I'll just sleep on that."

Reed has followed me but starts to turn back to the stairs.

"Don't be silly. You're what, like, six two? You'll throw your back out sleeping on a loveseat. Or give yourself kinks in your neck."

He hesitates in the hall, and I grab his hand.

"Come on. I'll grab some extra blankets and pillows from the linen closet so we don't have to worry about sharing."

It'll also help ensure I don't wind up brushing against anything and losing my head.

We get the pullout ready for bed with two pillows and two blankets, and I lie down. Reed hesitates but eventually climbs in next to me.

Even though it's big for a sofa bed, Reed still takes up most of the mattress, and his arm presses against mine as we both lie on our backs, staring up at the ceiling.

"I'm glad you came to the party. You don't go out and have fun much. And I know Henry enjoyed it."

I don't take my eyes off the vent above me, focusing on the pattern the grates make.

"Me too. It's…work is demanding." Reed sighs. "Henry had a blast. He didn't want to leave. Between you and the other kids, this was basically heaven for him."

"And I know Johnny was super pumped that you could come."

Reed turns over onto his side facing me. "It was great to hang with him again. And damn, I didn't know he and Stevie were getting so serious."

I mimic the position change, rolling onto my side so I can face him and talk. It's like being at a sleepover.

But I never wanted to kiss anyone at the ones I used to have. That's not the case right now.

"Yeah. They're great together. I know they'll be really happy. And with me around to help, you'll be able to see Johnny more often, which will totally make his day."

"Having you around has done much more than just allow me to see Johnny. Not that visiting with him isn't reason enough."

"Thanks."

The sofa bed is less than comfortable, and I adjust again, trying to find a spot for my hips. Looking back up, I'm a bit closer to Reed than before.

"I mean it, Mae. I'm so lucky to have you around, and Henry adores you."

"He's a great kid. I'm glad I get to spend time with him."

"I know he loves hanging out with you. If today weren't evidence enough. Seeing him so happy and playful is amazing. I almost forgot kids could be like that."

A sting radiates through my ribs as I consider how hard it must be to be a single parent.

Raising kids is work enough, but to do it alone? That's a lot.

"I really like being there to help. Hanging out with Henry is a blast, if rough on the knees."

I briefly consider telling Reed that *he* should be spending more time with him, too, but now's not the time. Plus, he did bring him out tonight, which is a step in the right direction.

I move onto my back again, but a spring digs into my spine, and I know I can't stay in this position for long.

Maybe I can just wait till Reed's asleep? I don't know what I'll do if I keep staring into those hazel eyes.

A shuddering exhale slides out. This was a bad idea. I shouldn't have asked Reed to join me.

It's way too tempting.

A loud groan comes from the bed as Reed shifts, and I try to move back where I was and give him some space.

"Sorry. This thing isn't super comfortable." He chuckles quietly.

"Maybe you would have been better on the floor." I smile at the ceiling.

"It certainly would have been quieter."

We both laugh, and then Reed also tries shifting to his back. His arm is right up against me, the heat from his skin burning into my own.

But the squeaking bed is so loud, and when I hit a particularly noisy spring, I quickly pull off it, rolling onto my side and right into Reed, who's also struggling to get comfortable.

We're nose to nose, his face inches from mine. My heart pounds in my chest. I can feel every single beat as I stare into Reed's eyes.

I struggle to take shallow breaths, warmth melting through my core, and I clench my legs together.

In the dark, I can just make out Reed's gaze dropping to my mouth, and then his lips press into mine.

My eyes blow wide, and then I quickly return the kiss. Reed's lips are soft as his hands find my face, and he pulls me in, brushing his tongue against mine.

Arousal burns hard in my veins, and I press myself closer to him, wanting every bit of his body on me.

After all this time, I'm finally kissing him, and it's better than anything my sixteen-year-old self could have imagined. Then, I'm suddenly there, remembering how it felt to want him more than anything, knowing he was almost twice my age.

My older brother's hot best friend is kissing me, and my fantasies did not do his skills justice.

Chapter 8

Reed

Mae's tight little body presses against mine as I explore her mouth with my tongue. Fucking hell, the taste of her.

It's everything, and I just want more. I knew this was going to happen, and I tried to keep my distance.

I was going to sleep upstairs, but there's something about Mae. I just can't resist her.

Sliding my hand down her neck, I find the swell of her breast hiding behind that oversized sleep shirt she borrowed from Stevie. I find the hem, pulling the thing up so I can feel Mae's skin on mine.

Her flesh is warm, and as I smooth my thumb across her breast, I feel her hard nipple, eager and wanting.

Mae moans into my mouth, and her leg wraps around my hips. *Oh, fuck yes. I want everything you have, little one.*

But then Mae's hand comes to my chest, and she pushes herself back.

"What is it?" I whisper, gripping her side.

"We can't. You're my boss, for Christ's sake. And Johnny's best friend. That's way too many lines to cross. We shouldn't."

I exhale, dropping my head to break her stare. Pulling back, I swallow hard, hating that she's right.

I'd completely lost control. It's a good thing one of us could still think straight.

"Okay. Yeah. You're right. I'm..." I nod. "I'm just going to roll over. I'll stay over here."

"Okay. I'll, um. Yeah. I'll do the same."

We both flip to our other sides, and I briefly glance down. I'm rock-hard, and it's going to be really difficult to fall asleep now.

But Mae's right. She really is. We can't do this.

Eventually, sleep claims me, but my dreams are filled with images of Mae letting me do everything I want to.

"REED."

The quiet whisper pulls me out of unconsciousness, and my eyes fly open. Did I just hear my name?

My mind clears, and I remember I'm sharing the sofa bed with Mae. Is she up? Did *she* whisper my name?

I turn over, the couch creaking, and as I face Mae, I see she's awake.

"Did you say my name?"

She stares, her gaze flickering between me and the space between us. "Yes. I..."

I shake my head. "What?"

Mae doesn't answer. Instead, her hands cup my face, and she kisses me, her tongue diving between my lips.

Moaning, I'm able to stop for just a moment. "I thought you said we shouldn't?"

"I know. I...I don't care."

It's all the answer I need. I crash my lips against hers again, pulling up her shirt to caress Mae's breasts. They're too perfect, and lust roars through my blood like a drug.

"Fuck, Mae. You feel so good."

I smooth my hand down her curves, gliding back up to pinch her nipple between my fingers. She arches into me and moans.

"I've fantasized about this since I was sixteen." Mae pushes her breast harder against my palm, and I squeeze.

Nuzzling into Mae's neck, I kiss her skin, playfully biting. "Really? And what exactly did I do during these fantasies, Lil Bit?"

Mae's hand flies to my hair, gripping as she groans. I pull back, meeting her eyes.

A charming blush floods Mae's cheeks, and I stroke my thumb across her bottom lip. She can't hold my gaze, and I smirk.

I tip her chin up. "Come on, tell me."

Mae's voice is a soft whisper. "Everything."

She bites her lip, and her eyes blink up to mine.

"I think I can help with that."

Rolling on top of Mae, I push between her legs, the pullout groaning in protest. The large shirt covering her has to go, so I slide my hands up her sides, lifting it over her head and tossing it to the floor.

"God, you're stunning."

Mae blushes all the harder, and my erection throbs. I lower my head, kissing her, then move my lips down her neck and chest until I reach her full breasts.

"I've wanted you, too, Mae. This week has been torture."

"Really? I thought it was just me." Her eyes are worried, and I rake my gaze across her bare skin.

"Not at all. I've been imagining this tight little body beneath me for years."

Her ample curves look gorgeous in the room's low light, and I suck her nipple into my mouth, grasping her other breast with my hand.

She arches into me as I circle her nipple with my tongue. The tight bead responds to my caresses, hardening further, and I slip my hand lower toward her waistband.

"Oh, fuck, Reed." Mae's voice threatens to reach upstairs.

"Shh, Lil Bit. We need to keep quiet if we're going to make this work."

She giggles and nods as I slide my hand into her shorts, her eyes fluttering closed.

Dipping my fingers inside her panties, I can feel how ready Mae is for me. Her slit is wet, and I press a finger in.

Mae moans, her hand covering my own as I tease her entrance. Swirling my tongue around the tip of her breast, I flick lightly at her clit, and Mae's legs clamp down around my hand.

"Oh God, Reed. I don't know if I can be quiet."

"Try, Lil Bit. I don't want any more interruptions. I've waited long enough to have you."

Pressing in, I thrust my digit deep, fingering Mae hard and slow. She rocks her hips, rubbing herself against me.

"That's my girl. God, you're so wet."

The couch creaks, the springs screaming with every bit of movement. It's sure to wake up the whole house at this point.

"Come here."

I lift Mae up off the bed and lower her onto the floor. I seize my opportunity and drag Mae's shorts and panties down her legs, revealing her to me.

She's beyond gorgeous. Her curvy little body, the one that's been haunting my mind, is perfection.

Sinking between her legs, I dive in for a taste, dragging my tongue through her seam. She arches up off the floor, biting her hand to stay quiet.

Mae's other hand comes to my head, her nails digging into my scalp, and I probe deeper, pressing my tongue inside her.

"Oh, Reed."

I smile against her, twirling my tongue around her clit. I slide a finger back in, thrusting as I continue the work with my mouth.

Her legs begin to tremble, and I can tell she's close.

"That's so good, Lil Bit. Come for me. I want to feel your little body squeeze down around me."

Mae's legs squeeze around my head as I take her over the edge. Her pussy flutters against my mouth as she comes, and I draw it out until she's gasping.

"Fuck, Reed."

I smirk at her. "Oh, I'm not done with you yet, Lil Bit."

"That stupid nickname. Don't you think I've outgrown it now?" She eyes me as she pushes up onto her elbows, a devilish grin spreading across her lips as I crawl up her body.

"Didn't you know? It stands for a little bit naughty."

I press a hard kiss to her lips, reaching down for my throbbing erection and pulling it free through the zipper of my slacks.

Sliding the tip across her slit, Mae moans against my mouth, and then her head falls back as I circle it around her entrance.

As slowly as I can, I rock my hips forward, sinking into Mae's tight pussy. She groans, wrapping her arms around me.

Once I'm fully inside her, I hold Mae up with one arm as I thrust in and out. My muscles burn as I move, the sting adding to the delicious pressure building in my shaft.

"Oh God, Reed. This *is* so naughty, and I never want you to stop."

Smiling, I nuzzle into her hair, fucking harder. It's been so long since I've enjoyed anyone, let alone someone so young and beautiful.

I could have missed out on this. *A bit of good luck for a change.*

My body dwarfs Mae's small stature as I sheathe myself up to the hilt and rotate my hips. She moans low in my ear, and I can tell she can barely contain the sound.

My adrenaline surges as I enjoy how incredibly risky this is. We could get caught, and Mae is nearly half my age.

Johnny's little sister. Ha, and I thought I'd just end up kissing her.

It's too fucking good, and I want more.

Quickly pulling out and flipping Mae onto her stomach, I pull her hips up and take her from behind. She just bites back a yelp, and I lean forward, wrapping my hand around her mouth.

"Is that good, Lil Bit? Do you like being dominated by your boss?"

Mae whimpers as I thrust in hard, then pull almost all the way out. I slide my hand to her throat, letting her answer.

"Yes. Oh God, yes. I know I shouldn't, but I don't fucking care." She groans as I push in up to the hilt. "I've wanted this forever."

"That's my good girl. Come again for me."

Pummeling into her, I grip Mae's hips and give her everything I've got. She struggles to remain quiet, moaning as another orgasm overtakes her, her pussy squeezing around my shaft.

My pace becomes frantic as I slide in and out of Mae. The feel of her wrapped around my cock is better than anything I could have imagined.

I've wanted her for so long, dreamed of taking this little body and making it mine. I want her to yield beneath me as I take everything she has.

It's all I can take, and the sensation of her clamping down around my shaft once more tips me over the edge.

My release powers through me like a freight train, and I empty my seed deep inside Mae's warm pussy.

Our heaving breaths and Mae's trembling finally still. I pull free, loving how my cum is running down her leg.

"Fucking hell, Reed. I…yeah."

I chuckle. The blissed-out sound of her voice is like music to my ears.

"Let's get back in bed."

Lifting Mae up, I pull the shirt back over her head. After finding a washcloth in the downstairs bathroom, I help her clean up and pull on her panties and shorts. We flop back down on the squeaky mattress, and Mae snuggles under my arm as we fall asleep.

Johnny's little sister. Fuck. Things just got really complicated.

Chapter 9

Mae

A beam of sunlight smacks me right in the eyes as I roll over, and I wince. My body aches, squeaks resounding under me as I try to get more comfortable.

Then memories of the night before come flooding back.

I jerk into a sitting position and look down. My borrowed clothes are a rumpled disaster, and I can feel the tenderness from our *activities* between my legs.

Reed is still asleep beside me, and his clothes are as disheveled as mine. I pat the top of my head, and the bun I threw my hair into last night is a lopsided mess.

As I suppress a giggle, I hear a door upstairs creak open. *My brother!*

Scrambling out of the sofa bed as quickly as I can, I dash for the bathroom, snagging my dress from last night up off the floor as I run.

When I get inside, I examine my reflection. *Yup, I look* great. *Ugh.*

Peeling off Stevie's clothes and vowing to toss them right in the laundry, I turn on the shower and step inside. The cool temperature helps wake me up, and I rinse the evidence of sex down the drain.

As the water heats, I chuckle to myself. I can't believe I actually slept with Reed. I've wanted to for, well, forever, and the fact that it happened in my brother's house, no less, leaves my brain spinning.

I step out, snagging a towel from the rack, then do my best to make myself presentable. When I leave the bathroom, I hurry to the laundry room before seeking out my brother in the kitchen.

Once there, I see Reed chatting and having coffee with Johnny and Stevie. They smile over at me, and Stevie offers a cup of coffee.

"Oh, yes please."

"I'm sure we'll all be needing the caffeine today. It was a late night. But so fun!"

Stevie sounds happy, if tired, and I thank my damn lucky stars that it doesn't look like she or my brother know what happened.

Reed's eyes catch mine for a moment, and we both struggle to hold back a smirk. I have to break eye contact all too quickly because I'm seconds from giggling to myself.

"It was fun. I should have a birthday every weekend." Johnny smiles and sips his coffee.

As Stevie puts some eggs and bacon on, she rolls her eyes. "We could also just have more get-togethers. It doesn't have to be someone's birthday for our friends and family to come hang out."

No one misses how she cocks a brow at Reed, and I smile as I bury my face in my mug.

The food smells divine, and it's just what we all need to ease our hangovers. After scooping up some breakfast on a plate, I sit across the table from Reed next to Johnny and dig in.

"Thank you, Stevie. This is perfect."

"Of course. But I wouldn't turn down some help cleaning up as payment." She raises her brows at me.

I nod and offer a salute. "Aye, aye, captain."

We all laugh, and then I'm staring at Reed again. I can see his eyes flicker to my cleavage as he takes a bite of eggs, and my cheeks burn ever so slightly.

"How about you, Reed? Are you willing to stay and help?" Johnny asks.

"I would, truly. But I need to get back to Henry. Heather will want her house back."

I smile over at him, taking another gulp of lifesaving coffee. "What are you guys up to today? I know Henry has mentioned going to the park at least once a day this week. You could take him. It would be an easy way for him to play and you sit on a bench and relax a little."

Reed grins back but then shakes his head. "Unfortunately, we can't. We have some family we have to visit today. His grandparents. But maybe another time."

My heart squeezes. It's probably an important trip, one that Reed planned, but I still don't like seeing Henry's desires always put on the back burner.

"Well, just be sure to go before it gets too cold."

Reed nods. "I will. Maybe next weekend."

We all finish eating, and when I excuse myself to the bathroom again, I'm surprised to see Reed just outside the door when I come out from swishing some mouthwash.

"Oh, hi. What's up?" I pause in the doorway.

"Up? Oh, just me."

Reed pushes me back into the bathroom, closing and locking the door behind us. I can feel his erection as Reed presses me against the wall.

"Reed, what are you doing?"

His hands roam over my body, hiking up my dress and finding the wetness growing between my legs. My head falls back on a moan.

"I had to get one more taste. Tomorrow seems way too far away."

His hushed words cover my skin in a layer of blossoming arousal that leaves my knees weak. His fingers dip inside my panties, sliding deep as he strokes my sensitive core.

"Keep quiet, Lil Bit. Keep quiet and come for me."

Reed moves his fingers with quick, decisive strokes while applying pressure to my clit with his thumb, melting me into a puddle of bliss in seconds. It's beyond impressive how fast he can work me up to an orgasm.

I whimper against the incredible sensations, wishing I could cry out.

"That's a good girl. You take my orders so well."

I swoon despite myself. Reed's dirty talk is thrilling and goes straight to the heart of my arousal.

He unzips his slacks and pulls his cock out, grabbing my hand and wrapping it around his erection. The velvety skin slides gracefully under my palm as I stroke him.

Reed's pants are still in place, and there's something about the desperate, quick dalliance of this moment that makes it that much hotter.

I work quickly, pleasuring Reed with firm caresses that bring him to the edge in moments.

"That's it. Now finish me, Lil Bit. Let me feel those plump lips around my shaft."

Sinking to my knees, I take him into my mouth, enthusiastically licking his length and sucking him into the back of my throat until Reed comes.

His hips jerk as he empties himself, and I glide my

fingers across my clit, another orgasm washing over me in seconds.

"Goddamn, Mae. You're too fucking perfect."

Standing back up, I smile at Reed, pulling my dress back into place as he tucks himself away.

"I'll leave first. Just wait in here for a minute or two. Okay?"

"Yeah. Go. I'll see you later."

Reed sneaks out of the bathroom, and I sit down on the toilet, waiting to hear him say goodbye to Johnny and Stevie.

When he's left, I slowly exit the bathroom and sneak back to the kitchen to start doing the dishes. It gives me the perfect cover, and as Stevie and my brother return, they just thank me for helping.

Fuck. You need to stop taking risks like that!

I'VE FINISHED THE DISHES, and now the three of us are roaming the house to collect all the empty glasses and cans. As I patrol the living room with Johnny, Reed's plans for Henry today nag at the back of my mind.

"Hey, Johnny. Have you noticed that Reed doesn't spend much free time with Henry?"

My brother laughs. "He doesn't spend much free time with anyone. In fact, he doesn't have much free time."

"Well, yeah. But don't you think that of anyone Reed should be hanging out with his own kid?"

Johnny tosses another empty Solo cup into his garbage bag and then leans back against the couch.

"Yeah, of course. But Reed's been through a lot, and remember, he's navigating parenthood on his own."

Snagging a couple of beer bottles, I slide them into my own bag, straightening to ease my aching back.

"I remember. Reed's wife died."

"It was a terrible car accident, and Reed has never stopped blaming himself for not being with her the day it happened. She was alone with Henry."

My eyes fall to the floor. I can't imagine losing someone so close. And to lose your mom at such a young age.

"It was a little while ago, right?"

Johnny sighs. "It was three years ago, but I'm not kidding when I say it destroyed him. Reed hasn't been the same since then, and it took him years to get where he is now. I was worried he might…it was bad, Mae."

A sting reverberates through my heart, and my eyes well up. "I can't imagine."

"Yeah. I don't want to. Reed went from being an incredibly happy family man to a single father with extreme trauma overnight."

The room hangs in silence for a moment as we both find more garbage and toss it in our bags.

"I don't know if he'll ever really recover from it. I know that's why he throws himself into his work." Johnny nods to himself. "But that's why it's so great he has you now. Your help will allow him to have the support he desperately needs."

"I want to help. I really do, Johnny. But he needs to meet me halfway. His son misses out on so much because Reed is always at work. I just wonder, how long is Henry going to have to pay the price for his guilt?"

Johnny comes over and puts a hand on my shoulder. "Just do your job, Mae. There's a lot going on with Reed, and we can't expect him to change overnight. There's some stuff you don't understand, okay? Just know that if you keep helping and being your awesome self, he'll be able to dig himself out of the ditch that much quicker."

"Okay, okay." I smile, but my eyes fall to the floor. "I'll try."

Chapter 10

Reed

How I've made it through Monday and Tuesday without so much as a kiss from Mae is beyond me. However, it seems work has a way of interfering quite a bit.

I'm still in shock that I actually slept with her. And I didn't lie; it was far from the first time I thought about it.

Johnny's party had been so amazingly relaxing and fun. It's been ages since I allowed myself to have a good time, and after the kids were thoroughly distracted, chatting with my old friend was a special treat.

It would still have been a total win if that had been where the night ended. The fact that I finished it with Mae tangled in my arms, pleasantly worn out after fucking her, is like a gift from God.

Everything about her seems like it was specifically designed to drive me wild. From her long hair to her sumptuous curves to her tiny stature compared to my own.

Mae is completely my dream girl.

And for the first time in a while, I'm really considering just how much I work.

I know it's a lot. Henry and Heather have made that abundantly clear, but Mae has also started to show me how much better I can be at everything if I take the time to step back every once in a while.

Still, work is important, and I chose a job that doesn't have typical nine-to-five hours.

I also pick up my fair share of extra shifts. I don't necessarily need to be at work *quite* as much as I am now.

I just always feel like I have to be here, helping. What if I miss something like I did before? With Clara.

You're missing time with Henry.

I've heard it from everyone at this point, and I just don't know anymore. But something nagging claws at the back of my mind.

Henry is Clara's son in so many ways. He looks just like her.

I sigh. I need to get out of my head because this wallowing isn't helping.

Thankfully, I've got time now to sit down and finish paperwork in my office at the hospital. It's a tedious part of the job, but one that has to be done, and I hate having to take it home with me.

I'm about halfway through the massive stack when I get a page. Looking down, I see it's a call from the ER.

"Looks like I'm going to work."

But as I take a closer look at the message, my heart stops. Henry has been brought to the ER.

Everything around me narrows into tunnel vision. My blood pounds in my ears, and my stomach clenches like I might be sick.

Thoughts race through my head so quickly I can barely

focus, but I gather myself enough to run out of my office and down to the ER as fast as possible.

Images of rushing down these same halls to the ER to find Henry and Clara there surface in my mind. It's too similar, and blinding panic blocks out everything else around me except what's straight ahead.

I run into other doctors, cutting around corners so tight I almost fly face-first into the walls.

The words of that fateful phone call ring in my mind, and my thoughts start to spiral.

What if Henry's been in another car accident? What if he's being rushed to surgery?

What if I'm already too late?

He could be gone already, leaving me alone.

As much as I try to tell myself to stop and take a breath, I know this is a panic attack, like all the others I've had, and I can't stop it. It's already flowing too fast, and my brain can't find its way to a place of calm.

Adrenaline and cortisol are pumping through my veins, clouding my judgment and making my hands shake.

When I reach the ER, I find Mae sitting with Henry. He's perched on a hospital gurney, his skin pale and his eyes red.

I can see he's holding his wrist, and another doctor is there, standing in front of the bed.

I just make out Mae's words to Henry. "Shh, it's okay, Henry. You'll be alright. Shh. You're safe, buddy."

I rush over, pulling up next to the attending doctor and snatching the clipboard out of his hands.

"What happened?!" My voice cuts through the quiet surrounding Mae and Henry, sharp as a scalpel.

Mae's eyes flick up to me, and she squeezes Henry against her. "He's okay. He hurt himself at school."

Pushing closer, I examine my son, finding the site of his

injury in his left arm. I need space, so I move Mae off the gurney and go through the rounds, checking Henry's radius and ulna.

"Dad, wait. I want—"

"Shh, bud. Let me look at it, okay? I need to see how bad it is."

From behind me, I hear Mae's voice cut through the fog hanging around my head.

"He fell off the monkey bars at school. The teacher said he landed on his wrist and knocked the wind out of himself. Henry says his side still hurts a bit, too."

I lift Henry's arms gently, examining his ribs. He hisses as I prod the area.

"You could have broken a rib, Henry. We'll need X-rays, and I want to check his wrist, too. See if he's broken the ulna."

I'm speaking to the doctor behind me like he's a nurse, but I can't bring myself to care right now. Everything is too much. *God, how could I have been absent again?*

Sobs spill out of Henry as I order the necessary tests. I set his arm back down, trying to get him to look at me.

"Hey, look up here, buddy. Take a breath. You need to calm down."

Henry shakes his head, wincing as he causes himself more pain. I try to hold him still.

"Bud, you can't move like that. You're going to hurt yourself."

He cries harder, and I sigh. Mae steps up from behind me and sits next to Henry again.

"Hey, it's alright. Shh, I know, buddy. It's scary. But I promise you'll be okay. You're in a safe place, and your daddy is here to help."

She strokes his hair, letting him lean into her.

"I know you didn't mean to fall. Nothing is your fault.

It was just an accident, okay? That happens. I've fallen down a ton, trust me."

Henry looks up at Mae, sniffling and wiping under his eyes. Mae dries more tears with her sleeve.

"Really?" His big tear-filled eyes look up at Mae.

"Oh, yeah. I've fallen off my bike. I even sprained an ankle when I was chasing after a dog. And right before I started nannying for you, I got a concussion!"

Henry giggles shakily.

Mae smiles at him, offering another hug. "You're so lucky to have a daddy who's a great doctor. He'll fix you up. Right?"

Her eyes meet mine in an expectant way, and I'm stuck standing there like a deer in the headlights.

She knew exactly the right thing to say to him, and I just make him cry harder. *What the fuck is wrong with me?*

Why doesn't Henry see how much I care?

"Of course, bud. You'll be fine."

Henry glances at me, offering a slight nod. I gently rest my hand on his other shoulder, patting softly.

"You're okay. Everything will be all right."

I'm not sure if I'm talking to him or myself.

Henry calms, and the attending doctor, Dr. Holmes, lets me know he'll ensure all the proper tests are run.

"Just stay with your boy. I've got it handled, alright?"

I just nod.

Sitting behind Henry on the bed, I glance at Mae. She smiles tenderly, her eyes that horrible blend of pity and concern.

If it weren't for her being here, Henry would still be crying, still upset. And I don't know why that bothers me so much.

Chapter 11

Mae

The unexpected trip to the hospital plays out as well as I thought it might. Reed is a disaster worrying over Henry, and his go-to response of full doctor mode doesn't sit well with his son.

Eventually, Reed seems to calm down a bit, and so does Henry. They x-ray his arm and ribs, which reveals no broken bones, just bruising.

We all breathe a sigh of relief, and Henry apologizes again for falling. The poor guy feels like he ruined everything.

"You're okay, buddy. Don't worry. No one is mad. We're just glad you're okay."

I smooth my hand down Henry's uninjured arm as I rock slightly. No matter how old you get, when you're hurt, all you really want is a snuggle.

Usually from your parents, but I'll do in a pinch.

"Shh. I know you must be tired. You can doze off on my shoulder. We'll get you home soon."

After a few moments, Reed comes back in, saying Henry is released to go home. I nod down to where he's sleeping on me, and Reed offers a tight smile.

"He fell asleep?"

"Yeah. It's been a long day for him. I'll help you get him to the car."

Reed nods. "Thank you. I've actually been relieved for the rest of the evening. Dr. Holmes is covering."

"Oh, that's great." I smile. It truly is good that Reed can come home and be with Henry.

"Would you…would you please come back with us? If Henry wakes, I'm sure he'll want to see you there."

Reed's brows pinch together as he asks, and I can sense the trepidation lingering there. He doesn't seem to enjoy asking for my help like this.

I noticed how dejected he looked when Henry wanted me with him. It's exactly what I've been warning Reed about.

"Yeah, of course. I'll follow you there."

WE RETURN HOME to Reed's, having loaded up Henry in the car. As I drove behind Reed on the way here, I couldn't help but dwell on all the things I've been trying to tell him.

His son needs him around more often. It's a simple fact, and if it doesn't happen soon, Henry's going to continue putting his trust in other people.

When I pull up, I see Reed lifting Henry out of the car. His sleepy eyes hover open for a split second, and then he lays his head back down on Reed's shoulder.

I open the door for them, and Reed walks in and down

the hall to the living room. He sets Henry on the couch, who stirs, and then Reed goes into the kitchen.

"Hey, buddy. You're home."

Henry rubs his eyes as he looks around. "Why am I downstairs? I just want to go to bed."

"I'm not sure. Let me ask your dad."

I step away, patting Henry's knee, and find Reed in the kitchen.

"Hey, Henry is really tired. Should we just take him up to bed?"

Reed is pouring some children's Tylenol into a measuring cup. "I want him to take a little bit of medicine before we do. It'll help him sleep."

"Oh, okay."

I follow Reed back out to Henry, and he sits on the couch near his son, who's already started to fall back asleep.

"Hey, bud. Can you take this for me, please? Your medicine from the hospital will wear off soon, so you need more."

"I don't want to. Go away." Henry swats at his father's hands.

Sighing, I step forward, sitting on Henry's other side.

"Hey, come on. Just take a bit of medicine, and then we'll bring you right up to bed. Okay?"

"It's gross." Henry frowns.

"It's not gross. It's sweet. Look." Reed dips the tip of his finger in the cup and licks off the sticky clear liquid.

Henry eyes him. "Hmph. No. I just want to sleep."

"Buddy, please." Reed's shoulders sag.

"Henry—" I take the cup from Reed "—open up for me, okay? You don't even have to do the work."

After a moment, he does, and I pour the Tylenol down the hatch. Henry swallows with a grimace.

Reed reaches under his son, lifting him up and heading for his room. "Alright. Let's get you upstairs."

I follow them up and watch from the door as Reed turns on the nightlights in Henry's room and lays him down in bed.

"I want Mae to tuck me in," Henry grumbles with closed eyes.

"I can't, bud. I need to go. I'll see you later, okay? You were very brave, Henry."

"But, Mae."

"No, buts, mister. Get your rest."

I close the door, leaving a crack open so Reed can see, and then go back downstairs. I know Reed needs to be the one doing this, even if neither of them realizes it.

Sitting at the kitchen table, I wait for Reed to finish putting Henry down. I'd like to talk to him about this business with Henry before I head home.

I hear the door close, and Reed comes down the stairs, looking more tired than Henry did. He walks around the island and reaches for a bottle of wine from the rack above the fridge.

"I don't know about you, but I need this."

With a chuckle, I nod, and Reed pours us two glasses of red. It smells delicious, and I have to imagine it's much more expensive than the stuff I buy.

Reed sits down across from me, taking a sip and sighing. I drink some, and the flavor is better than anything I've had.

"This is so good."

Reed looks over with a smile. "Thanks. It's something Italian. I've had it forever, but tonight felt like as good a time as any to crack it open."

Silence fills the kitchen as I wait for Reed to say something. He has to know he needs to address what happened today.

Finally, after two more sips, Reed sighs and breaks the tension.

"I'm sorry about today. If I snapped at you."

I cock a brow at him.

"Okay, I know I snapped. I'm sorry. I was…fuck, Mae, I was terrified. I had no idea what happened when that page came through, and my mind conjured up every worst-case scenario."

I know he was upset, but hearing Reed confess that he was genuinely scared sends a pang through my heart.

"I'm sorry, Reed. If I would've had a moment, I would have texted sooner, but I drove straight from the school to the hospital."

"You did the right thing. You got him there. It was just…it made me think of things I've tried really hard to forget."

The accident.

"I don't exactly know what happened. Was this similar—"

Reed shakes his head. "No, it was nothing like the accident. But my mind didn't care about that, I guess. I just saw Henry was in the ER, and I went into a complete panic. Every day, I worry that something might happen to him when I'm not around. That I'll miss it again."

Reaching across the table to take Reed's hand, I try to show nothing but empathy on my face. "You can't be everywhere at once. You're not a superhero, and no one expects you to be. Accidents do happen, and that can be awful, but today it was alright. He just fell. Kids fall. Try to remember that."

"I wish I could in the moment. But when the adrenaline spikes, I can't think straight, and all I can do is remember running into the ER, only to be too late. I want to forget that memory so badly."

My heart aches for Reed. I can see the pain he's in clear as day on his face, and I want nothing more than to help in any way I can.

Reed's not a bad person. He's trying so hard, and if I could just get him out of his own head, even for a few minutes.

"Can I help you with that?"

His eyes fly up to meet mine, his brows shooting to his hairline. But then Reed's features soften, and his stare bores into me.

His grip on my fingers tightens, and I see a little bit of the Reed from Johnny's party.

"And how exactly are you going to do that, Lil Bit?"

I roll my eyes briefly. That nickname is turning me pink from head to toe.

But then my stare goes to the table between us, and I take a shuddering deep breath.

"You shouldn't have to feel like this. I can take your mind off it. Do you want that?"

Reed lifts my chin, my eyes finding his, and he licks his lips before speaking. "I want that. I want you. I've been thinking about it all week."

He stands from his chair, taking my hand and pulling me up. Reed's fingers squeeze my sides as he presses my body up against his.

"Please, Mae. Help me forget."

My heart pounds in my ears as Reed's desperate, needy tone ripples down my spine. He's never struck me as the type to beg, but right now, that's all I can see—a man begging me to make him feel something besides fear.

"Anything you want, Reed. Take it."

His lips crash into mine as he pulls me even closer. I moan against his mouth as his tongue explores and tastes.

Reed's hands roam over my body, his pace frantic. As he pinches one of my nipples through my shirt, his other hand snakes through my hair, gripping it tight.

Fire races through my veins as Reed takes control of my body. I'm quickly turned around, and he bends me over the table, grabbing my ass and squeezing.

The jeans I'm wearing are thin, but not thin enough. I want to feel Reed's skin on mine. I go for my button, but he pushes my hands aside, doing it himself.

With deft fingers, Reed unfastens my pants and pushes them down my legs. I step out, and then his hands tease my center over my panties.

I'm already wet for him, arousal pooling deep in my core as Reed's hands toy with me. His hips meet my ass, and I can feel his erection through the thin fabric of his scrubs.

He sinks onto his knees behind me, pulling my underwear aside as he licks up my seam. I bite back a moan as his tongue pleasures my aching sex, my hand flying to his head as I lift my knee onto the table.

Reed's fingers join the teasing, and he slips two inside me, pumping as he flicks my clit with his tongue. I'm seconds from coming already.

As he sucks me between his lips and moans, the vibrations rumbling through me, Reed finds my G-spot.

I orgasm hard, barely able to contain the cry that wants to burst free.

He pulls back, lightly slapping my ass. "So good, Lil Bit. Goddamn, your pussy is divine."

I adore his dirty talk and spin around, pulling him up and switching places with him. Now, on my knees, I look up into his gorgeous hazel eyes.

"My turn."

The corner of Reed's mouth lifts in a cocky grin, and I bite my lip. Silver streaks are just starting to form at Reed's temples, and I clench.

He's even hotter than he was when I was a teenager, and I'm obsessed. He's always been the reason I was attracted to older guys.

I've always fantasized about Reed.

I reach up for his scrubs, untying the knot at his stomach and letting the blue fabric slide down his legs. His erection is straining beneath his boxer briefs, and I free him through the hole.

"Yes. God, I've been thinking about you on your knees, taking my cock. Swallow me down, Lil Bit."

I happily oblige, wrapping my lips around the head of his shaft and sucking. I watch Reed's eyes flutter closed, his head falling back on a low moan.

Taking him in my mouth, I lower down all the way to the base, barely able to handle his impressive size. Reed's hands go to my hair as he grips and rocks his hips, dragging himself back and forth across my tongue.

Reed's pace increases as he thrusts himself in and out, fucking my mouth. I struggle to breathe as he pummels me, but I'm all too happy to show him how badly I want to make him feel good.

I grip the base of his erection, pulling back to take a breath. Reed's leg twitches as I use my tongue to tease the sensitive spot on the underside of his shaft.

Rolling my tongue across the tip, I toy with his opening as I massage his balls. He grunts above me as the pleasure builds, and then I'm suddenly pulled to my feet and pressed back to the table.

"Don't move."

Reed quickly stalks across the room to his wallet and

pulls out a condom. *Oh, that's a good idea. Probably should have done that the last time.*

He slides the protection over his erection and then meets my eyes.

"Give me that tight pussy, Lil Bit."

Reed grips my legs, lifting them over his shoulder as he has me cross them at the ankles. His cock swiftly dives deep inside me, and he rotates his hips.

"Oh, fuck, Reed. Yes, please."

He pulls out almost completely and thrusts back in as deep as he can, and I'm barreling toward another orgasm. Reed's fingers find my clit as he pumps into me, and it's enough to send me flying over the edge, never wanting to come back down.

I do everything I can to stay quiet, and Reed's other hand comes to my mouth, quieting my moans. It shouldn't be as hot as it is, but I don't care.

Reed's actions are a frenzy of desperate energy as he completely loses himself to the passion. Faster and harder, he fucks deep as his fingers bring me to shattering new heights.

Another release overwhelms me as Reed barrels into me, his pace never faltering.

And then his hand is in my hair, pulling me forward as he pushes in as deeply as possible. I groan, the near pain magnifying the way it feels to have him claim me so entirely.

"Say you're mine."

Reed thrusts in hard, his movements slowing, and the force of it pushes me back on the table. The grip on my hair tenses, and he pulls my forehead to his.

"Say it."

Another hard shove of his hips, and I'm whimpering as even more tension builds.

"I'm yours. I'm all yours."

"That's my good girl."

His thumb slides across my chin and pulls my mouth open. He pushes his finger inside, and I suck.

"Such a tiny, little thing, and you're all mine."

Reed's pace starts back up again, and I'm practically flooding with wetness as he takes me.

He's right, too. Reed towers over me, his large six-two frame dominating me. I love how it feels to have him crowd me and boss me around like this.

If possible, Reed drives into me harder, and I can tell he's close. Reed tenses as the sensations overwhelm us both, thickening even further inside me.

It sends another orgasm racing through me, and as I clamp down around him, he joins me, coming as his hips jerk.

The release drags out, and it's several moments before Reed finally stills. As he slides himself free, Reed turns, reaching for a tissue off the counter and pulling the condom off.

He quickly throws it in the trash and then turns back toward me. His lopsided grin makes me giggle.

"Well, fuck." He smirks with a laugh, rubbing the back of his neck. "We should probably shower or something."

I stand up, a little wobbly, and wrap my arms around his waist. "That sounds like an excellent idea."

Chapter 12

Reed

After the incredible sex, and I mean fucking incredible, I escort Mae to the downstairs bathroom, and we shower. The warm water feels great, and I'm so much more relaxed than I was before.

Having Mae here all the time would certainly make my days more enjoyable.

We get dressed and then head back to the kitchen for some water. Sitting across the table from her again, I smile, but Mae looks nervous.

"What's wrong?"

"I know this is a weird time, but I'm not sure there will ever be a good one."

Well, that's ominous. I raise my brows. "A good time for what?"

"I want to talk with you about something that might be a little uncomfortable. Is that alright?"

I swallow hard, my gaze going to my hands, and I sit back in my chair. Is this the relationship talk?

It feels a little soon for us to be going down that road, but I understand why she might want to define things.

"Okay."

"I'm worried about Henry."

Oh. Never mind, then. Shit, I thought she was going to ask if we were dating. That's a relief.

"It was just a little fall. He'll be okay. I know exactly what he needs to heal."

Mae shakes her head. "No, not that. I'm worried about how disconnected you guys seems to be. He's always so disappointed when you don't make it home when you say you will, but worse, he's coming to expect it. When something like today happens, Henry isn't sure he can rely on you to be there."

The emotional high I had been enjoying after the fantastic sex completely falls flat. I clench my fists as I cross my arms, huffing out a sharp breath.

Looks like I've been blindsided again, and I really don't like where this is headed.

"I was there today. I got to Henry in seconds."

"Well, yes, because it was the hospital, but what about when he has games or is going through something challenging at home? Henry has started seeking out other people to reassure him when dealing with big emotions. That's why he didn't want me to leave when you examined him."

My blood rushes through my ears. I know Henry had been more responsive to Mae's consoling, and I wasn't looking for a reminder.

"So it's my fault that my own son would rather have you around?"

"That's not what I said."

"It's what it sounded like to me." I push up from my chair, walking to the sink.

I do *not* want to have this conversation. Things had actually started to feel better. Why is she even bringing this up?

Mae has no idea what I've been through or how hard I work. And I'm just supposed to sit here and listen to her call me a bad father?

"Reed." Mae follows me, her voice pleading. "It's just that he doesn't spend much time with you. You're constantly picking up double shifts and staying late at the hospital. Henry feels like he always comes second to your job, and that's rough for a kid."

I turn toward the sink, washing some of the plates Henry had used earlier this morning and trying to ignore Mae's words.

"Reed, you can't put this off. You need to be more present for him, for you both. You have time to get your relationship back on track, but not long. Trust me, I've worked with kids for years and studied a lot to help them as best I can. Everything points to Henry building up more and more walls to isolate himself from disappointment. That could really affect him as he gets older."

Tossing the small plastic plate into the sink, I spin around, facing Mae.

"Studied? You're a *nanny*. I hired you to be a nanny. Not to diagnose my son with some made-up issue because I have to work or pretend like you're his mother."

Mae steps back, her hands fisted and resting on her hips. "That's not what I was trying to do."

She walks across the room before turning back to me. "I care about Henry. Quite a bit, actually. And I know *both* of you would be happier if you prioritized your son more often. You obviously knew you needed help when you hired a nanny, so let me help."

Sweat dots my brow, and I can't look at those pleading

chocolate-colored eyes. I face the sink again, turning on the water and pretending to do anything other than just watch it run.

"It's hard to see a situation objectively when you're in the middle of it. I know you guys have been through a lot, so I understand why it might be hard for you."

I don't turn, closing my eyes tight as water rushes from the faucet right down the drain.

"You understand? Like hell, you do. I don't appreciate being told how to raise my child."

"Reed, that's not—"

I spin around again. Mae has no clue what she's talking about. She's not a parent, and she's never lost a spouse.

"You just don't get it. I don't have a normal nine-to-five job. I'm not clocking in at some bank or calling it a night after waiting tables. I'm saving lives. I'm making a difference in the world. And it actually matters if I miss a shift. The hospital can't just find a substitute like I'm a fucking kindergarten teacher."

Mae's mouth falls open, and she gasps softly. "So teachers don't make a difference? I guess I must be pretty far down the ladder, then, since I just take care of your kid and your house all day."

She reaches for her jacket and purse hanging on a chair near the island, then hurries toward the door.

"You know what, Reed?" Mae turns and glares at me. "If you actually cared about making a difference, you'd be there for your son. Because right now, he barely notices whether you're here or not."

I feel like I've been punched in the gut, complete with the nausea and pain ricocheting through my stomach.

"Get out."

"Oh, trust me, Dr. Finnigan, I'm gone."

Mae jerks open the front door and lets it slam behind

her as she leaves. The sound is too loud, rattling the entire house, and I worry Henry will wake up and find out what happened.

But as I stand in the silence of the kitchen, nothing changes. Henry never comes out of his room, and all I can think is that I have no idea if he's a heavy sleeper or not.

I know nothing about my own child.

Chapter 13

Mae

The door to my apartment slams behind me as I enter. It's barely an excuse for a studio, and at the moment, I hate it.

Which feels a lot worse when I'm already so fucking mad that I had a good scream in the car. Some primal therapy, anyone?

I fling myself onto my tiny bed, burying my face in my pillow and giving the yell-it-out method another go, but I'm still just as pissed at Reed.

"How could he stand there and say that? I work so hard for him and his son. Just because I'm not some fancy doctor. Ahh!"

My phone buzzes on the nightstand near my head, and I pick it up to check the notification. It's a Face Time call from my parents.

"Really? What time is it?"

I look over to see it's not especially late and then remember they're in a different time zone. *Ugh. Fuck. I don't want to talk right now.*

Putting on my best fake smile, I swipe to answer.

"Hi, guys."

"Mae!" My mother's voice trills through my phone, and I turn the volume down.

Based on the background, my parents are outside on the beach, and there's a loud whooshing sound I'm guessing is the wind.

"Baby, we miss you so much! How's the new job going? I hope no more devil children!"

Mom has way more energy than usual, and my guess is that she's already half in the bag. Dad chuckles behind her, and I stifle a groan as I watch them living it up in the Cook Islands.

"Nope, no devil children." *Just a devil boss.* "How's vacation?"

Mom and Dad start talking over each other about how beautiful it is and how good the food has been. They're clearly having the time of their lives, and I'm more than a little envious.

"So, dear, how's the financial planning going? Did Johnny give you good news about starting school soon?"

Does two years count as good news? "Yeah. He was great. I can practically smell the books now."

"Oh, honey, that's wonderful!"

Yeah, I know I shouldn't be lying to my parents, but the idea of bursting their beach bum bubble makes my heart sink.

"Yup. I can't wait for you guys to be back home, though. I miss you. And you missed Johnny's party."

It was probably a good thing they weren't there. They'd have caught on to the Reed and me situation way easier than Johnny.

Or maybe they could have prevented me from

nannying for the jerk, and I wouldn't have to be so angry right now.

"Oh, we know, babe." Dad takes the phone. "But these were the cheapest tickets, and we really wanted to make this anniversary something special."

"I know. I'm glad you did, but hey, I have to get going. Long day tomorrow. Talk to you soon?"

"Of course, babe. We love you so much."

I smile, rolling my eyes. "I love you guys, too. Have fun!"

Waving for the video, I end the call and toss my phone down next to me on the bed. *Ugh, guess it's time to find a new job.*

I HAD CRASHED SHORTLY after the video chat, and when I wake up, Thursday morning greets me with sunbeams rudely glaring in my face.

"Ugh. Fine. I'm up, okay."

I stretch my arms over my head and decide to check for new jobs now. Get it out of the way and all that.

As I pull my laptop onto my legs, I bring up the agency website, my cursor hesitating over the search bar.

I don't want to keep nannying. That was the entire point of me taking this position, but I also know I'm never going to find something that pays as well.

Nannying can pay so much better than retail or food service, and those are the only other types of jobs I'm qualified for at this point. I specialize in kids, but I can't be a teacher yet.

"Still need that degree."

When I finally open up the page for job postings in my

area, I see my previous family is still looking for a new nanny to replace me.

"Ha! Good luck. Your kids are terrible. Make sure you add 'put last nanny in the hospital' to your notes."

I chuckle at my own joke, but then I find myself actually considering giving them a call. They paid pretty well, and I'll have sparse competition for that particular position.

"No. No demon kids. You're not that desperate." I stare at the family's name on my screen. "Yet."

Ringing cuts through my hunt for a new position, and I see that Johnny is calling me.

"Dude, you have terrible timing. I'm trying to find a new job."

"I heard. I just got off the phone with Reed. What the hell happened?"

I sigh, switching the phone to the other ear as I scroll. "I don't want to talk about it. I just need to focus on finding a new position, not on how rude Reed was."

"Mae, what did—"

But then I hear shuffling, and Stevie's voice replaces Johnny's.

"Hey, hon. Sorry about the job. But I know just how to take your mind off it. Throw on some old clothes and I'll swing by. Okay?"

That's definitely not what I was expecting, and I look down at the clothes I fell asleep in last night.

"I'm not busy. Why not?"

"Great. See you in fifteen."

Sure enough, Stevie is over to my place in about fifteen minutes, which gives me just enough time to put on a worn out pair of leggings and a paint-stained T-shirt before brushing my teeth.

"Hey, girl. You ready to give me a hand? Nothing like a little physical labor to clear your head."

I laugh, slipping on some old sneakers. "Sure. Can we stop for coffee on the way? I'm going to need caffeine if I'm going to be any help."

"Of course! Let's go."

After a quick stop for some java to go, Stevie drives me to a house she's staging across town and lets us in with her key. The enormous new home still smells like paint and cleaning supplies.

"Ew. It smells terrible in here."

"Ah, you get used to it. I also light candles before the open house. Okay—" Stevie claps her hands as she surveys the room "—there's some furniture all shoved into the living room, and we need to move it into the proper place."

"Alright, can do."

The house is clearly going to cost a fortune. There are tall ceilings that put ten-footers to shame and a massive chandelier in the entry hall.

A staircase just past the front door spirals up to the second and third floors, and the open space it creates is lit with an impressive array of windows.

White is still the only paint color on the walls, which I absolutely hate, but there's also tons of gorgeous natural wood trim and accents that warm the house up.

After asking Stevie about it, I learn it's a five-bedroom, four-bathroom home with a finished basement and expansive backyard, which I sneak a glance at through the glass patio door.

The place is stunning and exactly the type of home I want to live in if I ever manage to get my shit together. Being jobless, yet again, blares through my mind like a siren, and I frown.

When Stevie finds me in the kitchen looking out the back door, I quickly school my expression into a smile.

"Let's start with the living room and dining room, and we'll see what kind of time we have after that."

Stevie gestures down the hall, a cheery grin lighting up her face.

I nod and follow her into the living room, where all the furniture to stage has been stored.

We carry the heavy-ass dining table to the other room after laying out a beautiful rug that reminds me of a mosaic, then haul in all eight of the chairs.

Stevie even has me set the table, using a lovely set of white dishes from a box in the corner, along with matching silverware. Adding a bouquet of fake flowers and hanging a few paintings completes the look.

"So, now that you've had a moment to clear your head, what *did* happen? I'm not Johnny, so you can trust me to believe you."

I sarcastically chuckle, straightening the fork of a nearby place setting.

"I tried to talk to Reed about Henry. About how much he works and how it's affecting his son. He was less than receptive."

Sighing heavily, I walk back to the living room to help Stevie move the couch up against the far wall.

"What did Reed say?"

"That he hired me to be a nanny, not Henry's mother or psychologist."

There's a matching stuffed ottoman, and I push it in front of the sofa. The luxurious green velvet is incredibly impractical but makes the room look grand and expensive.

"Ouch. Do you think you overstepped?" Stevie furrows her brow at me, concern shining out through her eyes.

"Maybe. I tried to be as tactful about it as possible, but

Reed was immediately defensive and said several hurtful things. I should have just listened to Johnny and stayed out of it."

"Here." Stevie gestures to the cushion next to her as she takes a seat. "Sit down."

I do, offering a sad smile as she wraps an arm around my shoulder.

"Tell me what exactly you said."

"Okay, well, I'm paraphrasing a little, but essentially, I said that Henry is coming to expect disappointment from Reed because he consistently prioritizes work. He's looking for other people to ease his hurts when he's upset, and if this continues, there could be some real damage done to their relationship and Henry's development."

Stevie nods and meets my eyes head-on. "You did the right thing. I can tell how much you care just listening to you, and if that's what you tried to get Reed to understand, and he responded by being defensive, that's on him. Not you."

"Thanks. I really needed to hear that."

"Always glad to help my favorite almost-sister-in-law."

I laugh, and we squeeze each other in a hug.

"Back to work!"

Stevie pulls me up off the couch, and we start right back up, moving all the little side tables and even more rugs to their final spot in the house.

There are way more paintings than I would have thought could fit on the walls, and several lamps that we scatter throughout the two rooms to provide additional light.

What surprises me the most is they've programmed an Alexa for each of the rooms and put color-changing lights in every socket.

"You guys seriously go all out for these stagings."

Stevie laughs. "Well, the Realtors want it to look homey and inviting. We need to show the potential buyers just how amazing living in this house could be. And with high price tag houses like this one, it's not way off base to assume the buyers will want or already have this type of stuff in their homes."

"You are clearly very good at your job because this place is still mostly empty, and I want to live here."

"Ha ha. Why, thank you." Stevie does a little bow, and I toss one of the small pillows at her.

As we finish hanging the pictures in the living room and adding a bunch of small decorations, like a wooden tray on the ottoman with a small vase and a stack of books on the end table, I've almost completely forgotten about how mad I was.

"Alright. We made really good time. I should invite you with me on the regular. Let's hit the kitchen next. We can put up the—"

The chime of the doorbell cuts through Stevie's instructions.

"You expecting the real estate agent or something?"

She looks toward the hall. "No. Not at all. I should have the house to myself for the entire day. Hmm."

We head for the front door, and I can't help but smile proudly at everything we've accomplished. As I walk past, I also eye the numerous mirrors we hung up.

They're good for bouncing the light and making the space look bigger.

I remember Stevie's words, and I'm still considering adding a few mirrors to my studio to see if it actually works.

"Think that mirror trick can make my apartment feel less like a matchbox?"

But as I walk up behind Stevie and she opens the front door, it's not a Realtor coming to speak with her.

It's Reed.

Chapter 14

Reed

This morning has been a disaster. Sitting on the chair next to Henry on the couch, I can't help but dwell on the fact that, for the first time in I can't remember how long, I'm the one that had to call off work.

The hospital took it fine, the on-call doctor saying she could find someone to cover the shift in no time.

I'm just so used to it being the other way around. I'm the one that pulls extra shifts and goes in on my days off to help.

Being on the receiving end of a favor feels strange and unwelcome, but as Clara would say, "You're terrible at asking for help."

I sigh. Henry seems happy enough.

He was thrilled to hear I'd be spending the day with him. After the shock wore off, of course.

And I am blatantly refusing to examine that reaction any closer. After Mae stormed off, and I was forced to call in with no babysitter in sight, I've had nothing but time to think.

I can't think too hard about Henry's reaction, though. I don't want to consider how it might back up her ridiculous claims, and frankly, I'm still too pissed.

"Dad, can I have more milk, please?"

Henry doesn't even look over from his show to ask, just holding up his empty cup.

"Sure thing, bud."

I go to the fridge for more unsweetened almond milk and shake my head as I look at Henry propped up with pillows on the sofa.

He's not in too rough of shape, but the kid definitely has some bumps and bruises that benefit from rest and ice.

An image of Mae in the hospital bed abruptly surfaces in my mind, and I remember her comment about my prescribed care.

I shrug the thoughts away, pouring myself another cup of coffee before delivering Henry's beverage.

"Here you go, kiddo."

"Thanks, Dad." He looks over at me for a moment. "It's weird you're not at work."

"Yes, it is. But you need a few days to rest before going back to school."

"Okay."

His attention returns to the TV, and after watching a few episodes of his favorites, I can tell he's getting bored.

I have no idea what to do with him, however. Everything I can think of won't be good for someone who's injured and needs to take it easy. And we can't just keep watching TV.

Even I'm getting sick of it.

Depositing my mug in the sink, I lean over the counter,

putting my head in my hands. *This is so stupid. I have no idea how to entertain my own kid.*

Sighing, I look over at him. Henry's little head pokes up, just visible from this side of the couch.

When he was a toddler, Clara would hide behind it and pop up when he searched for her. They'd be laughing and giggling like crazy, the game entertaining young Henry for several minutes.

A horrid sting sets up shop behind my ribs, and it's almost like I can see her crouching there. Her blond hair would be pulled back in a ponytail, and she would be dressed in clothes that favor comfort.

She spent her entire day with him when he was small. Even when we started Henry in preschool, she was always the one to drop him off and pick him up.

Tears threaten to break free as the memories tear through me. Clara would have made today special, thinking of something particularly fun to do that didn't require much physical activity.

"What would your mom have done?" I whisper.

But overwhelming sadness blocks out any creative idea I may have had, and I come up with nothing. *At least I know I have to feed him.*

"Henry, you want something to eat?"

"Oh, yeah. Can I have a bowl of Cap'n Crunch?"

"Of course, buddy."

I whip up my morning specialty, a bowl of cereal with probably too much milk, and Henry eats it in no time. We switch up the entertainment to a movie, and about halfway through, he falls asleep.

As I try and fail to follow the plot of this odd anime movie Henry chose, there's a knock at the door.

Moving quickly and quietly, I hurry to the door to see who it is. I'm not expecting anyone.

Swinging the door open, I see Johnny on my front porch. When he turns around from his pacing to face me, I'm met with one of the deepest scowls I've ever seen him wear.

"Johnny, what's up?"

I step out onto the porch, closing the door behind me. I don't want to wake up Henry.

That's when dread crawls over my skin. *Holy shit. Did Johnny find out about Mae and me?*

Anger burns across his face, and it's just the type of look a brother might wear if someone defiled his sister. *Fuck, I'm going to lose my best friend, and I'm not even seeing her anymore.*

Images of punches thrown and the shattering of our tight bond bubble up in my head.

"You know, Reed, you have a lot of nerve." Johnny crosses the porch toward me, jabbing his finger in my chest.

Oh God, here it comes.

"Why the fuck did you fire Mae? She's an excellent nanny. Kids are, like, her whole life."

My shoulders sag with relief, but then the tension returns as Johnny continues to glare at me.

"Seriously? You're here because of that? Mae having her big brother fight her battles for her?"

Another stiff jab pushes into my pec. "Fuck off, Reed. Mae doesn't know I'm here, and she wouldn't like it, either, so don't go shooting your mouth off about it."

"That's quite enough, Johnny. Who I choose to watch my son isn't your business."

Johnny shakes his head as he frowns. "That's bullshit, and you know it. We're talking about Mae, so it is my business why you kicked her to the curb like yesterday's trash."

I cross my arms over my chest, glaring right back at

him. "Fine. You want to know? Mae overstepped, spouting nonsense about disconnection from my son and telling me I work too much."

"First of all—" Johnny cocks his head at me, looking down his nose in my direction "—you do work too much. You have to know that by now. Second, can't you see she was just trying to help you? Mae's extremely devoted to child care. She even wants to become a teacher, so she's made it a point to learn as much as she can about development before even starting college."

"Well, I didn't hire her for that, and I made that abundantly clear."

"You're acting like a selfish prick. You just can't hear that maybe there's something you could do to help your obviously strained relationship with Henry."

"Back off, Johnny."

I eye him hard, but the asshole just keeps pushing.

"No. You're punishing Mae because she's the first one to finally have the nerve to tell you that you're avoiding anything and everything to do with Henry. You throw yourself into work so you don't have to deal with the accident, and it's leaving you completely disengaged with your son."

Johnny shakes his head, meeting my glare this time with the pity I don't want.

"Henry looks just like Clara. And you can barely look your kid in the eyes. I know it's hard, but this—" he gestures inside the house "—isn't how to deal with it. I should have said something, too. But I was too chickenshit before Mae was courageous enough to speak up and risk angering you. You won't get this time back. He's only going to be this young once."

He walks up to me, putting a hand on my shoulder, and I clench my jaw.

"Henry deserves a father who's around, showing him how much he loves him all the time. Losing your wife, Henry's mom, was a terrible fucking accident, and there was no way to be prepared for that. But it did happen."

My anger bleeds into the grief I've been holding on to for three years. Clara was the better person of the two of us, and I'm utterly lost without her.

I think back to the little kid asleep on the couch inside, and the pain that roars through my heart makes it hard to breathe.

"You have to fill two roles, be both parents now, and there's nothing easy about that." Johnny offers a sorrowful smile. "But you're not alone. We're all here to help. You just have to ask."

"I've never been particularly good at that."

"I'm well aware, dude. But this is it. The time is now. You need to do this. Take a step back from the go-go-go pace you've set for yourself and find your son again. He's not gone. You didn't lose him, yet. But you could."

Crying in front of anyone isn't one of my favorite pastimes and doing it in front of Johnny feels particularly shitty. I've always been the first to take on life's big milestones in our friendship.

I was the first to pick a major in college, the first to start seriously dating someone, the first to propose and get married, the first to have a kid, and the first to suffer such a significant loss.

And I guess there really is a first time for everything, because I'm also now the first one to start tearing up on the goddamn porch.

All I can do is nod.

"You need to make this up to Mae. Firing her was a dick move that you did only because you were feeling defensive."

"Are you telling me to hire your sister again or you won't be my best friend?" I crack a tiny smile at him.

"Damn straight, asshat."

"Dad!"

Henry's voice cuts through the silence of the porch, and I sniffle, wiping my face.

"I need to go check on him."

Johnny nods, stepping to the porch stairs. "I get it. You've got some stuff to think about. But I'll be expecting the good news from Mae. You hear me?"

"I do. We'll talk later."

"Alright. Go be a dad. That's the whole point, after all."

He jogs to his car, and I head back inside the house.

Johnny's not wrong. I have a lot to think about, and apparently, some lunch to make.

Chapter 15

Mae

"Reed?"

"Mae!"

Before I have time to process, Henry is hobbling over to me with a large iced coffee in his hands. He holds it out to me with a massive smile on his face.

"This is for you! It's a double espresso caramel macchi…macchi…macchi something."

I can't help but smile at him, and I take the drink. "It's macchiato. My favorite."

Reed still stands at the door, another coffee in a drink holder, and I eye him.

"How'd you figure out my favorite drink?"

He nods his head, a guilty expression raising his eyebrows. "I asked your brother."

"I see." I set the caramel treasure down on the coffee table, glad there's a coaster to absorb the condensation already dripping from the cup.

"I assume that's how you figured out I was here."

"Yup." Reed chews on his lip before meeting my eyes again. "Can we talk?"

I hesitate a bit too long for Stevie's liking, and she steps up behind me, putting her hands on my shoulders.

"Of course, she can. I'll hang out with Henry. You want to fluff pillows, buddy?"

Henry eyes her like she's asked him to watch paint dry.

"It means you get to punch them."

"Oh! Heck, yeah."

Stevie laughs, rolling her eyes for Reed and me before escorting the ten-year-old to the bedrooms.

I sigh. "Let's chat outside."

"Alright."

Reed steps back onto the porch, and I follow him out, closing the door behind us.

As Reed walks up to the railing and leans against it, he mumbles to himself.

"Having a lot of important chats on porches today."

"What?" I cock an eyebrow.

"Never mind."

Tension on the porch is so thick I can almost feel it surrounding us, but then Reed clears his throat and looks up at me.

"So, what did you want to talk about?"

He rakes a hand through his hair. "I'm sorry."

I smile sarcastically. "Hmm? What was that?"

Reed releases a hard breath. "I'm sorry. I overreacted. I know you were only trying to help. I just…I wasn't prepared for parenting advice or hearing about my fractured relationship with Henry."

"Thank you. I honestly didn't know if you had it in you to apologize."

He looks briefly wounded but then nods. "That's fair. I

said a lot of stuff I shouldn't, so I understand if you're done with me, but…"

Reed's eyes fall to the wooden deck beneath our feet as he steps on a particularly squeaky board. I can see he's struggling with the right thing to say, but I am *not* helping him through this.

If Reed wants to make this better, he's going to have to start with a bit of groveling.

"I want you to come back."

Our eyes meet once more, and I hold his stare.

"Please come work for me again. Henry adores you. I need you. And if I'm going to get better at this balance thing, I need some help. I'll also double your salary."

My mouth falls open as my heartbeat soars. Did he just say *double* my salary? Did he just admit he needs help?

Spinning visions of bills and savings accounts fly through my brain like Dorothy's house in the twister. Double my salary would half the time it'll take until I can start working toward my teaching degree.

I'd be able to start school in just a year, and I do love Henry. He's the best kid I've worked with.

But I can't let myself be charmed by an amazing salary and Reed's distractingly good looks.

"I have stipulations."

"Of course. Hit me."

"No more yelling at me when I'm just trying to help."

"Done."

"And no more last-minute double shifts. It's too hard on Henry and me when you change plans so late in the game. Plus, it makes getting him to sleep a disaster. Your son can hold quite the grudge."

Reed sucks in a deep breath, his eyes finding the middle distance between us. But then he slowly nods.

"That's going to be hard, but okay. I'll try my best to

give you both a better heads-up when plans do change and avoid staying too late if I can."

It's not exactly a yes, but it's something. *And what about the sex?*

"What would this mean in terms of the *thing* between us?"

My heart swells in a way I'd rather it didn't. I know we only slept together twice, but I've been crushing on Reed since I was sixteen.

I've had feelings for him for a long time, and adding the sex just made them more complicated.

I know I want to keep going there with him. Even now, it's like my body is on fire just being around him.

But if that's going to mess with my financial situation, I can pull it together.

"I'm not sure. I wasn't exactly prepared for that to happen once, let alone twice. But..." Reed shakes his head. "I just don't know."

I swallow that down, a part of me sinking into the floor boards, but that's not the important thing right now.

At least, that's what I'm telling myself.

"Alright. But I need some time to think about this. I won't lie and say I don't desperately need the money, but this is a big commitment."

"I understand that. Take some time." He shrugs. "Try to get back to me before Monday if that's possible, though. Finding child care at the last second is certainly a challenge."

I can't help but smile. It's good for Reed to have some alone time with Henry, and if he realizes how hard it can be to entertain a kid, that's even better.

"I can do that. I'll send Henry out."

Reed nods, turning toward the stairs and gripping the handrail. Abruptly, he spins around.

"Actually, Henry has a standing monthly sleepover at his aunt Heather's place tomorrow night. Would you like to join me for dinner? We can chat some more, and you can fill me in on all your remaining stipulations."

I stare at Reed's hopeful face, considering. He's been remarkably open, and Reed's even made sure to interject a bit of self-deprecating humor.

Maybe I should give him another chance?

"Okay. You can pick me up."

"Great."

I smile tightly and go back inside the house. When I find Stevie and Henry, they're having a ball, tossing pillows onto the bed from across the room.

"Alright, bud. Your dad's waiting."

Henry plops the pillow he's holding back on the bed, coming to give me a big hug.

"Will I see you on Monday?"

"I'm not sure, buddy. We'll see."

"Dad's been really good today, and he promised to take me for ice cream after this, so don't stay mad."

"Did your dad say I was mad?"

"Yeah, he said that he 'pissed you off really good.'"

"Ha!" Stevie and I both chuckle.

"Okay, kiddo. I'll keep that in mind. Now, go on!"

Henry squeezes me again and then takes off for the door. When it slams behind the boy, I'm left wondering what the hell I should do.

"Well, that was something. Bringing you with me today has certainly upped the drama factor of my typical day."

"I'll say."

I sit on the bed, quickly remembering that it's been staged and the provided mattress is hard as a rock.

"I don't usually have this much excitement following me around, either. Unless, of course, you count nearly being killed by those twins." I sigh. "What am I supposed to do about this?"

Stevie sits beside me. "What did Reed say?"

"That he'll pay me double. That he's willing to work on being around more. Hell, Reed even apologized."

Her eyes go wide, and I laugh with a nod.

"I know! But that doesn't mean Reed will suddenly start changing. And he was beyond rude the other day. It's just complicated."

"It's a good sign, though. It's hard for anyone to apologize, and I can imagine it's especially so for Reed. He's never asked for Johnny's help with anything, even though Reed has definitely needed it."

I stare at the generic off-white carpet covering the entire upper floor. There's a faint pattern created on it, and I can practically hear the salesperson's voice saying, "It'll hide the dirt better."

Stevie puts a hand on my shoulder, and I glance up at her with a forced smile. "He came and apologized. Actually knew he did something wrong. It's a step in the right direction. You're right, too, though. He won't change overnight, but it looks like you're having a positive effect."

"I hear you." I stand up. "I'm going to go think for a bit, if that's alright."

"Of course. Get out of here."

"Thanks, Stevie. Maybe you're right. Maybe our fight was just the push Reed needed."

"Here's hoping, babe. Here's hoping."

Chapter 16

Reed

"Alright, bud. Got all your stuff?"

I look back at Henry through the rearview mirror. Heather is waiting on the front porch, and I'm actually going to be on time for dinner.

"Yup. Will you tell Mae I said 'hi'?"

He unbuckles and leans over to grab his little duffle packed with games and a couple sets of clothes I managed to sneak in.

"I will. I'm sure Mae will be glad to hear it."

I step out of the car and help Henry out. Walking him to the house, I smile at Heather, who's promptly smooshed into a huge hug.

"Hi, Henry. Why don't you head inside and say hi to Uncle Mark? You can help him in the kitchen."

"Okay!" Henry quickly darts to me and gives me a hug. "Bye, Dad! Love you!"

And then he's off like a bullet. I can't help but smile.

"So, Reed, how've you been?" Heather folds her arms

over her chest. "I haven't gotten nearly as many last-minute babysitting requests lately."

I roll my eyes, nodding. "No. I've got some help. I hired a nanny. It's actually my best friend's sister."

Heather pegs me with her patented "well, damn" face, and I stare at the sidewalk as I rub the back of my neck.

"Yeah. You'd like her. Mae gave me quite the talking to. My ass is still sore."

"Ha! She give it better than me?" She smirks.

"A bit. Well, Mae just didn't hold back at all. She really let me have it, from the hours to me leaving Henry hanging."

"Hmm." Heather nods, her smile only getting bigger. "Sounds like a pretty cool chick. I think I would like her. What about Henry? Does he get along with Mae?"

"Get along? He adores her. I have my work cut out for me between you two." I think about how Mae makes every moment with Henry look effortless and fun. "Clara would have liked her, too."

My voice is quiet, but I know Heather hears me when a tiny gasp escapes her. When I look up, tears brim in her eyes.

"You never…I'm really glad, Reed. Truly. I hope this is the change you both need."

Heather's voice doesn't hide her emotions, and I can feel that familiar burn in my chest when I think of Clara. It will always hurt, but today, there's gratitude in there, too.

Mae isn't totally on board with coming back to work, however. I still need to meet with her tonight, and hopefully that goes well.

"I'm meeting her tonight, actually, to talk things over. I was a total ass and have a lot to make up for. It's just a lot of change, and you know how much I *love* that."

Sarcasm rings through my words, and Heather knowingly raises her brows at me.

"I do. But try to have an open mind. This could be just what you both need to find a better balance."

"I'll do my best. Thanks for watching Henry. He loves these sleepovers."

"Of course. I'll see you tomorrow morning." She starts for the door. "Hopefully, with good news."

MAE'S HOME is in a very different part of town. As I park in front of the large building, I can tell they've crammed as many studio apartments into the space as possible.

It's a gray concrete-like brick, and the yard, if you can even call it that, is a slim patch of browning grass that surrounds the property. A thin, chain-link fence surrounds it, and the gate squeaks terribly as I pass through.

I buzz Mae's number and wait for her response.

"Hey. I'll be right down."

I wait a few minutes on the sidewalk that runs up to the door before Mae arrives, looking like something out of my wildest, most wicked fantasies.

I thought she looked impressive at Johnny's party, but I can't find the words for how she's dressed tonight. When I told Mae to dress for a high-end restaurant, she clearly understood the assignment.

Her dress is black again, but this one isn't nearly as sweet as the other one. It's form-fitting and slinky in all the best ways.

With a large slit up the leg, the black fabric cinches in around Mae's waist. The top looks like it can barely contain her ample cleavage, and it ties around her neck and back, leaving much of her smooth alabaster skin visible.

As she comes to stand next to me, we look like the perfect pair, heading out to a fancy dinner at a five-star restaurant.

"You look incredible." I smile, my gaze raking down Mae's body.

I remember that tight little body well, and it's achingly difficult to keep my thoughts from wandering into dangerous territory.

"Thank you." Mae nods at my suit. "You look pretty good yourself. It's a nice change from the scrubs. I mean, I haven't seen you in a suit since…"

"Johnny's party."

A delightful pink creeps up Mae's cheeks as we both remember precisely what happened the last time Mae looked good enough to eat. *Fuck, Johnny would be really pissed at me for this.*

I know I've already dug that grave, however.

We've already slept together twice. A few more times shouldn't make it worse.

"Yeah." Her eyes fall to the ground. "Should we go?"

"Yes." I hold out my arm. "Right this way."

Mae chuckles, taking my arm as I lead her to the car and help her in. Coming around to the driver's side, I fire up the engine, and we're off across town in a flash.

We're both fairly quiet throughout the drive, and I can't keep myself from staring at the swell of Mae's breasts, where they rise and fall as she breathes.

"So, where are we going? You just said it's a fancy restaurant." Mae looks over, her tiny purse clutched between her hands.

"It's called Le Ciel. It's this gorgeous rooftop restaurant at the top of the Nuit Luxueuse Hotel."

I've been there a few times, mostly with Clara, and it's still strange even to me that I want to bring Mae there.

But maybe that's the whole point? I'm trying to bridge the gap between the past and my future.

Hopefully.

"That sounds incredible. I hope I look alright." Mae smoothes her hand down her dress.

"You look perfect."

She briefly smiles at me, but then her gaze falls back to the dashboard. Tension has been the mood since I picked Mae up, and I'm more than ready to move on to the more relaxed and fun part of the evening.

Arriving at the hotel and taking the elevator up to Le Ciel, Mae and I are taken to the private table I requested near one of the enormous windows.

The wide span of glass that encircles the restaurant offers a breathtaking view of the city at night, and the twinkling lights below are like stars.

"This place *is* gorgeous. I can't believe I'm eating here. Oh, God. What am I even going to order?"

I pull out Mae's chair as she speaks. She sits down and immediately goes for the glass of water waiting on the table.

Trying to stifle a laugh, I take my seat across from her and retrieve my napkin, spreading it across my legs.

"Order whatever sounds good. We can do an appetizer and then some steak if you're a meat lover. The lobster is excellent if you enjoy seafood."

"Lobster? I can't say I've had much of that in my life. Maybe once while on a date that wasn't nearly as elegant as this one."

I quirk a brow. "So it is a date, then?"

Mae blushes, and it goes straight to my cock. "Well, yeah. This isn't exactly a business meeting, now, is it?"

"Actually, I've had a few dinners with colleagues here. It's a favorite after a grueling medical conference. And we're talking about business, aren't we?"

Nodding, Mae takes another sip of water. "Yes. We are."

"So. Do you have an answer?"

"I do." Mae pauses, and my heart beats so hard that I worry she can hear it. "I'll come back. I love being with Henry, and if you think you can hold up your end of the bargain, I'd like to be your nanny."

A sigh of relief rushes out, and I smile. "Oh, thank God. I was so nervous."

"I'd say I'm sorry for making you wait, but I'm not. My last little punishment for your rudeness."

I narrow my eyes at Mae, playfully glaring. "Fair enough. But I think I've taken enough licks at this point."

"You sure about that?" Her eyes darken, a lustful haze coloring the chocolatey brown, and then Mae laughs, the sound singing through my nerves. "Okay. Sure. Lobster it is."

I hadn't seriously considered our little tryst, being too preoccupied with ensuring Mae would return as my nanny. Still, I knew we'd fall back into each other if she agreed.

Mae is too sublime for me to ignore, not after all these years of being curious or my very real memories of just how spectacular she tastes.

"Good evening, Monsieur. Mademoiselle. I'm Claude, and I will be your server tonight. I've requested fresh bread for the table. May I get you anything else to start off your meal?"

"Yes. Could we please have an order of the black truffle and parmesan baguette bites and the oysters?"

"*Oui*, Monsieur. Excellent choices. Will you be having wine this evening?"

I look to Mae, and she nods. "Sure. Yes. Um, red, please. I'm not a big fan of white."

With a smirk, I nod at the server. "A bottle of the 2015 La Landonne, please."

"Very well, Monsieur. I will send the sommelier to the table and return for your entrée selections. Bon appetite."

The meal is fantastic as always, and throughout dinner, Mae and I relax, chatting about hilarious ER stories and some of the worst offenses she's seen from the kids she's nannied for.

"It was everywhere. I couldn't get to all of it by the time their parents got home, and man, was it fun explaining to them why there was Marshmallow Fluff on the ceiling."

"Wow. I feel incredibly lucky that Henry hasn't done anything like that. Though there were definitely times when I'd come home to find his mom and him up to something ridiculous. I remember a time they turned the upstairs sink blue."

"With what?"

"Food coloring. It also got all over Henry's hands. Science experiment or something."

Mae smiles, sipping her wine and closing her eyes as she enjoys the taste. She's been doing it subconsciously every time she drinks, and it's adorable.

"Mmm, that makes sense. Henry does seem to love science. He's got a fair coming up, if I recall."

"Yeah, I think I saw the form in his backpack."

The conversation is flowing easily. The wine probably helps with that, but I can also relax around Mae, like her presence alone is comforting.

It occurs to me that I've talked about Clara a little, and I'm surprised the sting deep in my chest doesn't prick quite as hard. It almost feels nice, reminiscing about Clara's humor and carefree spirit.

"I think he asked if you'd help with his project. Do you think you can manage that?"

Mae smirks at me, resting her chin in her hand as she leans on the table. The soft light of the restaurant makes her skin glow, and I find myself staring again.

"I'll try. I'm definitely no expert. Unless his project is about sutures and setting bones."

"Unfortunately, I think he's picked something to do with electricity. So you're out of luck, Reed."

She giggles lightly, taking another bite of her lobster. Even the way she wraps her lips around the fork is sensual, and I'm straining behind my fly.

"Well, shit. Here's hoping Henry doesn't electrocute me. Unless, of course, it works like the Energizer Bunny and I can keep going and going."

Mae's head falls back as she laughs, the slender column of her neck exposed, and my eyes trail down to her breasts.

"Oh, God. I can just imagine you all hopped-up like that damn pink rabbit. Too much, dude."

"Oh, I don't know." I drink my wine, relishing the dark flavors as they swirl on my tongue. "I can imagine one place having that kind of stamina might be nice. I am forty, after all."

The gentle flush painting Mae's cheeks from the wine deepens.

"You don't have anything to be worried about, Dr. Finnigan. Your *stamina* is just fine."

A lust-fueled silence hangs over the table, creating a quiet bubble where it's just us, and the rest of the world falls away.

"This restaurant really is amazing. The entire hotel. It'd be nice to stay here."

My heart thunders as I meet Mae's beautiful eyes. I've been risky and bold before, but nothing like booking a room before I even knew if my date would be into it.

I pull out the room key and slide it toward Mae.

"I actually did get a room for this evening. Since Henry is staying with Heather, I thought maybe we'd make an evening out of it."

"That was a bit presumptuous of you, wasn't it?" Mae raises her eyebrows at me.

"A little. Okay, a lot. But I just had a feeling…and I didn't want to miss the opportunity."

"Well, it looks like this time—" Mae lifts her glass, swirling the wine around and breathing deep "—it's big risk, big reward."

Chapter 17

Mae

I'm a brazen hussy enjoying a moment worthy of Lifetime romance movies, and I couldn't care less. I absolutely want to go to the hotel room with Reed, even if I know it's a terrible idea.

From the moment I decided to work for him again, I've had two things on my mind—getting Henry and Reed into a true father-son rhythm and enjoying every naughty second I could with Reed.

I know the relationship question was still very up in the air when we last spoke, and I know that it's the last thing I should be thinking about.

But even though I fought against it, being around Reed makes my walls come tumbling down.

I mean, I didn't wear this dress for nothing. In the back of my mind, I hoped that Reed would make a move, and Le Ciel is the perfect place to do it.

With a smile, I reach across the table and take the room key. The card fits perfectly in the front slot of my wallet, and I take another sip of the savory wine.

"Alright, then."

Reed's eyes sparkle with delicious mischief, and I can't wait to see what trouble we can get into now that we'll have the entire space to ourselves. No kids, no brothers, and no interruptions.

"So, does that mean we can take some of this food downstairs? Every bite has been incredibly good, and I don't want to leave behind a single crumb."

A chuckle makes Reed's smile stretch wider, and goddamn, is he gorgeous when he laughs. It's the best thing I've seen him wear, and the suit is impeccable.

"Of course, I'm sure they'll give us something to take it in. Do you think there's room for dessert?'

He leans forward in his chair, his elbows resting on the table as he eyes me. I mimic the posture, allowing my cleavage to press against the tight fabric of my dress.

Reed's eyes dip lower, and I run my fingers across the thin strap. "I do love sweets. What did you have in mind?"

Reaching across the table, Reed's fingers intertwine with mine, and his gaze flicks between my eyes and the thin fabric keeping me hidden.

"They have a delicious chocolate mousse. It has marshmallow meringue and toasted almonds."

I lean onto my hand, my face moving closer to his, and smile. "Perfect."

The single dessert arrives with two spoons meant for sharing, and Reed offers the first bite to me. The decadent flavors are rich and creamy, the smoky marshmallow taste reminding me of smores but so much better.

"You've got a little chocolate on your lip." Reed gestures to my mouth.

I lick my lips slowly, egging on the building tension that

has my core burning in the best way. With a smile, I playfully lean forward, gesturing to my lips.

"Did I get it?"

Reed's hand goes to my face, his thumb dragging across my bottom lip. His gaze pierces me, pinning me in place, pulling me in, and leaving my breath short.

"Looks like. Is it good?"

He's still holding my chin, and I nod. "Amazing. But I don't think I'm quite satisfied."

"Still hungry for something sweet?" Reed's eyes flick to my mouth.

"No. I think I want something," I whisper, leaning to his ear, "hot. Take off all your clothes hot."

The server arrives with our boxes just in time to see Reed quickly help me out of my chair.

"The food was excellent, Claude. Would you charge it to room 1436, please?"

The server nods. "Of course, Monsieur. So glad you enjoyed your meal. We look forward to seeing you again."

With that, we practically sprint through the restaurant for the guest elevators, and I'm only slightly sad we had to leave that fantastic dessert on the table.

As we hop into the lift, we're blissfully alone in the gleaming metal carriage, and Reed pulls me to his chest, crashing his lips to mine. His tongue darts between my lips, exploring and tasting.

His hands roam over my body, finding the slit in my skirt and reaching around to take a handful of my ass. It's then Reed notices this dress has some very wicked undergarment requirements.

"You're not wearing anything under here, Lil Bit."

Reed's fingers ghost over my slit, and I stifle a whimper.

"You are a naughty thing, aren't you?"

Answering him is an exercise in futility because Reed's

fingers continue their assault as his mouth finds my throat, pressing kisses and gentle bites into my flesh.

"I couldn't. Everything showed, even a thong."

A low growl rumbles through him as Reed's lips move down the front of my chest, finding my nipple through the fabric.

"Well, remind me to thank the designer."

My head falls back as a moan bubbles up, and Reed presses me to the elevator wall.

The cool metal is a sharp contrast to the inferno raging through my blood, and goose bumps ripple across my arms.

It's a swirling array of barely-there touches between my legs and Reed's teeth lightly biting my nipple when the elevator dings.

He scoops me up in his arms, carrying me through the doors as soon as they open and down the hall. Even in just the vestibule, the hotel has decorated way more than necessary, and massive pots of flowers sit to either side of a large arch that leads to the rooms.

Reed carries me to where the hall divides, and we follow the sign for rooms 1400 to 1440.

As he finds 1436, Reed nods down to my purse.

"Care to open things up? My hands are occupied."

I smile, biting my lip, and pull the room key out of my wallet. The whirring sound of the lock opening seems to take forever, but then we're finally inside.

My eyes open wide when I take in our surroundings. This is clearly a five-star hotel, and they've spared no expense in making this suite feel like you're in the lap of luxury.

The main area is a living room that puts my studio apartment to shame. At the far wall, there's a massive balcony patio already set up with a bucket of champagne on ice and a trail of red rose petals.

"How is this here?"

I study Reed's expression in wonder as he sets me down, and I head straight for the balcony.

"I called room service when you went to powder your nose."

"I believe the exact phrase I used was 'freshen up' because I was trying to speak politely in the ritzy restaurant."

Reed laughs. I turn to the glass double doors, opening them wide and letting the evening breeze flood into the room.

The stars are shining as the city glows across the horizon. It's absolutely breathtaking, and I know I'll never forget this experience.

And we haven't even fucked yet.

Reed's arms circle around my waist, and he nuzzles into my neck, pushing my hair off my shoulder.

"Quite the view, indeed."

"I know. I've never seen the city like this." I grin, watching the twinkling lights.

"I was talking about you."

Heat flares through my cheeks, and Reed spins me around, kissing me. I'm already buzzed from the wine, and the feel of his silky lips claiming me is doubly intoxicating.

Stepping back, Reed takes my hand and walks me inside.

"Come on, you haven't even seen the best part."

I follow him through the living area to a set of large French doors, admiring how it almost feels like we've traveled to Paris. The colors, the decor, it all speaks to that charming vintage feel of the city's earliest years.

Opening the double doors, I gasp as I see the massive

expanse of bedroom and adjoining bathroom. The bed is beyond huge, with cream-colored linens and fluffy pillows piled high against the ornate wooden headboard.

There are more rose petals and a tray with chocolate-covered strawberries. I'm also impressed by the sweeping sheer fabric canopy that hovers over the bed, heightening that sense of plush, soft extravagance.

Turning to the right, I see another set of doors, but these ones are open and reveal a massive bath built right into the floor and taking up the whole room. It's already filled with steaming water, and the gentle hum of the jets sound as they create inviting bubbles.

There's also an airy glass and stone shower in the corner and another door tucked into the back, which must go to the actual toilet.

"So, Lil Bit, what would you like to enjoy first? The bed or the bath? I should also mention the jets are adjustable, and there's a handheld sprayer."

My brows shoot to my hairline. This is way too incredible and way too nice for plain old me.

"Oh, God. I don't know. It all looks so magnificent."

"Well, I do have a thought."

I wrap my arms around Reed's neck, grinning like a fool.

"I want to see that curvy body of yours wet and glistening." Reed's hand slips under my dress again, and I moan.

My eyes flutter closed as he smoothes over my skin with a feather-light touch. "Bath it is, then."

"Perfect. Though it does feel like part of you is wet already."

Heat flares through my cheeks, but I love it. I never want this night to end.

"Help me out of this dress?"

"Oh, fuck yes."

Reed and I work quickly to free me from the tight fabric while stripping him down to nothing as well. When we're gloriously naked, Reed lifts me up once more, this time wrapping my legs around his waist where my slit rubs across his shaft.

As we kiss, he walks us to the tub, the frantic caresses desperate and needy. Stepping down into the water, I sigh as the hot bath washes over my skin.

Some type of fragrance or incense fills the room, making it smell like a dreamy evening in Paris. Notes of rose and spice bloom through my senses.

The jets massage my muscles as Reed rests me on a seat, allowing me a few moments to enjoy them as he rains kisses and nibbles across my neck. But we're both too revved up to enjoy them for long, and Reed grabs a golden tan sponge from the ledge, squeezing water down my hair and chest.

I'm soaked from head to toe and grateful for the warm air of the bathroom. Reed showers himself similarly before blowing across my nipples, making the already erect flesh that much harder.

The abrupt chill compared to the warm water around me creates a delicious swirl of sensations. Then Reed's hands are around my waist, hoisting me up onto the ledge of the bath and spreading my legs.

He plunges his tongue between my folds, circling my clit, and I fall back onto my elbows. I'm on the brink of orgasm in seconds before Reed pulls back, licking up my thigh.

"Goddamn, Lil Bit. Your fucking taste. I can't get enough of it."

My heart swells, and then he stands straight, making eye contact with me as he strokes his erection. Watching him pleasure himself is wonderfully naughty, and I bite my lip as his grip moves up and down his hard cock.

The head glistens, and I'm practically salivating for a taste of my own. But Reed dives back between my legs, his fingers joining his tongue as he works me right up to the edge.

I know he's still stroking his length as he tastes me, and the thought is enough to send even more wetness flooding through my core.

"Fuck, Reed. Please. Please make me come."

His fingers thrust hard as he sucks my clit between his lips. I slide to my back, grabbing his slick hair and squeezing.

"Mmm."

The vibration of his hum buzzes against my sensitive skin, and I cry out.

"Yes! Oh, please, yes!"

Reed sucks hard until his mouth breaks contact, and I whimper, desperate for more. He blows across my pussy, that chilly sensation so intense against the heat welling up inside me.

"Come for me, Lil Bit. I want you trembling against my tongue."

He finds my clit again, flicking and stroking it with the tip of his tongue before his fingers find the magic spot at the top of my walls, and his "come here" motion sends me spiraling.

My orgasm crashes down around me like a wave, and I'm drowning in the ecstasy of it all.

As I finally come up for air, Reed smiles down at me, pulling me up and to the tub's edge. He presents his glorious shaft inches from my lips.

"Your turn, Lil Bit."

Chapter 18

Reed

Mae slides me between her lips, taking me all the way up to the hilt. It's bliss, and I rock my hips as she starts sucking, moving her head back and forth.

Her tongue slides against my shaft as she works my length from head to base, breathing hard. I fist my hands in her hair, fucking faster until Mae pulls back.

"Such a good girl, taking my cock so well."

She smiles up at me, swirling her tongue around the head before gliding it down my shaft and teasing the underside. I buck as she pays particular attention to the sensitive ridge along the head, sweeping her tongue across the dripping precum at the tip.

Burning need courses through my veins, and Mae sits up straighter, taking my dick in her grip as she slowly licks every inch of my erection. The slow, precise movements as she strokes her hand up and down make my brain scramble, and I'm dying for release.

The teasing licks at the tip start up again as Mae grips

my cock, finding my balls with her other hand and massaging gently.

Even better, a rhythm builds as she strokes and takes me deep into her throat, testing her limits. Her hands swivel around me as Mae moves them up and down, sucking on the head before sliding me completely inside her mouth.

"Fucking hell, Mae."

The encouragement goads her further, and Mae licks and tugs gently on my sack as she strokes my dick. It's nearly painful but right on the edge, making my passion boil all the hotter.

She glides her lips back and forth across my length, then pats them with the head. The playful slaps are thrilling, and my climax is poised in my shaft, begging to shoot free.

Sounds of her lapping at me fill the room as I bask in Mae's expert abilities, her tongue and mouth taking me to a whole new level of hungry desire.

Gripping her hair, I pump slowly as she swallows me down. The way she takes me is like nothing else, and I know I'm pushing her to the limits.

She doesn't seem to mind in the slightest, continuing to give me the best damn blow job of my life. As I pull back, dragging across Mae's tongue, my dick glistens from her work, and she licks it up, and rubs her lips up and down my shaft.

As Mae takes every inch of me again, she looks up, meeting my eyes. The fire and passion burning behind them are palpable, and I smooth my hand down her cheek as she takes my erection down her throat.

It's magnificent, but I'm ready for so much more.

"I need your pussy."

I pull her forward and into the bath, then scoop her

legs around my waist as she lays back against the ledge. My cock slides to her entrance, wet and ready for me, and I push in.

"Oh, Reed!"

Her legs clamp around me as I sheathe myself as deep as possible, thrusting in and out, nearly mindless with lust. Mae's tight pussy squeezes as I fuck, and I slide my thumb to her clit, rubbing with just enough pressure.

Marveling at how her breasts bounce with each pump of my hips, I grab a handful, pinching her nipple.

Water sloshes as I continue to plunge into her, our maddening rhythm bringing both of us so close to release. It's like our bodies were made for each other, and I sink deep, circling my cock inside her to hit every delicious inch.

I pull her up and out of the water before turning her around, placing her hands on the ledge for support, and taking her from behind. The swell of her curvy ass glows in the soft golden light, and I smack one of her cheeks.

"All fucking mine."

Mae leans over the edge, and I lift one of her legs, driving myself inside her hard. Her moans and cries echo in the large bathroom, and the freedom of getting away with her makes the experience that much better.

Her flexibility is a dream, and I love how her body completely opens itself to me. This gorgeous young vixen is all mine, and I've wanted her this way for so long.

I'm well her senior, and I know that's technically a *thing*, but goddamn, at this moment, it's so incredibly hot. Working this sweet girl to madness over and over again as she stretches around my cock.

I don't hold back, fucking hard and fast. Finding Mae's slit with my fingers, I flick her clit again and she orgasms.

"Reed! Oh God, yes!"

The shackles I'd put around myself the other times we had sex are gone, and I fuck with abandon, relishing the way Mae has given everything she has to me.

She's not only let me take my fill of her, but she also wants it as much as I do. I can feel her clench around me, her core begging me to fill her up.

Snaking my hand through her hair, I wrap the long brown locks around my fist, pulling Mae's head back. She arches, and the little water droplets coating her skin glitter like gems.

"Don't stop, Reed. God, please take me."

Pulling her up, I hold her against my chest as I pump slowly. Mae moans low and long, and I turn her face to mine over her shoulder.

Kissing her hard, I slowly let her return to the ledge, my lips trailing down her skin until I can no longer reach her. Directing her leg back onto the marble, I grip her hips, anchoring myself as my thrusts speed up.

"Do you like that, Lil Bit?"

"Oh, fuck yes." She rocks back against me, always hungry for more.

"Is this the best you've ever had?" I buck into her hard, jostling her on the ledge.

"Yes!" Mae's ass slaps against me, and I lay down another smack, gripping her. "It's all you, Reed!"

Her pussy squeezes, right on the edge of another orgasm, and I'm barreling toward my own release. Slipping free, I continue to fuck Mae with my fingers.

"That's so good, Lil Bit. Come again for me."

"Reed…I…oh, fuck."

She comes once more, and the sensation of her walls clamping down around my fingers, fluttering and weeping with arousal, is enough to drive me over the edge. I adore how her whole body surrenders to the pleasure.

My sweet, naughty Lil Bit.

I stroke my rock-hard cock and quickly follow behind, grunting low as I rain my release across her slit. The sight is wonderfully filthy, and my orgasm drags on until I've coated Mae's lips in my cum.

Ragged breaths blend with the sound of the jets as we come down from the incredible high. I pull Mae in for a kiss before guiding her onto my lap in the bath.

The steamy water, kept warm by the tub's impressive controls, sloshes over our skin. Mae rests her head on my chest as we relax.

There's no hurry to go anywhere or quickly get dressed, and I'm so fucking glad I booked this room. However, I should have put some condoms in the bathroom instead of just in the nightstand.

"That was incredible. You…" Mae looks up at me. "This was perfect."

I smile. "It was. And we're in no rush. Relax for as long as you want."

She snuggles in. "I think I will, but I'll admit, that bed looks mighty appealing."

Laughing, I grab the sponge and some soap, lathering up her body and getting Mae cleaned up.

Once we're done, I carry Mae to the bed, slipping in alongside her. Rolling onto my back, Mae wiggles under my arm and promptly falls asleep, her sweet face happy even as she dreams.

There's a budding warmth that ignites me from within, but this one I can't attribute to lust. It's something else that I haven't felt in three years, and suddenly, my heart is hammering behind my chest again.

I took Clara here. Not to this room, but we were here. And now…

A prickling unease fights for control over the happiness

I've found with Mae. She's not my wife, and she's not Henry's mother.

Should I even be feeling this way about someone else?

It's odd, and my anxiety peaks. I feel as though I'm navigating stormy seas on a rowboat without a map.

I want to think that Clara would be happy for me. That she'd want me to get out of this terrible rut and find love again, but I just don't know.

Would she feel betrayed? Would she disapprove of me dating someone after her death?

Dating. Uh-huh, that's what you're doing.

I sigh to myself. I'm very aware that Mae and I aren't dating in the traditional sense, but I also can't deny that I'm having the time of my life with her.

I don't want to be alone forever, and Henry adores her.

That burn behind my chest picks up as I think about Mae with my son. It's an optimistic hope, making me feel like a kid wishing for his favorite toy on Christmas.

I want that life, that happiness. I want it so badly.

Images of Johnny's shocked face float up to the surface of my mind. There'd be no way to avoid telling him if Mae and I were in a proper relationship.

That's a scary enough thought to nearly have me leaving the bed. *God, she can't tell him. Not now.*

Johnny would *not* take it well, and I have absolutely zero intention of letting it slip that I'm banging his sister until we've had the "relationship talk," if we even do.

Could we do that?

There's still a pang of nagging guilt in the back of my mind when I imagine dating Mae or even marrying her someday. But I can't be expected to stay alone forever, right?

Mae rolls over in the bed, and with my arm free, I get up and start pacing around the room. This mental back-

and-forth with myself is annoying, and I should be sleeping.

Maybe Johnny wouldn't lose his shit if we both told him.

I'm still thinking hard as I step onto the wraparound balcony from the bedroom's patio door. The cool night air tickles across my skin, making me shiver.

I can't stay out here for long, but for a few moments, the crisp breeze and stillness of the city calm my frantic mind.

"We could tell him together. It would be great to have my best friend and girlfriend already comfortable with each other."

The wind shifts, chilling me more than I like, and I step back inside, returning to the bed and lying down with Mae.

"Maybe. Anything's possible, right?"

She doesn't answer, of course, being asleep and all. Still, as I finally drift off, I can't help but wonder if a happy life with Mae and Henry could actually be possible.

Chapter 19

Mae

I wake up that morning with Reed in the bed next to me, and I love the feeling. I'm pleasantly sore, and I feel like we're right back where we started, hopefully with an even better outlook.

I love Henry so much, and I want him to have the best relationship possible with his dad. I want Reed to work toward making sure that happens.

My semiconscious musing is interrupted, however, when Reed's hand slides up my leg beneath the covers.

"Good morning." I look back over my shoulder with a smile.

"Good morning, indeed. Care to make it even better?"

I roll to face him, pushing him onto his back as I trail kisses down from his mouth to his collarbone. Gripping his erection, I move on top of him, hovering just above the head.

"Just a second, Lil Bit."

Reed reaches into the nightstand and pulls out a

condom. I nod, and watching his hand roll down his cock is alluring.

When we've got more time, I'm definitely interested in watching him stroke himself until he gets off.

He finishes putting the protection on, and I take his erection again.

Rubbing it across my slit, I warm things up for myself, and Reed moans low in my ear, his hands roaming over my curves.

It doesn't take long for my body to crave Reed, and I lower myself onto his cock, rocking my hips back and forth as I take control for once.

Reed's eyes pinch shut as the sensation overwhelms him, and I plant my hands on his chest to ride his dick. This position drives Reed especially deep, and when he's bottomed out inside me, I circle my hips, loving the way he rubs against every sensitive spot.

His hands move up to my breasts, taking them both and squeezing. My head falls back on a moan, and I arch back, grinding his erection deeper.

"That's it. Ride my cock, Lil Bit."

As I move to start my rhythm once more, Reed pumps his hips quickly, fucking me as he holds my hips.

The frenzied pace has me barreling toward an orgasm, and I bite my lip. I can just imagine how it looks having Reed thrust into me like this as my ass hovers above him.

Filthy images flash through my mind of our amazing time together, and it thrills me. I lower down to kiss him, and Reed roughly pulls my head to him.

The animalistic way he kisses me, takes me, is so good. I lose myself to the pleasure, my orgasm roaring through me. Reed pulls back and smiles.

"Such a good girl. Turn around."

I do, spinning to take him reverse cowgirl style, and

Reed pistons his hips into me with such strength I immediately come again.

Planting my feet so I can raise my hips again, Reed grips me, thrusting up into my pussy like before.

It's so damn good, and then Reed snakes his hand down to my clit, stroking as I ride him. I clamp down around him, and Reed moans through his release, emptying himself.

The room calms down, and I slide off Reed, totally blissed out.

"Starting mornings this way is so much better than an alarm clock."

"Ha! That it is. I'm going to get cleaned up. Call for room service, would you? Anything you want."

"Oh, it's bacon time, baby."

Reed laughs, heading for the shower, and I pull up the room service menu on my phone before calling and ordering way more than we'll ever eat.

THE REST of the morning goes amazing, with eggs and waffles being delivered to the door with a healthy portion of bacon, of course. We sip coffee before switching to the mimosas I had them bring up, and then it's time to get dressed and go get Henry.

I'm excited to see him again, but coming up with a reason for my appearance takes us a minute.

"I'll just say that I picked you up. Wanted to give Henry the good news with an in-person surprise."

Reed smiles like it's no big deal.

"Okay." My smile is less confident, and I really do wonder how much longer we can keep this up.

However, I don't want it to stop any time soon, and right now, I'm just happy with where we're at.

We drive over, and when Reed rings the doorbell, Henry rushes to the door, surprise painted on his young face.

"You're on time! No work today?" And then Henry's eyes land on me. "Mae! You're back!"

He tears out through the doorway and launches himself into our arms, doing his best to hug us both simultaneously. It's enough to make my heart swell and it warms me from the inside out.

A woman comes out after him, and I have to assume it's Heather.

"Why, hello there. You must be Mae." She looks to Reed. "And that must mean she accepted your apology."

I smile, offering my hand for a shake, which Heather accepts. "Hi, nice to meet you. I am, in fact, Mae, and I did accept his apology. There was sufficient groveling."

"Oh, I would have paid to see that. Well, nice to meet you, too. I'm Heather."

We step back from the shake cordially, and I look between Reed and her. "So, Heather is Henry's aunt. Your sister, or…"

Heather seems to freeze, her eyes going to Reed, who quickly swallows and then puts on a smile.

"No." He shakes his head. "Henry's mom's."

"Oh!" My eyebrows shoot to my hairline, and I feel my cheeks go pink. "I'm so sorry. I didn't mean to…"

"You're fine, Mae. We should all be comfortable talking about my sister."

She glares ever so slightly at Reed, and I have a feeling she's been another person in his life to challenge him. I like that.

"Thank you, Heather, for watching Henry. You're

always there when I need you, and I don't tell you enough how much I appreciate that."

Heather and I stand there in shock for a moment, but then Henry is over having to stand around and quickly snaps us all out of it with an adorable sigh.

"Can we go now?"

Reed looks over, squeezing the boy in a quick hug. "Of course, bud. What would you like to do? We have the whole day."

"Really!?" Henry bounces up and down with glee. "Can we go to the movies? I want to see that new one with the kid spies."

Reed glances at me before nodding. "Sure. Did you want Mae to come, too?"

"Um, duh."

We all laugh, and then Reed, Henry, and I pack ourselves into the car. We stop off at my place to grab a change of clothes and head off to the nearest theater. It's not a long drive, and Henry keeps us thoroughly entertained with his stories about subjecting Heather to science experiments.

I have a feeling Reed's going to owe his sister-in-law a new set of pans.

"Thanks for coming, Mae. I know you probably had plans, but I had a feeling Henry would want you to tag along." He glances over as he drives. "Plus, I really didn't want to have to endure this movie without another adult."

Laughing, I shake my head, and Henry squints at us, confused.

"So, what's your go-to movie snack? I'm, of course, a popcorn with ridiculous amounts of butter kind of girl, but I'm also a fan of Sour Patch Kids."

With a grimace, Reed frowns. "Ugh. That sounds like a recipe for a stomach ulcer."

"And I would still die happy. What about you, Henry?"

"I like Reese's Pieces and popcorn."

"Ooh, salty and sweet. Good combo."

The laugh that ripples through Reed is genuine and unforced, and my heart positively sings as the sound fills the car.

"Well, I guess I'm the weirdo, then."

"Why do you say that?"

But before Reed can answer, Henry chimes in. "Dad likes a small, unbuttered popcorn with just a smidge of licorice."

I can tell Henry is actually quoting Reed's concession stand order, and I laugh hysterically as I imagine the two of them trying to get their food at the movie theater.

"That sounds utterly disgusting."

We pull into the parking lot, and in just a few minutes, we're inside, and I've convinced Reed to update his "old man" order.

"Come on. Processed butter is the whole point. Just live a little."

"All right, all right. We'll take a large, extra butter popcorn with salt and a pack of Reece's Pieces. Oh, and I guess three medium sodas."

I smile like I've won the lottery and take my cup from the cashier to fill up at the fountain beverage station.

I go for a mixed flavor Sprite with blueberry and lime, and Henry goes for a Dr. Pepper, to which he adds cherry flavoring.

"What's it going to be, Reed? A water?" I tease him relentlessly as Henry grabs way too many napkins. Although, knowing him, they might all be necessary.

"While that would actually be a good idea, no. I'm getting a root beer. It's always been one of my favorites, and I don't usually let myself enjoy it."

"Root beer, huh? That is somehow more 'old man' than a water."

With his son well out of earshot, Reed steps slightly closer and whispers under his breath. "You're going to get it now, Lil Bit."

God forgive me, but I absolutely cannot wait to see just what he means by that.

Once all the food and drinks are purchased, we go into the theater with Henry and find a seat about halfway back and right in the middle. It's the perfect spot in the house, and thankfully, Henry sits right between us.

After all, a dark movie theater? I'm not sure even I would have the restraint. The outing goes great, though, and the movie's not half bad.

There's tons of slapstick comedy, and the bit where the kids actually have to save their parents is really fun.

We laugh, having a great time, and when the credits roll, we're all up and ready to head back home.

The trip back to Reed's is another round of funny anecdotes about Henry's time with Heather, and the more I hear about how she is with him, the more I'm glad that he's had a strong, loving woman in his life.

When we reach the house, we decide since lunch was essentially popcorn and candy, eating isn't something we need to do, so we play cards.

The best part is that Henry picks the game and he deals.

We're two hands into War when Reed's pager goes off. I eye him, wondering, but he just nods slightly and walks over to where it sits on the counter.

"Are you on call?"

"No, I'm not, actually. Let me just give them a quick call."

My pulse quickens in that way when you know you're

about to be disappointed, and Henry and I wait while Reed phones the hospital.

"Hey, I got your page. Is it an emergency?" There's a pause as Reed—all of us, for that matter—listens for a response. "No. Oh, Jenny can't make her shift. Well…"

Reed looks over at Henry, who just waits calmly like he has so many times before.

"I'm actually not available to come in. Yeah, I know I usually don't hesitate to help out. Is Dr. Taylor available? Yes, you should call him. He'll probably jump at the chance. Okay, great. Thanks."

Reed hangs up, and before I can say a word, Henry launches himself at his dad.

"Thank you. For not leaving."

I can see the emotion welling behind Reed's eyes, and my heart pinches from the fullness straining it.

"I'm going to get better at that, bud. Okay?"

"Okay, Dad." Henry steps back and points at the table. "Can we play some more?"

"Of course, Henry. Anything you want."

As he sits back down next to me, I smile over at Reed. It's all Henry has ever wanted. All I want. Just more time with him, and for once, he's actually trying.

Chapter 20

Reed

As I join Mae and Henry at the table once more, there's a war going on that has nothing to do with the card game. I'm struggling so hard between feeling guilty and feeling accomplished.

I feel guilty because I said no to the extra shift when I could be saving people. But I also feel guilty because the look of joy on Henry's face says it all about how neglected he's been.

Also sitting behind that guilt is the pride I get from actually choosing my son this time around because I've been so bad about doing that.

And here we go again on the guilt train.

Ugh. This is much harder than I thought it would be.

Thankfully, Mae has a way of making rough situations even out. She directs Henry and me to try Uno since we've played War at least five times now.

It's been ages since I've played, and the cards from my deck are stiff and glossy. No one's been using them because

Henry knows how to play solitaire by himself, but there isn't much you can do with Uno alone.

We deal out the deck so each of us has an equal amount of cards, and then Mae refreshes us on the rules again. I've completely forgotten about the reverse and take four cards, and weirdly, this deck seems to have blank wild cards that you can write on your own.

"What's this?"

I hold out the once-blank card that I've been dealt and frown.

Henry sits up straighter, smiling, and reaches for the card. "That's one that we wrote on before we started using the deck. My mom and I did a bunch."

"Oh, that's awesome, Henry." Mae smiles, taking the card and looking closer. "Wait. This says take everyone else's cards even if you're about to go out."

Henry laughs, running a hand through his hair like I do, and the pinch in my chest at thinking about Clara eases.

"Yeah, that was me. I wanted a super win card. But Mom only let me make one."

Mae joins in with her own chuckle. "I can see why."

The card ends up going to Henry, and we begin the game with Mae.

After a few turns around our little circle, I have the most cards, being completely hit with Henry's homemade wild card. Henry still has three cards and Mae only has two cards remaining in her hand.

Yeah, I'm not going to win this.

As I consider which color to make it, Mae winks at me like she has a trick up her sleeve, and I'm quite intrigued.

I choose blue, knowing she doesn't have that color because I have about ninety-nine percent of them, so at least Henry will stand a better chance of winning.

Mae goes first, laying another wild on top of mine so the whole thing was moot, and declares it to be yellow. I have zero yellows, and we've played a bunch of them.

You sneaky devil.

It shifts to Henry, who lays a card down slowly and then shouts over at Mae as he makes his play.

"You didn't say Uno!"

Mae looks shocked, but I can tell it's an act, and she sighs, picking up the pile of cards, all but guaranteeing that Henry will win.

Sure enough, Henry lays a yellow, says "Uno," and in the next round, he wins. When I look over at the clock through the laughter, I see what time it is.

"Oh, buddy. It's way past your bedtime. Let's go brush your teeth."

Mae and I get Henry upstairs and have him ready for bed in a few minutes. He's a bit harder to put down than usual, and I have a feeling it's because he's having way too much fun.

We read a book and then, with the swirling stars lighting up his room, we both head back downstairs.

Mae finds her way to the couch, lying back like she's just as tired as my son was at the end of our game. She sighs, kicking her feet up on the table, and I walk over to her, grinning.

"Well, that was quite the day, wasn't it? Thanks for coming with us."

"Of course, it's what I'm here for." Mae smiles up at me, dropping her feet back onto the floor.

"Mostly, yeah. But you didn't have to, and today was so much better because you were here."

I sink to my knees in front of the couch, just to the side of her legs.

"Well, thank you for saying no to the extra shift. Did you see how excited Henry got?"

My eyes fall to the floor for a moment, caught up in the memory of how happy I could make my kid just by hanging out.

"I did. That was…great."

Mae adjusts on the couch, scooting up slightly, and my purpose for being on the floor comes back into focus.

"How quiet do you think you can be?"

I look up at Mae as I lift one of her legs over my shoulder, situating myself between her thighs.

"Fuuuck." She drags out the word, and I smirk. "I can try."

"You better."

At that, I find her slit with my mouth. She's still wearing her pants, so I rub against the fabric to warm her up. She arches back on a hiss, squeezing the edge of the couch cushion in her hand.

I love to watch the way her knuckles turn white and how her eyes pinch shut as she loses herself to the sensations, and I nuzzle into her, teasing her, thoroughly enjoying myself.

Only testing her resolve for a few moments, I slowly reach up and find the edge of her leggings and panties, pulling them both down over her curvy hips and revealing that glistening pussy of hers.

Mae sucks in a breath as the cool air around us hits her bare skin, and I tease her with just the tip of my tongue. Her fingers tangle in my hair, and then not even I can stand waiting any longer.

Dipping my tongue between her folds, I sink it deep inside her, swirling and licking in long caresses as I use my thumbs to spread her open.

A tiny squeak escapes her, and her hand quickly goes to

her mouth to cover any other sounds that might end up breaking free.

My erection throbs behind my fly, and I know this is going to get too hot and heavy to keep quiet in the living room. I pull back, licking my lips, and Mae whimpers.

The delectable sound is enough to have me desperate, and I pull her up off the couch and into my arms. I carry her to my bedroom, where we can lock the door and have a bit more privacy.

As soon as she's on my bed, I pull the rest of her clothes off, and my mouth goes right back to the tasty little treat waiting for me.

Mae arches again, pushing herself against my lips and tongue, and I reach up for her breast as I feast on her.

It's not long before she comes, and I love the way her pussy flutters against my mouth. As her release recedes, she sits up and pulls my mouth to hers.

She kisses and tastes in a maddening frenzy, totally high on the lust fueling us both. Her small hand goes to my cock, stroking up and down before helping me out of my pants.

When we're both naked, Mae cocks a brow at me and nods down at my straining erection.

"Can I see?" She's breathing hard, her chest heaving. "Can I see what you like?"

I catch her meaning quick enough, and holding her gaze, I reach down for my dick and stroke, doing everything I would if I were alone and trying to make myself come.

Mae's hand goes between her legs, her knees dropping open as she pleasures herself. Watching her work, the arousal taking over her expression, and the sounds she makes is deliciously filthy.

I'm nearly coming in just a few moments.

A deep moan starts up as Mae crests to another orgasm, her eyes rolling back. I lean toward her, dragging just the tip of my cock against her slit.

She watches as I stroke, and then she takes over. The feeling of her hand clenching around me, her fingers gripping my cock, sends fire racing through my veins.

I reach for a condom in the nightstand as she continues to grip me. I roll the protection down quickly before sinking myself completely inside Mae's tight pussy.

Her legs wrap around my waist as I thrust in deep, filling her completely as I slide every inch inside her. Pumping hard, I rock us up and down on the bed, barreling us toward that perfect moment when we both forget about everything outside of what we're doing.

Mae is so much smaller than I am, and I love the way I can fold her legs up onto my shoulders and completely take over her body. She's undeniably flexible, and I fucking love it.

I bottom out inside Mae, rolling my hips in wide circles to rub the head of my erection against the easily stimulated nerves inside her. She tries to arch up, but I'm holding her legs too close to her body, and there's nowhere for her to go.

Wanting more of this feeling, of the way she yields beneath me, I pull back to flip Mae onto her stomach and then grab her hips, yanking them back so I can sink into her again.

She stifles a cry behind her fist, clamping down on her knuckles to dull the sound. I fuck hard and fast, increasing our pace as I claim her.

I plant my foot on the bed next to her, offering myself even better leverage as I drive in and out of her. Wrapping my hand around her hip, I dip lower, finding Mae's clit and lightly patting.

"Fuck, Reed. Oh, God." She mumbles the words as she buries her face in the covers.

"Sweet Lil Bit. You just love how I take you." I smack her ass, keeping it somewhat gentle to avoid being too loud. "Don't you?"

"Yes. Oh, hell yes." Mae grips the blanket, thrusting her hips back to meet mine each time I push forward.

Her channel hugs me, bringing my release ever closer with each movement. I feel her clamp down, the climax overtaking her, and I rub that tight bud at the apex of her thighs faster.

She shivers as the orgasm takes over, and the rhythmic flutters of her pussy drive me over the edge. I come with everything I have, my cock pulsing as I empty myself.

The jets seem to shoot from me forever, but eventually, the tremors die down, and I slip free.

Needing to clean up, I snag a tissue from the nightstand, pull the condom off, and take it to the master bathroom.

Mae flops to the bed, pulling the sheet over her as I rinse off, and I can't stop the laugh as I see her snuggled up in my bed, seconds from passing out.

That'll be a tough one to explain to Henry, but I can't bring myself to move her or make her leave.

As I get in bed beside her, I pull Mae under my arm and breathe deeply, loving the way she smells.

"Thank you, Reed."

"For the sex? You're quite welcome, but it was certainly a team effort."

Mae giggles, and my heart squeezes at the sweet, delicate sound.

"No, for staying with Henry and me tonight."

"Oh." I smooth my hand down her arm. "Yeah. It was fun, wasn't it?"

"It was." She yawns. "I know it's difficult. But it was really great. So…thank you."

"I'll do my best to keep it up."

I close my eyes, leaning my chin against her head.

"I'd like that. Henry would, too."

"I like you, Lil Bit."

"Hmm." I can hear the smile in her delighted moan, and I know she's quickly falling asleep.

Exhaustion takes over for me soon enough, and I relish how it feels to have this woman in my arms as I fall into unconsciousness.

This is going to work. We're going to figure this out, and it's going to be amazing.

Hopeful dreams spin in my mind as I drift off. It's the first time in a while I'm actually looking forward to having zero plans tomorrow.

Chapter 21

Mae

After the absolute wonder that was our evening getaway and that first day of coming back to work for Reed, the past two weeks have flown by. It's been fantastic, picking up with Henry right where we left off.

I'd missed him, and every day, he continues to show me how great a kid he is. Reed is showing some improvement, too.

I stay late nearly every night, and while we can't be as loud in Reed's bedroom, the sex is still incredible. All in all, there's only one thing that could make things better.

Reed and I still haven't talked much about my concerns for Henry, and I can't shake the nagging feeling that we'll need to have that talk sooner rather than later.

For now, I've decided to just enjoy this. I requested a lot from Reed when I agreed to take my job back, and I can't expect him to change overnight.

At least that's what Stevie and Johnny keep telling me.

Still, I know Henry needs more time with his dad, and the pressure of nearly always being the one to entertain him is starting to exhaust me.

All I want to do is sleep lately, and I seriously do not have time for that. Though it could be all those late nights with Reed.

Maybe I just need something to break up the routine a bit. I'm sure Henry would love a change, and doing something fun as a family is exactly what he and Reed need.

Looking over at Henry, who's finishing up his homework at the kitchen island, an idea springs to life.

"Hey, I have a plan for when you're done. You up for something different?"

Henry glances up with a huge smile, and I chuckle. A twinkle of excitement shines behind his eyes.

"Yes! I'm almost done."

"Okay, well, finish up so I can tell you."

Henry goes back to scribbling down answers to his math problems with record speed, and I search for some nearby places that'll be open late.

After just a few minutes, Henry perks up, shouting, "I'm done!"

"Ha ha. Awesome. So what do you think about going swimming? We can run over to my place and grab my stuff before your dad gets home. It'll be a fun surprise, and maybe we can even hit up your favorite restaurant?"

A flurry of hoots and ecstatic movement throws the otherwise quiet kitchen to an earsplitting decibel, and I shake my head as Henry runs laps around the island, screaming "Oh yeah" like the Kool-Aid Man.

"So, I'll take that as a yes?"

"Yes! Let's go! Let's go! Let's go!"

Before I can answer, Henry dashes upstairs, and I run

to catch up. He's throwing clothes over his shoulder when I arrive at his bedroom door, and I quickly snag one out of the air before it hits me in the face.

"Dude! Slow down. Do you even know where your suit is?"

"It's in here somewhere!"

I can barely hear him because Henry's practically inside his drawer, and I grin. Piling up the discarded clothes, I look over his kneeling form to where I've seen his swim trunks folded on the top shelf of his closet.

I pull them down and then clear my throat so Henry will stop what he's doing and look. He spins, taking in the shark-printed trunks, and smiles.

"Whoops. But yay! Let's go!"

Henry snatches the swimwear out of my hands, running out of the room. I lean my head out his door and call after him.

"Put these clothes back, young man! And we need your towel!"

Sprinting back in, Henry helps me put the clothes away, and I finally have a moment to ask him what else he usually brings.

"Do you use goggles or anything?"

"There a bag under the stairs where Dad keeps all that stuff."

I shake my head. "This would have been useful information before you took off running."

"Sorry." Henry frowns with a fake look of embarrassment, and I can't help but love him just a little more.

If I do ever have kids, I hope they're just as cool as this one.

Ruffling his hair, I snag a towel from the linen closet as we head back downstairs. I grab the swim bag, and Henry follows me to my car.

"Alright, let's go get my stuff, and then we'll come back here to surprise your dad."

It doesn't take long to reach my house, thankfully. Traffic can move at a snail's pace if you hit the road too close to rush hour, and Henry and I sprint up the walk toward my building, laughing boisterously.

"Alright, I don't want to hear anything about water bottles when I open this door." I stick the key in the dead-bolt and turn. "I'm aware it isn't the biggest place, but it's mine, you know?"

Henry laughs. "Okay, okay. Let's just get your swimsuit so we can go get Dad."

"After you, buddy."

I swing the door open, escorting Henry inside where he can wait at my tiny excuse for a kitchen table. I'm pretty sure it's supposed to be patio furniture.

Jogging to my closet, I snag my bikini and a towel, lifting up my pant leg to see if I need to touch up my shaving.

It's good enough, and I decide to slip the suit on under my clothes so I don't have to worry about changing at the YMCA.

As far as bikinis go, it's nothing impressive. In fact, I've had it since I volunteered as a lifeguard a few years ago. The reddish-orange fabric is cut much more like a sports bra than some sexy suit that's all strings and cutouts.

Sliding up the bottoms, I notice I'm a little bloated, and I sigh.

"Must be that time of the month soon."

I still look okay and just have to remember to suck it in a little if Reed is looking.

"You done in there?"

"Yup! Coming!"

I pull my jeans on, tugging my T-shirt over my head

and readjusting my ponytail. I don't usually wear makeup anyway, and now I'm extra glad I opted out since we'll be getting in the pool.

As I walk out, Henry is in my fridge, rummaging around like a looter.

Sneaking up behind him, I whisper in his ear, "What are you doing?"

Henry jumps, and I giggle as he has to steady himself by gripping the refrigerator door.

"Mae!" His eyebrows are up to his hairline. "I was thirsty. And all you have is water."

"This is true. But I'm all done, so let's head back, and we can snag something at your house before we leave."

Henry keeps me entertained with his assessment of my apartment while driving back. I'm particularly tickled when he says my decorating style reminds him of a "hippie," which is pretty accurate if you consider all the macramé and upcycled furniture.

As we drive past a sign on the highway, I notice a warning about an accident on the exit just before the one we need, and I silently hope everyone is okay.

Besides a bit of a backup thanks to the wreck, we get to Reed's quickly, where I'm sure I'll find Henry something to drink as we wait for Reed to come home.

We shouldn't have to wait too long after six, which Reed has been doing an okay job of abiding by for his arrival time. But as the minutes tick on, and Henry and I have played one too many games of War, I glance at the clock. It's seven.

"Mae?" Henry eyes the time with me.

"Yeah, buddy?" I smile, trying to hide my frustration.

Henry looks at the fridge. "I'm really hungry. Can we just eat something?"

"Yeah. I'm hungry, too. I'll fix up some noodles. Sound good?"

Henry nods, walking over to the TV and turning on one of his favorite cartoons. He won't say anything, but I can *feel* his disappointment.

His faith in his father has just gone down another notch.

As the pasta boils, my cell rings on the counter, and I pick it up to answer.

"Well, hello. Let me guess. You got held up."

I know my tone is short, but I'm just as upset as Henry.

Reed sighs. "I'm sorry. I got help up at the ER because there was an accident. Two cars hit head-on. Drunk driver."

Remembering the highway sign, I exhale sharply. "Oh, man. I actually saw the warning about that on the I-15."

"You did?"

Turning off the gas, I cover the noodles so I can drain them, putting Reed on speaker.

"Yeah. Henry and I were coming back from grabbing my bathing suit. He finished up his homework, and I thought it might be fun to go swimming at the Y. If you make it back soon, you'll still have time to join us."

I pour the noodles into the colander waiting in the sink, and the steam rushes into my face.

"I'm still slammed here, and it doesn't show any signs of slowing down. Friday nights can be crazy. I can't take off yet. But I'll be sure to compensate you for staying late."

A few boiling droplets sprinkle onto my skin, stinging something fierce before I wipe my arm with a towel.

Reed's not coming.

"Don't worry about the pay, Reed. We just wanted to have some fun with you, but it's fine. I'll put Henry to bed tonight."

"Mae—"

But I don't want to hear more excuses, so I just hang up.

I glance over at Henry. He heard the entire conversation.

"Dad isn't coming home anytime soon, is he?"

"No."

The pain on Henry's face burns worse than the scalding water. He's paying for his dad's late nights—again.

"But that's not going to stop us from having some fun! Let's eat up, and then we'll swing by the Y and swim till nine."

That's a late night for Henry, but there's no school tomorrow, and I won't have him miss out on a new experience because Reed is stuck at work.

He sits up straighter, hopping off the couch and joining me at the island to scarf down dinner.

Afterward, we drive to the YMCA, and I meet Henry in the massive pool once we've stashed our stuff in the locker rooms. We play a rather aggressive version of Marco Polo, and I launch him across the pool from my knees several times.

Despite everything, we have an incredible time, and I realize it's been a while since I've actually had so much wholesome fun.

When I've definitely had enough, Henry swims over to some other kids playing in the pool, and they start up a game of chicken. I recline back on a nearby chair, exhausted beyond measure, and can't understand how Henry still has it in him to swim so hard.

My stomach rumbles, the noodles not sitting well, and I excuse myself to the locker room to use the bathroom. Henry doesn't seem bothered by the food at all, and I worry that I'm coming down with something.

This is not the time to be sick. And Reed is such a stickler about germs, he'll probably make me call off if I have so much as a cold.

Splashing my face with some cool water, the churning in my gut backs off. I look in the mirror and notice that bloating again.

"Oof. This is looking like it's going to be a rough period."

It's not the first time I've had stomach issues because of it, but I still worry I might be sick.

"Ugh, whatever. Just get back out there."

Waving at Henry, I sit back down on my lounge chair and check the time on my phone.

"Fifteen minutes, Henry!"

"Okay!"

As we wrap up our outing, I give Henry a big hug. The night wasn't a total waste, and I know he'll sleep like a rock.

Right on schedule, Henry falls asleep in the car on the way home, and I feel terrible having to wake him to get him inside. There's no way I can carry him, though.

We make it as far as the couch before Henry begs to lie down, and I chuckle, deciding to let him sleep there. It's a struggle to get him to go change in the bathroom, but I know neither one of us will like it if we fall asleep in our wet suits.

I pull out the drying rack from the downstairs laundry and drape our towels and swim stuff over the dowels.

When I've pulled my jeans and tee back on, I lie down on the other end of the L-shaped sofa across from Henry. I think he's fallen back to sleep before Henry looks over at me.

"Mae, do you think Dad will be home tomorrow?"

"I think so, bud. There was an accident tonight. Remember? I'm sure your dad knows how much you want to see him."

"Okay. Thanks, Mae. Swimming was fun."

"Anytime, kiddo. Anytime."

Chapter 22

Reed

Shutting the door as quietly as possible, I slip inside the house, my body aching from head to toe. That was one of my longest shifts on record, and the idea of sleep sounds so good that I might actually cry.

I set my bag down by the door, sliding off my sneakers and yawning. I make it to the living room sofa before I stop in my tracks.

Henry and Mae have passed out on the couch, and I see towels and bathing suits hanging up on a rack from the laundry room.

The familiar scent of chlorine hangs in the air, and as I come around to the other side of the couch, I have to stifle a laugh at seeing Henry's hair.

Thick locks are sticking up in every direction, and his thin leg is swung over the back of the sofa. He's been known to fall asleep in some interesting positions, and this one definitely takes the cake.

With a smile, I pull off the spare blanket from the

nearby chair and lay it over Henry. He only stirs slightly, a slight snore cutting through his heavy breathing.

They clearly had a blast, and my chest pinches as I recall what Mae said before she hung up. I was supposed to be there.

But, like always, duty called, and getting away meant leaving people without a doctor they sorely needed. At least, that's what I want to believe.

They could likely have handled it without me. *It's not like you're the only doctor there.*

Mae's familiar words ring in my mind, and I sigh. She's right, of course. The hospital has a huge staff.

Looking over at her, I see she's curled up into a ball on the couch, making herself as small as possible.

"She's probably cold," I whisper.

I find another blanket for Mae, covering her with it as I fight the urge to tuck her hair behind her ear. I don't want to wake her, not for anything.

I can see how much she did with Henry while I was working, and she more than deserves her rest.

Quietly, I head down the hall to my bedroom.

Unconsciousness quickly claims me as I lie back on my pillow, happy that at least Henry got to have fun, even if I couldn't be there.

SUNLIGHT SNEAKING through the cracks in my blinds signals morning has arrived, and I drag myself out of bed. I'd kill for a bit more sleep, but I know I have to get downstairs and help with Henry.

As I reach the kitchen, I find Mae and Henry attempting to make breakfast.

"Morning."

Henry looks up, smiling. "Hi, Dad! We're making pancakes. Do you want to help?"

I walk to the coffee pot, which I'm thrilled is full of fresh steaming caffeine-infused liquid, and pour myself a cup. This is going to be a three cup kind of day, I can tell.

"Sure, buddy." I step up to the counter, eyeing the eggs, flour, sugar, and bowl set up in front of Henry. "Where do we start?"

Mae comes up behind Henry, setting down the milk and nodding at the fridge. "I picked up some bacon earlier this week, if you'd like to make that, too?"

"I will never turn down bacon." I smile.

"Never?! What if it had poop on it?!" Henry giggles, and I frown playfully.

"Ooh, that's a hard one. Can I clean it off?"

"Gross!" Mae and Henry cry out simultaneously, and I can't stop my own laugh from erupting.

"Alright, alright. I'm kidding. So, I don't see any mix. Are we making these pancakes from scratch?" I raise an eyebrow at Mae.

"Yup. It's not that hard. Just need to grab the baking soda and salt."

Mae retrieves the remaining ingredients from the cupboard and proceeds to walk Henry and me through the basics of mixing pancake batter from scratch.

"Always mix your dry ingredients first."

I watch as she measures out the flour, baking soda, sugar, and salt into little cups that Henry adds, one by one, to the large mixing bowl.

"Okay, now use the fork to swirl it all together. Just try to mix it up really good."

He does alright for a while but then gets a little carried away, and a bit of the white fluff spills onto the counter.

"Whoops."

Mae smiles, shaking her head as she scoots the mess to the edge of the marble and into her hand.

"Now what am I supposed to do with this?" She holds up her fist, shaking it at Henry.

Turning my back to get another cup of coffee, I suddenly feel the light dusting of something raining down my neck.

I spin around, and Mae playfully points at Henry, who laughs hysterically, shaking his head.

"It was her!"

"Mae. Now please don't encourage that kind of behavior." I eye her hard and then go back to the coffee pot.

Another smack of flour hits my face as I turn around, and my mouth falls open.

"You did *not* just throw flour in my face!"

Mae wipes the white dust coating her hands onto her shirt. "Who, me? Couldn't be."

Tense silence fills the kitchen momentarily before Mae bursts out laughing.

She's the most beautiful thing in the world when she laughs, and I find myself quickly losing the battle to remain in control of this cooking extravaganza.

Mae sprinkles more flour on Henry, who promptly smears some on her arm, and I fling a little off the counter toward my son.

Nailing him right on the cheek, I laugh, and he readjusts his sight to launch some in my direction. I try to duck, but soon, it's a flour free-for-all in the kitchen, and we all wind up dusted in the soft white substance.

At this point, I'm laughing so hard I can't breathe, and then it hits me that this morning has gone so similarly to others when Clara was here. She was always the funnier one of us both, the gentler, more spontaneous partner and parent.

While there's a familiar sting of grief twisting in my gut, there's also a happiness I haven't enjoyed with Henry in a long while.

A genuine light sparkles behind his eyes, and suddenly, he looks like a kid again. I often forget that he's just seven.

He's so mature, and maybe that *is* because he was forced to grow up faster than expected because of the accident.

But right now, he's just a sweet kid laughing his ass off as we try, and mostly fail, to make pancakes.

Emotions swell in my chest, constricting my throat, and I fight hard to keep them locked behind the walls I usually have up. Being with Mae and Henry like this is a precarious situation, and I can't help but worry it'll come tumbling down.

"Alright, alright. Truce! Let's mix the wet ingredients into this new batch of dry, and we'll see about actually cooking them this time."

Henry giggles, but Mae is successfully able to add the eggs and milk with just a dash of vanilla. "For flavor," she remarks.

"Dr. Finnigan, think you can handle flipping?" She looks to me, and I nod with a fake salute.

"Aye, Captain!"

We all laugh, and then Henry lets out a tiny sigh as he fiddles with the odd balls of flour and water he's created.

"I wish you could be here every day, Mae. This was fun."

He's not wholly paying attention to what he's said, but Mae's eyes flick to mine as we both consider Henry's words.

She smirks softly at me, her brow raised, and I smile back.

There's something going on between us that isn't just about sex. We *both* know it.

What would it be like to actually pursue that fully? Ever since the hotel, I've been thinking about it on and off, and I'm still completely stuck in a state of indecision.

I just don't know. It all feels so fast and intense. I don't remember feeling like this with Clara.

Of course, I didn't meet her the same way I met Mae. And it's not like Mae was a total stranger before nannying for me.

She's Johnny's baby sister. I've known her for years.

And I still can't tell if that's a good thing or a bad thing.

I can't deny that waking up with her in the morning and spending my evenings buried between her legs are some of the best I've ever had. Plus, watching her with Henry is like watching two old buddies be silly together.

I adore it.

But this was absolutely *not* the plan. I'm swamped at work, and I hired a nanny because I needed to make this less complicated, not more.

All of this is just happening so fast; it's too much like being on a roller coaster in the dark, unable to see the turns coming up.

Without control, anything could happen. I could lose Mae in any number of ways, and I'll just be left here to deal with everything again.

I can't do that to myself.

I'm not sure I'd survive it again.

I take the bowl of pancake mix from Mae and face the stove, pouring thick circles into a hot pan and focusing on flipping. *That* I can handle.

Chapter 23

Mae

After being so disappointed last night, this morning with Henry and Reed was a very pleasant surprise. The flour thing had been a desperate attempt to get him to lighten up, and boy, did it work.

The raucous laughter filling the house was sorely needed by all of us, and watching Reed and Henry connect again threatened to make me cry.

Ugh. What's up with me? I'm likely to cry over a Kleenex commercial at this point. Jesus.

Eating up the few pancakes that survived our impromptu food fight, I smile happily at Henry as he shovels forkfuls into his mouth, dripping with syrup.

"Slow done, dude, you're going to choke."

Finally swallowing the mass of pancakes, Henry reaches for his milk and washes it down. A massive burp rips out of him, and all our eyes go wide.

"Henry!" Even Reed can't keep the laughter from his voice. "What do you say?"

"Excuse me!" He wipes his mouth with a napkin and sits back. "I'm full. Can I go play in my room?"

Reed shakes his head with a smile. "Yes, buddy. Just put your plate in the sink, okay?"

Henry snatches it up and runs it over to the sink before he dashes upstairs like his pants are on fire. I giggle, finishing up my helping of flapjacks and cleaning up after myself.

I look back at the counter, tracking the flour handprints and footprints scattered about. "This place is a disaster. But it *was* fun."

Snagging a roll of paper towels and some kitchen cleaner, I wait for Reed to finish before taking his plate and spraying down the island.

"I definitely haven't laughed that hard in a while."

I put his plate in the basin, and then Reed quickly comes up behind me; I'm trapped between him and the ceramic front of the farmhouse sink.

As I spin around, Reed's eyes hit mine with an intensity I haven't seen in some time. There's a war going on inside his head, and I practically see the cogs turning.

"How do you do that, Mae? How do you make everything seem so effortless and carefree? It's like there's nothing a bit of effort and cleanup can't solve. How did you come into my life and make everything feel so different?"

Any hope I had for finding an answer swiftly dies in my throat because the next moment, Reed's lips crash into mine. His kiss is a passionate fury, a silent plea against my mouth to give him more, endlessly more.

It isn't like our previous kisses. This one is explosive, a powder keg sparked by an errant flame, threatening to burn down everything around it.

My body heats, molten lava flowing through my veins,

and my hands quickly fly to Reed's face. This is so unexpected and risky, but Reed's obvious craving for connection quickly infuses me with the same desperation.

His hands go to my waist, pulling me hard against his firm body. Reed's grip is greedy, and I wonder just how far this moment is going to go.

Henry is just playing in his room. He could be out any second.

But as Reed's tongue caresses mine, a hungry growl rumbling through his chest, I have trouble caring about anything outside this moment.

"Oh my God!"

Reed and I both jump as Stevie's voice blares through the kitchen like a freight train.

Turning to see both her and my brother just a few feet away from Reed and me, my stomach flip-flops as Stevie claps her hands over her mouth and giggles.

"Well, how long has this been going on?"

Her tickled attitude is not reflected by Johnny in the slightest. His mouth couldn't hang farther open, nor could his eyebrows shoot any higher.

"I..."

Stevie just continues to hide a laugh behind her hands, but as soon as I think Johnny might actually be frozen in shock, his brow furrows, rage billowing over him.

"What the hell is this?!"

I've never heard my brother so angry, and I freeze, stuttering over nonsensical words.

"Please—" Reed holds a hand out "—keep your voice down. Henry is right upstairs."

Johnny pushes forward, jabbing a finger at Reed despite Stevie's attempts to keep him back. "That didn't stop you from putting your hands all over my baby sister!"

I roll my eyes at him. "I'm not a baby."

"Honey, hear them out. We don't know what's going on between them." Stevie steps up to Johnny, putting a hand on his shoulder.

"Clearly!"

"Johnny, get ahold of yourself. I'm allowed to do what I want." I try to get his attention, stepping in front of Reed, but my brother's eyes won't break from him.

"It's nothing to be upset over." Reed walks closer to Johnny, still holding his hands out. "It's just a case of close proximity and loneliness. Neither of us planned for this to happen. The chemistry is intense, and neither of us has been with anyone in a while. A classic case of 'office romance.'"

My heartbeat stutters, and now it's my turn to stare at him in shock.

Just an office romance? Chemistry? Is that really all I am to him?

Nausea claws up my spine, clawing at my insides, and I'm seriously concerned I might bring up the pancakes we just enjoyed eating. Rage quickly follows it, however, and I clench my fists.

"Is that really all it is to you? Just some office fling?"

Reed turns, but he just stands there and gapes at me. I raise my brows at him, demanding a response.

Nothing.

The queasy feeling in my stomach churns harder, and the telltale sting in my eyes signals the tears are on their way.

I was really just a convenient hookup.

"Office romance?" Johnny fights against Stevie's hold, and the concern on her face sends panic shooting through my nerves. "You bastard! Need I remind you that you're supposed to be my best friend?"

I step back, shrinking toward the fridge where no one is

blocking the exit. I'm such an idiot. *I…I thought we both felt…damn it.*

The burn on my lips still tingles, and I can't stop myself from reaching for them. Does Reed really not care about me at all?

Just a moment ago…no. I've had enough.

Pushing past the island, I grab my purse from the entry table and reach for the door.

"Where are you going?" Reed's voice cuts through Johnny's stream of insults.

"I've overstayed my welcome. I'm leaving."

"Mae—"

But I don't wait to hear what he's going to say. I fling the door open and leave Reed to deal with my brother. *Have fun with that.*

Chapter 24

Reed

"Mae!"

The door slams in my face as I try to follow after her, but then Johnny's at my back, holding me in place by the arm.

I glare at him. "Let me go."

Johnny throws my arm out of his grip, pushing me back, and then he shoots a warning at me. "Don't. Don't go after her. You need to give my sister some space and tread carefully."

I scoff at him, rolling my eyes.

"With both of us."

Meeting Johnny's stare, I can't keep the anger back any longer. That's not how I wanted to break the news, and it's *not* what I wanted to say.

The "office romance" thing was a kneejerk reaction because I was put on the fucking spot, and now I can't explain myself to Mae.

"You just gonna walk all over Mae's life and take control? She's a grown woman."

Johnny crosses his arms over his chest, shaking his head as Stevie tries to soothe him. Getting punched in the face seems pretty damn likely right now.

"I don't want to see her get hurt. I know exactly how closed off you are and how much *good luck* you've had with dating over the past three years. I'm protecting her."

"Protecting her? You sure you're not just protecting your image of her?"

Stevie has to physically restrain him at this point, keeping him from coming right up in my face. I know I should back off, but every ounce of tension that's been coiled inside me for the past few weeks has boiled over.

"Why exactly should I think Mae is different from any of the other flings you've had? I won't let you treat her like she's disposable."

He can't possibly think that poorly of me?

"Disposable seems a bit harsh, don't you think? I lost my wife, Johnny. You don't know what that's like."

But Johnny's glare doesn't break.

"I know you've stuck your dick in anything that moves with zero regard for their feelings ever since. Sometimes, I wonder if you work at a hospital or a sex club."

I clench my jaw so hard I worry I might crack a tooth, then exhale forcefully.

"I don't have to justify anything to you. What I do in my free time is none of your business."

"If what you're *doing* is Mae, it is my fucking business!"

Stevie can barely keep the two of us apart at this point, her hands pressing into our chests to keep us back.

I point toward the door, narrowing my eyes at him. "Get out."

Without another word, Johnny leaves. Stevie looks back at me mournfully and then follows after him.

Hearing their muffled voices outside the door for a moment, I glance up at the ceiling, running a hand through my hair.

A car door slams, and Johnny peels out of the driveway. *Thanks for keeping it down, asshole.*

I sigh, plopping down in a chair at the island. My phone is lying there, and I pick it up to call Mae.

It rings several times before going to voicemail, and it's the same thing after two more tries. I'm ready to chunk the stupid thing against the wall when a text comes through.

I need some space right now. I'll message when I'm ready to talk with you.

Tossing my phone back to the counter, I close my eyes and take a deep breath.

I just need to give her the space. As much as I want to explain everything to Mae, she's not going to listen right now, so there's no use in bothering her until she's ready.

"I'm sure she'll be fine by Monday. I'll just give her the weekend."

After a few minutes of staring off into nothing, Henry comes down from playing video games, saying he's thirsty.

He reaches into the fridge, coming out with a Gatorade, and looks around. "Where's Mae?"

"I'm sorry, buddy. She had to go take care of some stuff. But you've got me for the whole day." I try to sound enthusiastic.

"Will she be back tomorrow?"

My gut tightens. Henry doesn't seem too thrilled about spending the day with me. "No, probably not. But how about we do something fun?"

He sits across from me at the island, staring at me like he's waiting for a fucking miracle.

"Like what?"

I chuckle to break the tension, rubbing the back of my neck. "Whatever you want, bud. We could go see a movie or go to the park—"

"Ooh, can we go to the arcade?"

I furrow my brow. Henry's never mentioned *that* before. "Arcade?"

"Yeah. Devon, my friend at school, was talking about this cool arcade called Time Out that has loads of cool games and stuff. Can we go there?"

I nod. "Sure. Why not."

"Whoo! I'll get dressed."

Henry sprints back up the stairs, and I follow at a much slower pace. I'm still in my pajamas, after all.

As I find some jeans and a shirt, I think about all those classic shooting games I used to play. Maybe they'll have a few of those there, and I can blast away my stress via some zombies or something.

Once we're changed, I drive Henry to Time Out and agree to let him spend the entire day there. It's going to cost me a fortune, but the idea of going back home sounds about as fun as going to the dentist.

Sure enough, there are several shooting games, and Henry and I go crazy on all of them. He's having a ball and quickly hyped up on sugar from the unfathomable amount of junk food available.

Unfortunately, no matter how many zombie heads I shoot off or how many ropes of licorice I eat, the simmering frustration and regret continue to burn through my gut like an ulcer.

Johnny and I have never truly fought before. I hate it.

I hate everything about how this morning went down. But I shouldn't be surprised, right?

Just another case of bad fucking luck for Dr. Reed Finnigan.

At this rate, making it to Monday is going to take a freaking miracle.

Chapter 25

Mae

My fingers ache from where the plastic digs into them as I carry these heavy-ass bags of takeout. Nervous tension lingers in my veins, and I really hope this works.

I set the bags down on the porch and ring the bell. After only a few seconds, Stevie opens the front door, and I retrieve the food, holding it high.

"A peace offering. To make up for yesterday."

She offers me a gentle smile, taking the bags and sighing. "That was a lot, Mae. I had to hold Johnny back from actually swinging."

I frown at her, then bury my face behind my hands. "I'm so sorry. That…that sucks. Please forgive me?"

Stevie walks me down the hall to the kitchen, where Johnny is seated at the table. She presents my offering from Johnny's favorite Asian place and then wraps an arm around me.

"It's not me you need to be worried about." Only I

hear the comment, and then she excuses herself to give me and Johnny a moment to talk.

"Well, well, well. Look what the cat dragged in." Johnny glares at me.

"I'm sorry, okay? Really, I truly am. I didn't mean to start seeing Reed behind your back." I tentatively sit down across from him.

"It's not like you tripped and fell on his lips, Mae."

"I..." I slump in my chair, sighing out my embarrassment. "No. I didn't trip. But I didn't exactly plan for it, either."

He exhales hard. "Then what happened?"

"I'm not sure. Except..." I don't want to tell him this next bit, but I know it'll help him understand. "I've had a crush on Reed since I was a teenager. Ever since the first time you brought him over. And I know you saw some of that."

Johnny's eyebrows shoot up. "I just assumed it was a crush. Like all teen girls."

"It was! At first, anyway. But then I kept running into him and he needed a nanny; I was constantly around him, in his house, no less, one thing led to another."

I sigh, hanging my head where I bury it in my hands. "I should have told you. I know. I'm sorry."

The nauseous feeling from yesterday has never truly gone away, and as I sit at the table, the smell of Chinese food makes it worse.

"Then tell me this. Where is it going?"

I look up and meet Johnny's eyes. "I don't know. Things didn't really end on a great note yesterday."

My brother's jaw clenches. "If he—"

"Don't." I hold a hand up. "Don't do that. This is my situation to figure out. I'll deal with it. I don't want or *need* you to swoop in, all big-brother-protector mode."

Johnny scoffs, but I raise my brows at him. "I can do this on my own. We'll just see where it goes, I guess. Please, please be okay with that."

"Fine." Johnny throws his hands up, then reaches for a take-out bag and retrieves an egg roll. "Just take my advice, okay? Be careful."

"Not that I want to tell my brother this, but we're careful." I go for one of the crab Rangoons.

"Good. But that's not what I mean. I *mean* Reed has a long way to go when it comes to being emotionally available. He's not exactly been a commitment type of guy for a while. After Clara…I'm not sure he's ever really forgiven himself for not being there."

"What's that—"

"That's his story to tell. I just want you to know what you're getting into."

I sigh, but I get it. Johnny doesn't want to reveal Reed's secrets. Reed should be the one doing that.

"Okay."

We both nod at each other for a moment before Stevie comes in. "Care to take this to the living room? We can watch some bad TV."

Johnny cocks a brow at me as a grin spreads across my face.

"No, no, no. Do not make me watch—"

"The Bachelorette!" I yell out in unison with Stevie.

"Fucking hell."

Johnny grabs the bags while I help Stevie with the plates and silverware. We all head to the living room, and it's like I can breathe again.

I was seriously concerned that mending things with my brother would take a lot more than a quick chat and some takeout, but thank goodness, China Bon Bon eggrolls still soothe Johnny like they did when we were growing up.

After watching for a while, nature calls, and I start for the guest bathroom. Stevie stops me, yelling back over the sofa.

"Hey, that one is being renovated. We decided to change it up. Use the one upstairs."

"Okay!"

I bypass the powder room, sneak a peek inside to see it's been totally gutted, and head upstairs for the master bath.

Flicking on the lights, I notice a box on the large dual-sink counter, and curiosity gets the best of me. I pad over to find that it's a bunch of pregnancy tests, like a bulk box of twelve.

"Economical." I flip the thing over in my hand, looking at the back. "Johnny did talk about wanting to start a family with Stevie."

I set it back down, and just as I'm about to pull down my pants, my stomach does a flip-flop. *Take one.*

The thought is strange, out of nowhere, but then I remember how I've been feeling. Bloating, nausea, exhaustion—it's all there.

I've been telling myself it's due to my upcoming period, but I still haven't had it.

"Shit. When is that supposed to be here?"

Pulling out my phone and checking my calendar reminder, I see I've missed the notification for it.

Five days ago.

My stomach clenches hard, and a nervous pitter-patter steps up shop behind my sternum.

"Um, okay." I try to slow my breathing. "No. This is fine. We're just going to take this and see that it's negative. Easy peasy."

I take one of the pregnancy tests from the box and tear it open. It's not the first time I've had a scare, so I know the drill.

Peeing on the little pad, I make sure it's good and coated and then put the cap back on. I set it on the floor and finish things up while it cooks.

Rechecking the box, I see it's the typical two-minute countdown.

These aren't the digital readout ones. It's pink lines, but I guess they can show results earlier because it's not waiting for a certain threshold before it displays the word *pregnant*.

"Stevie wants her info fast, I see."

I don't risk setting a timer on my phone, and instead, I just stare at the clock for the one hundred and twenty seconds.

The clock changes from 6:37 to 6:39, and I know it's time to check it.

I don't.

For another five minutes, hell, it feels like five years, I just stare at it on the floor.

"Christ, Mae. Just look."

Shuffling toward the test, like I'm in a horror movie and it will attack me, I pick it up and check the lines.

"Two. Two lines."

Scanning the instructions again in a feeble attempt to see if I've misread it, I nearly throw up.

"Pregnant." Panic swirls as I clutch the test. "Fuck. No. Wait. How, though? We've used condoms or at least pulled out. I'm on birth control!"

But dread crawls up my spine as I consider how forgetful I am about taking it. In fact, I can't even remember if I took it today.

"No. No! It's a fluke. I'll just—" I snag another test from the box "—I'll take this one at home. It'll be different."

Rushing back downstairs, I quickly tell Johnny and

Stevie I'm not feeling well, blaming the takeout, which Johnny takes as a personal slight.

Thankfully, they don't fight it too much, and I can fly back to my apartment to take the other test.

Running a few yellow lights, I make it back to my place in record time and head straight for the bathroom. But after another two-minute test and a five-minute stall, the second test shows the same two pink lines as the other one.

"Fuck."

I slump down to the floor, my ass hitting the tile hard. I drop my head to my knees, hiding from the world behind my arms.

"I'm on birth control. I mean, I take it pretty regularly. A few missed days now and then shouldn't be enough to get me pregnant!"

However, getting laid on the regular had never been a concern in the past, so being lax with my pill-taking wasn't a problem.

"The one place where I'm irresponsible for a few weeks, and this is what happens."

I stand up, examining myself in the mirror. *There's a cluster of cells in there that are becoming a baby.*

Do *I* want that?

My brain is scrambled. What does this mean for my savings plan? For work? For getting my degree and becoming a teacher?

I have a plan, one that I've actually been working toward really hard. No excess spending, no spreading my finances too thin.

"I have a plan!"

But then I see Henry's face as I close my eyes, and a strange pang reverberates through me.

I love him so much. He's a great kid, and I've always loved kids.

But I'm also so young, and I have no idea how the fuck Reed is going to take this. Our relationship isn't exactly on solid ground.

Would he even want to have another child? Would Henry want a sibling? Sharing the attention can be really hard for some kids.

My head spins, and that nausea I can now attribute to hormones rears its ugly head.

How am I supposed to tell Reed about this? Do I even have to?

"It's my body, after all, and this is way too much, way too fast." I meet my eyes in the mirror. "Reed is never there for Henry like he should be. At least, not enough. Do I even want a workaholic like him to be the father of my child?"

Tears prickle, and I don't bother wiping them away when they eventually slide down my cheeks. A new baby in Reed's life would probably be just an inconvenience.

Just like our non-relationship, apparently.

Sighing, I blow my nose with some toilet paper and determine some more bad TV is in order.

I have time. I don't have to decide what to do right this minute.

"And you have options. It's the twenty-first century, and you're a strong, independent woman."

But even as I say the words as confidently as I can, shaking my finger at my reflection, I don't feel like a strong, independent woman.

I feel confused and overwhelmed and exhausted.

And above all, I feel alone.

Chapter 26

Reed

Monday morning rolls around, and it's the first one in a while that I don't have to work. But I don't tell Mae that.

I want her to come to the house. I gave her the space, and now I want a chance to talk with her.

Though, I'll admit that a part of me also *doesn't* want to talk to her.

Confrontation isn't something I excel at or look forward to, and I'm beginning to see that avoidance is clearly my default.

Saying I'm out of practice when it comes to this relationship stuff is a massive understatement, and since Johnny left me with a lot to think about, I've done just that—avoided Mae, my feelings, everything.

The arcade with Henry was fun, and we even managed to go to the movies yesterday. Still, my MO for the entire weekend was distraction.

It occurs to me this *is* the closest thing I've had to dating someone since Clara died. Like Johnny said, I've kept stuff with women short and emotionless since I lost her.

I was doing it a bit subconsciously, but some part of me knew I was closing off the possibility of romance because I just couldn't face that again.

Losing a person you care about is just too hard, and not caring seemed like the easier route.

Avoidance.

Worse, just like Mae said, Henry was more than prepared for me to leave at any moment. He had even asked if work had paged me a few times when I was looking at my phone.

I said no, and we kept playing, but I also didn't tell him not to worry, that I wouldn't go in that day.

I didn't talk with him about why he didn't seem very excited to spend the day with me or why he's always ready for me to leave. I still haven't.

Avoidance.

Ripples flow across the surface of my coffee as I sigh. I take another sip, wishing the cure-all to life's mysteries and conundrums was as simple as some caffeine.

Henry's all ready for school, and just as I pour myself a second cup for the road, the front door opens, and Mae steps in.

My son dashes over to her, and she quickly wraps her arms around him in a hug.

"Hey, kiddo. Sorry, I'm cutting it close. Are you ready for school?"

Mae's voice sounds pinched, and while casual and easygoing has always been her demeanor, she looks particularly so. Tiredness clings to her.

"Yup. Dad's going to drive with us." Henry actually seems excited, and if it weren't for the circumstances, I might be, too.

"What?"

Excited isn't exactly the word I'd use for Mae. Her brow furrows as she looks to me, concern painted all over her face.

"I have the day off. Thought we could talk."

"All right."

She doesn't say a word after that, and the chore of getting Henry loaded up into the car is punctuated by of the most awkward silences of my life.

Mae is so distant, a wave of withdrawn energy flowing off her like a warning. I don't know how to handle it, so I just stay as quiet as she is.

I know Henry can tell something is up, so I try to chat with him through the drive. He brightens slightly, but Mae only stares out the window and nods occasionally.

The end of our nannying contract has been a very real concern all weekend, and it's made all the worse by Mae's attitude. Even more, I'm aware that'll come with an end to our *relationship*, too.

She's going to end this, and I've only just realized there's a this *worth saving.*

Drop-off goes smoothly enough, but I know as soon as I get back to the house, Mae will leave. So I pull over at the side of the road a few blocks down from the school.

"Is something wrong?" Mae looks around the car.

"No. I just…" I sigh. "Where's your head at today? You seem…off."

"What do you mean?"

Frowning at her, I adjust to face her in my seat. "What do I mean? You've barely said a word, and last we saw each other, some pretty big stuff happened. What are you thinking about? About Johnny finding out…about us?"

She doesn't look at me. "Reed, I…I don't know. I think I need more time."

"Okaaay." I drag out the word as I stare at the steering wheel. "So are you saying you want to keep this going or pump the brakes?"

"I don't know."

A frustrated sigh escapes despite trying to keep my cool, and I grip the wheel hard. "Look, I know things aren't perfect, but I'm willing to try. Create new habits with you and Henry. I want to do this right."

"Reed." Mae shakes her head as she continues to avoid eye contact. "It's not that simple."

"Nothing is simple." I bite back the harsh tone infusing my voice. "I'm trying to be open with you, and after everything, now you're going to block me out? I'm trying to do what you asked. Why won't you at least talk to me?"

Mae exhales hard, her tone clipped as she responds, "I have some personal stuff going on, okay? I'm distracted, and it's not like I was prepared to spend time with you today."

"So this is my fault?" I stop myself, taking a breath. "Sorry. What personal stuff? Maybe I can help."

She shakes her head, and all I can see as Mae continues to avoid looking at me is her eyes going wide.

"No. I'm not ready to talk about it."

It's like talking to a fucking wall at this point. "Fine. I'm just trying to help, you know? Just trying to 'open up' to you like you've been nagging me to do."

The car hangs in a brief silence, but my frustration is raging too hard for me to let it go.

"Why don't you just take the day off if you're going to be like this?"

Mae's eyes snap to mine for the first time as she glares at me. "Be like this? Are you serious right now?"

She shakes her head with a huff, gripping her purse with white knuckles. "I just said I'm going through some personal shit, and this is your response? God, you wonder why you suck at dating. How you stayed married is beyond me."

My gut tightens. I'm inches from losing it.

"The fuck does that mean?" I grit out.

"Fine. You really want to do this?" Mae smirks angrily. "You're an abrasive bully, Reed. Whenever things don't go your way, you just try to force it in the direction you want. My emotions are *my* concern. Just because I don't want to share my feelings right now doesn't give you the right to act like I'm the one being irrational. You have no idea what's going on, what I'm dealing with. And trying to force me to spill because you need to know right this second is *not* helping your case."

I don't respond, clenching my jaw hard to keep from saying something I'll regret.

Tears stream down Mae's face, and her body shakes as she fights to keep them in. With a sigh, she wipes them away, shaking her head.

"I shouldn't have brought up your marriage. I'm sorry. I know I snapped, but…you need to really think about how you speak to me, to Henry, and to everyone else in your life."

Her tear-stained face turns to mine, and facing the reality of how I've affected her makes my chest ache.

"I didn't cause the accident. Henry didn't. Johnny didn't. *You* didn't. You need to stop looking for someone to blame."

My head rears back like I've been slapped in the face, and my eyes burn.

"I—" I shake my head, closing my eyes, and reconsider my words. "I'm sorry, too. I…I don't know what I'm doing. And—and I don't like it."

Looking back up at Mae, her maple-colored eyes shimmer, and that pull I've always felt to her tugs hard. Before I have the presence of mind to stop myself, I reach across the car and press her lips to mine.

Mae leans further across the console, returning the kiss, and it quickly becomes frantic, a desperate plea for comfort among the raw nerves we've exposed.

My thoughts swirl, my emotions a whirlwind.

"Come back to the house with me. Please."

I'm begging. I'm begging Mae to be with me, and I don't fucking care.

After a moment's hesitation, Mae nods. "Okay."

Chapter 27

Mae

I don't remember the drive to Reed's house. My emotions are too much of a roller coaster to concentrate or think rationally.

All I know is that I'm desperate for the feel of Reed's lips on mine again, to feel him take me so entirely that I forget everything that's happened.

Thinking about the future, about potentially being someone's mother right now, is too much. I've chastised Reed for avoiding things, but that's precisely what I want to do.

I want to avoid thinking, avoid worrying.

For at least the next hour or so, I only want to lose myself to the feel of Reed inside me.

As we step into his house, I fling myself at him, dying to feel something besides confusion.

Our bodies crash together in a tangle of limbs as we frantically pull each other's clothes off. My jeans are thrust down my legs as I unbuckle Reed's pants, and then my shirt is over my head before I do the same to him.

Lips meeting with desperation, Reed guides me to the living room.

The blinds are drawn, and Henry isn't home. There's no holding back right now, and I thank God for it.

I need to lose myself in this. I need to forget.

"Reed." I pull his face to my neck. "Please."

His teeth bite into the flesh, not overly hard, but enough. It's exactly what I want—rough and all-consuming.

I reach around to the clasp of my bra, flicking it open and tossing it across the room.

"Mae." His hands roam over my flesh, finding my breasts as he pins me to the floor. "What have you done to me?"

Kisses trail down my chest and stomach as Reed sinks between my legs. The rug is soft and plush beneath me as Reed pulls my panties down.

"IT'S MADNESS. The way you affect me is like a drug."

Reed pushes my legs apart, looking up at me as he lowers his head, inches away from my slit. My core clenches as he teases me with anticipation.

"And I'm hopelessly addicted to you."

With that, his tongue plunges deep inside me, and my nerves light up. Electricity pounds through me, sparking every part of my body to life in but a moment.

His skills never cease to amaze me, and as Reed's fingers join in the work, I'm quickly arching up off the floor, pushing myself hard against his face.

Pain and pleasure swirl as he pushes deeper, his tongue

swirling around my clit. His other hand claws at my hip, holding me pressed to him.

I'm quivering from head to toe, and odd tears threaten to breach the surface. *More.* I need so much more.

I wrap my legs around his head, and Reed sits back, pulling my ass off the floor to rest on his chest.

"Come. Come, Lil Bit."

With hard thrusts, Reed fucks my pussy with his fingers, but the thing that throws me over the edge is when teeth find my thigh. He bites just enough, as hungry for me as I am for him.

"Fuck!"

I orgasm hard, clamping down around Reed, but he doesn't stop. He pumps harder, demanding more, and I come again, falling apart, and gasping for breath.

It's only been minutes, and already I'm throbbing from Reed's welcome assaults to my folds. Heat flares through my blood, boiling as it reaches my core.

"Goddamn, Mae. I want everything you have to give me. I want you crying out my name."

He shoves me back to the floor, flipping me over. Reed's large hand comes down hard on my ass, his smack ending in a caress.

Reed smacks again and again until my cheek burns, and I can imagine the pink handprint on my pale skin.

It's perfection, and I lose even more of myself to the extraordinary sensations.

Then he's sinking his fingers back inside me, his thumb pressing to my asshole and heightening the pleasure until I soar right back over that cliff.

I don't care if I crash on the rocks below. All I want at this moment is for Reed to take everything he wants from me.

My legs quiver, and my entire body shudders as Reed slowly curls his fingers. "Don't stop, Reed. Please."

"I won't, Lil Bit. I'm not stopping until you're begging for rest."

Flipping me over to face him once again and pulling my legs until I'm right in front of his crotch, Reed yanks me up to my knees. His straining erection is already dripping a long trail of precum, and I quickly wrap my mouth around it.

I suck in a frenzy, bobbing my head up and down his length, like my life depends on it. Reed's thick shaft fills my throat as I take him to the hilt.

"Fuck, yes, Lil Bit. Goddamn."

As he tests my limits, I reach up and massage Reed's balls. He bucks in my mouth, and I pull back until I'm sucking just the head.

The desire in his grip as he holds my head is intoxicating, and I let Reed fuck as hard as he wants.

It's nearly impossible to breathe, but I don't care. In fact, I *want* this.

The reprieve from my thoughts is just what I need; I'm only here with Reed. The world is utterly nonexistent.

He pulls out of my mouth, his dick bobbing, and spins me away, pushing my head to the carpet. Reed moves behind me, then lifts my hips into the air and licks up my slit again.

"My naughty girl. Tell me you want this."

"I want you, Reed."

Gooseflesh ripples over my back as Reed draws his nails across my skin from my shoulders to my thighs.

"Is this what you imagined? When you were all alone in your room. Did you fall apart around your hand to thoughts of my dick buried deep in your pussy?"

Heat flares through my cheeks, but I don't shy away from it. Not anymore.

"Yes."

His hips slam forward, driving his cock fully inside me. I cry out, filling the quiet house with my overwhelming passion.

It's delirium and euphoria as we thrust ourselves into each other with everything we have. Reed's erection pounds so deep and hard, pain and pleasure still blending to create something so much more intense than either of them alone.

That's exactly what makes it so incredible. He pistons faster, ramming into me like a jackhammer, and my hips burn where he grips me.

Then Reed's hand finds my breast as he leans over me, pinching my nipple hard.

"Ahh!"

"That's right, Lil Bit. Take it."

He slaps my backside again before tangling his hand in my hair and yanking my head back. My core burns harder than ever, and I feel the release ready to burst from my center.

My neck strains as Reed fists my hair, and soon I'm clamping down around his dick, coming hard.

He fucks harder, scooping an arm under my leg. It's times like this that I'm grateful I'm flexible.

With each thrust, Reed presses my face and shoulders into the carpet, and I grip the fluffy fabric for dear life.

Reed props my leg against his chest, reaching for my clit as he sheathes himself up to the hilt. Light pats against the skin scramble my brain, and another orgasm is ripped from me.

It drags on into eternity until I'm screaming.

"Reed! It's too…I can't…"

"You can. You're doing so well, baby."

The praise sings across my nerves like a soothing balm, and I angle my hips higher, letting Reed go deeper.

I feel him thicken even more, his release seconds away. I grip his hand where he's rubbing my clit, spearing myself on his shaft in time with his efforts.

Reed grunts low. "That's my girl."

He orgasms, filling me with his cum, and bliss bursts out from every inch of my skin. The pleasure is dizzying, and I become acutely aware of my heartbeat.

It's the most intense experience we've had, and as my trembling eases off, the sound of our ragged breaths drag my mind back to reality.

We're still here, still in the same situation as before, and a heaviness settles over my chest.

Reed slips free, sitting back against the couch as he catches his breath. The warmth of his body is replaced by cool air.

With the curtains blocking any sunlight from reaching us in Reed's living room, I feel like I'm sitting in a hopeless abyss.

Stinging starts in my eyes, and I struggle to keep them from leaking my emotions all over the place.

I'm pregnant. I could have a baby next year, thanks to getting carried away with the man sitting just a few feet away.

Lying naked on his expensive rug in the dimly lit room, I stare at Reed's profile. His eyes are closed as he leans his head back on the sofa.

We shouldn't have had sex again, not without talking first. But I know if I were presented with the situation again, I would still do it.

It's something about Reed. It always has been, and I think he's as lost in this as I am.

But did it mean something more to him than that? Or was it just pent-up desire for someone who's always been off-limits?

If Reed wanted me *this* badly, even after Johnny saw us together, what does it mean? Was this just another fling, or does Reed actually want something real with me?

Because as much as I might want to deny it, I want that with him. *Desperately*.

Chapter 28

Reed

Mae left in a hurry after we had sex again on Monday. I tried to stop her, but ultimately, I know I need to give her some time to think about everything we're doing.

To that end, I have to own up to this with Johnny. The guy has been my best friend since forever, and he deserves an apology.

After getting Henry to school, I work the first half of my split shift before taking my break to find Johnny at work.

I realize it's not the best place to have a heart-to-heart, but the idea of waiting a moment longer makes me anxious.

I'm thoroughly good at avoiding things, and even though it took me this long to realize that, I'm not going to let it get any worse.

As I drive to Johnny's office, I consider what Mae said yesterday. She's never had a problem calling me out on my shit, and for once, I try to consider her words before getting defensive.

A bully.

It's harsh, but I can see why she'd think that. I'm not exactly patient when things don't go according to my plans.

I sigh, staring hard at the red light in front of me.

It's the Clara thing, and instead of seeing that as an excuse, I understand it's just an explanation.

I'm still grieving that loss, and I'm doing all the wrong things to prevent it from happening again because losing her made me feel so out of control, so helpless.

I've *never* been good with that.

But all I've done is push people away, including my own fucking kid.

"He looks just like her." I steady myself with a breath as my eyes burn. "Like Clara."

Saying her name out loud stings, but I face it, letting the pain hit and then back off.

The light goes green, and I push down on the accelerator. After all, I can't stay stuck in this lane.

People would honk, and I'd affect their lives, too. So, as much as I don't want to see what the future holds—because it *could* be bad—I have to.

I don't have a choice.

Johnny's office is just a few blocks down, and I start thinking through what I'm going to say when I get inside.

"I was a dick. Mae is incredible, and she holds me accountable. She makes me want to be a better man." *Ugh.*

I roll my eyes. I have to do better than a line from a Jack Nicholson movie.

Throwing the car in park, I step out and head inside the financial offices. There's a receptionist at the desk, and I walk up to her.

"Hello, I'm looking for Mr. Marrington?"

The woman looks up and checks her screen.

"I'm sorry, Mr. Marrington is in with a client right now, but you're welcome to wait."

She gestures to the plush chairs behind me, and I nod, taking a seat. Waiting patiently is another of my weaknesses, and I find myself picking up one of the years-old magazines to pass the time.

It's all about markets, and it's actually pretty hilarious to see some of the predictions inside, knowing full well that many of those businesses went bankrupt. Guess you can't be right every time.

I only have to wait about fifteen minutes or so before a man comes out of the office down the hall, and I see Johnny shake his hand as he leaves.

Anger darkens his expression as he notices me, and I walk toward him.

"What are you doing here?" Johnny keeps his voice low, but I hear the rage simmering behind the whisper.

"Can we talk? I'd—" I close my eyes briefly before meeting his glare "—like to apologize."

Johnny's brows pinch together. "Wow. Didn't think you had it in you."

"Fair. I deserved that. But it's true. I came here on my lunch break because I didn't want this to fester any more than it already has."

It feels like an eternity before Johnny finally sighs and steps back into his office.

"Fine, come on in."

He gestures inside, and I go in, standing in front of his desk as Johnny sits behind his computer.

"Well, let's hear it." Cocking his eyebrow at me, Johnny smirks, all too aware that I despise apologizing.

"Ugh." I release a heavy exhale. "It was wrong not to

tell you about Mae and me. It was a complete dick move, and I should have done better."

He folds his arms over his chest.

"You're not going to make this any easier for me, are you?"

Johnny frowns, shaking his head. "Not a chance."

"All right. I deserve that. I was a jerk. I said shit I shouldn't, and I'm sorry. I'm crappy at this relationship stuff, and I've hurt both you and Mae by trying to avoid dealing with the situation."

Moving to one of the chairs by Johnny's desk, I slump down onto the edge.

"I know you just have your sister's best interests at heart. I swear I do, too."

"Ha." Johnny scoffs. "I'll believe that when I see it."

He sighs, raking a hand through his hair. "Look, Reed, I care about you. You're my best fucking friend, for Christ's sake, but you've burned a hell of a lot of bridges in your quest to figure out relationships. I know you've taken Clara's death hard, and I don't blame you for that. You should. But I don't want to see Mae be one of the people you leave behind in the ashes."

Silence hangs over the room, and I can feel my heartbeat in my head. A migraine pulls at the corners, and I have a feeling aspirin and a Coke are going to be in my future later today.

The creak of Johnny's office chair pulls my head up, and he comes around the desk to sit in the chair next to me.

"However," he says as he meets my eyes, "Mae is a grown woman. I don't get to make choices for her. No one does, including you. She can choose to date you or whomever she wants, and I won't stop her because that's not my place. If Mae decides to jump into this with you, that's her call."

"I appreciate that."

"But I swear to God, if you hurt her, I will end you."

I chuckle humorlessly. "Understandable."

Johnny leans forward in the chair. "I know you don't want this affecting our friendship. I don't either. But it might. If you disrespect or hurt her in any way or wind up seeing someone behind her back, I will never forgive that."

I hold my hands up between us. "I wouldn't expect you to."

"Good. Now, I'm not saying you can't ever break it off with her. I understand shit happens. But if you do figure out it's not going to work, you break up with Mae like a man. No texts or emails. You do it to her face. And *don't* drag it out. You can't jerk her around and lead her on. You have to be honest with her. And with me."

He levels me with an intense stare, his eyebrows raised, and I tip my head down in a submissive gesture. "I should have been honest. I know. I will from now on. I swear I've told you everything now."

"I hope for your sake that's true."

I stand up, reaching to shake Johnny's hand and holding his gaze. "Deal."

Johnny shakes, and before he breaks it, I add, "It's the least I can do."

"It's literally the bare minimum, dude."

He smiles, shaking his head at me, but I take it. I've had it coming, so I'll take whatever Johnny has to dish out.

I give him another nod. "Promise."

"You fucking better." He claps me on the shoulder a little harder than normal, then steps back, shaking his head again. "You really hooked up with my sister. You know how weird that is, right?"

"Nope. I'm not going to fall for that for one second." A relieved laugh escapes. "The only thing you'll hear me say is that Mae is incredible. If it weren't for her, I wouldn't have realized all the shit I need to deal with."

He pegs me with a sarcastic scowl. "Uh-huh."

"I'm serious. You tried to get through to me about the work-life balance. Heather did, too. Mae's been the only one who's actually gotten through to me. Made me want to do better."

"Huh. Who would have thought it would take my sister to get through that thick skull of yours." Johnny nods, narrowing his gaze at me. "Well, all right, then. But no more surprises. Deal?"

We shake again. "Deal."

"I've got to get back to work." Johnny playfully glares at me. "I know, I know. But hey, how about we do something fun soon? I have a day off coming up, and I won't pick up another double."

"Ha! I'll believe *that* when I see it, too. Message me."

Johnny pats me on the back, and I wrap a hand around his shoulder, mimicking the gesture.

With a deep exhale, I grin at him as I head for the door. "Smooth sailing from here on out. I know it."

Chapter 29

Mae

It's been a few more days since the last time I had sex with Reed, and things are actually going smoothly. As far as weeks with him go, this one has been pretty damn good.

I know he went and apologized to Johnny, which made me feel so much better, but I still haven't brought myself to tell him about the pregnancy.

In fact, I haven't told anyone, and I've never kept a secret for this long. I never had to.

I've also never lied to Johnny or kept him out of the loop, and it feels especially weird to keep this from him.

With the age gap, Johnny has always been more like a parent than my sibling, but he was the cooler parent I could talk to about stuff that was too embarrassing to bring up with Mom and Dad.

Like a black little storm cloud hanging over my head, the news hovers in the back of my mind. Reed has noticed, but he's doing his best not to push it because of how well it went last time.

I'm still in avoidant behavior land, though, and I know I can't put it off much longer. A decision needs to be made before I run out of time.

"What am I going to do?"

Stuffing the wet clothes into the dryer, I snag a fabric softener sheet and hit start. I need clothes for tomorrow, my weekly grind starting over again, even though all I want is to sit in this apartment and pretend like Sunday will never end.

Knock, knock, knock.

Whipping my head toward the front of my apartment, I wonder who could be banging on my door like there's a fire at 9 p.m. on a Sunday.

When I open up, I find Stevie outside in the hall. She's huffing breaths like she just ran up twelve flights of stairs, and her eyes are as big as dinner plates.

"Whoa. Hi, Stevie. What's up?"

She holds up a pregnancy test while she catches her breath, and after personal experience, I now know what a positive result looks like.

A wide grin stretches over my face. "Oh my God! Are you pregnant? Am I going to be an auntie?"

But then Stevie shakes her head, and my smile fades. "No. This isn't mine, Mae."

She raises her brows at me, and I freeze.

"Oh, come on. Is this yours?"

I blink, unable to even breathe, let alone respond to her. *Fucking hell. Did I actually leave that at their house the other day? Shit!*

"Um, look, I don't know who…I mean, it's not…" I'm a stammering mess, and Stevie just looks at me like I'm more than easy to read.

"Some poker face you got there." Stevie shakes her head. "Look, Johnny found the test, not me."

"What?!"

My heart hammers and nausea swirls through my stomach. I'm going to be sick right here in my doorway.

"If you would have told me…" She sighs. "I couldn't cover for you because I didn't know what was going on. So I just told Johnny the truth. Said it wasn't mine. Well, it didn't take him long to put two and two together."

I fall to the side, leaning on the doorjamb, heaving breaths to ward off the need to throw up all over Stevie's Dr. Martens.

"Oh, babe." She puts her arm around me. "Johnny's out of his mind. I've never seen him like this. And…"

Stevie hesitates, and as the tears roll down my face, I shout, "What?"

She jumps, flinching back before meeting my eyes again. "He's on his way to Reed's."

My stomach crashes through the floor, and my vision tunnels until all I can see is a wavy static clouding the floor.

"No, no, no. This isn't…" I stand up straight and meet Stevie's eyes. "Get me over there."

"All right. Let's go."

We make it down to Stevie's car in a flash, even the shitty elevator in my building knowing we're in a hurry and it reaches the first floor way faster than usual.

Once we're in the car and Stevie heads for the highway, she breaks the tense silence.

"Why didn't you tell me?"

"I didn't tell anyone. I wasn't sure what to do. It's not like I planned this." My heart is still thundering behind my ribs, and I thank God for Stevie's lead foot. "I was trying to weigh the options."

"Not to be rude, but I think you should've weighed them faster." Stevie changes lanes to pass a driver with the nerve to go the speed limit.

"Gee, thanks."

"I'm sorry, hon. Really. I wish Johnny would've stuck with his routine of never taking out the trash." She hesitates, her eyes flicking over to me before returning to the road. "What are you going to say?"

"I don't know."

The car falls silent again, and my brain turns over all the possibilities of what I'll find when we reach Reed's.

I didn't want him to find out like this, and I was so close to filling him in. At least, that's what I'm telling myself.

Reed did seem different over the past few days, and he'd actually gone to Johnny's work to iron out everything between them.

That was a huge step. We'd even talked about having a get together soon; Reed was going to turn down a double shift.

Tears prickle at my eyes, and I can't stop them. Slow yet steady trickles rain down my face as passing car lights flash against my window.

"I wanted to tell him. I…I think I want to try this with him, but now he's going to be blindsided."

"It'll be okay. We'll make them understand, all right? I'm right here with you."

But Stevie's words drift away as it starts to rain outside. The headlights of oncoming vehicles switch on, and I find myself staring at them until my eyes ache.

What am I going to say to Reed to make him understand? What am I going to say to Johnny?

Anger flares in my gut as I imagine him screaming at Reed in full big-brother-protector mode over there.

I've always hated it. Sure, there's something nice about having your brother stand up to bullies for you, but I'm not a kid anymore.

And that's the crux of it.

Johnny treats me like I'm still a child. I'm always just a baby sister to him.

Maybe that's why I fell so hard, so fast when it came to Reed. He never looked at me like I was just this dumb kid he had to take care of.

He looks at me like I'm a person.

Stevie exits the highway, and we take the right toward Reed's. As we pull up, I see the lights are on, and Johnny's truck is parked halfway in the driveway.

I hop out of the car and sprint toward the door as Stevie throws it in park. The front door is cracked open, and then I remember Henry.

Please, God, let him be asleep for this.

Just as my foot hits the porch, I hear Johnny's voice screaming from inside. *This is bad. Very, very bad.*

Chapter 30

Reed

I'm surprised at how well the last few days have gone, especially this weekend. I've actually managed to spend a lot of quality time with Henry, and it feels like a welcome change for both of us.

I wish Mae had been around, but I understand she's still sorting through some stuff. I'll admit that I hate how she's keeping it to herself, though.

She's been so buttoned up and still a bit closed off, but *New Reed* is trying very hard not to push his luck.

As I finish getting Henry into bed, I head downstairs to grab a much-needed drink. I forget how much children wipe you out when you're wrangling them all day.

Cracking open the fridge and snagging a beer, I twist off the top, and it's absolute bliss when the cool beverage slides down my throat.

"Oh, yeah. That's exactly what I needed."

I sit down on the couch, but as soon as my ass hits the cushions, someone is pounding on my door.

Is it Mae? Did something happen?

I hurry over to the door, flipping the lock and opening it wide.

Suddenly, I'm shoved back into my house and I stumble, then regain my balance.

"Johnny?"

"You fucking lying piece of shit!"

I step back, dodging Johnny's finger as he jabs the air in front of me. It hasn't been five minutes since I got Henry to bed, and now this.

"You can't just barge in here like this. Henry is sleeping. What's your problem?" I glare at him.

"Your fucking dick is my problem!"

Stepping to the side, I push the door in an attempt to keep the rain out.

"What are you talking about?" I look back over my shoulder at the stairs. "Look, I literally just got Henry to bed, okay? So can you just talk to me? He could hear you."

Johnny scoffs angrily before shoving me back as I reach out to calm him. The hard poke of his fingers burn on my chest.

"Ow. Okay, seriously, what the fuck, dude?"

His head falls back in bitter laughter before he snaps his gaze to mine. If I thought he was angry the last time we had a run-in, that's nothing compared to this.

Johnny's eyes are bloodshot as he screams, "You fucking prick! You're just going to stand there like you don't know. How could you?"

He shakes his head, but I'm still at a loss. "Do what, asshole?"

"Knock up my sister, dickhead!"

Everything slams to a halt, and I freeze like Johnny has actually slapped me in the face.

A familiar tunneling of my vision clouds everything in a fog, and my heartbeat is immediately racing.

It's a panic attack. I can tell, but I must have been hearing things wrong.

Mae's pregnant? There's no way.

"Yeah, nice act, but I'm not buying it." Johnny presses closer as he points at me. "Do you ever think of anyone else but yourself? Or do you just stick your dick in anything that comes along without considering how it might affect them? Hmm?"

My mind whirls, and I remember the *something* that Mae didn't want to tell me.

Fuck. Was that it? But we were careful. At least, I thought we were.

"Mae had plans, you ass! She doesn't have a fancy house and a fat bank account to afford this. But what do you care, right? You know, some people have to work their asses off to get where they are. She was finally getting back on her feet!"

Johnny starts pacing, circling back to me and inching closer with each round. His knuckles are white, and his fists hang in the air like he's only barely keeping himself from swinging.

I don't think that restraint is going to last long.

"But you probably don't know about that, either! Mae took care of our gram all on her own without telling anyone. She put off school to help, and now this? What are you going to do, hmm? How exactly are you going to support her since you couldn't be bothered to wrap your fucking tool?"

A crack of thunder sounds outside, and the tapping of heavy rain fills the quiet as I stand there like a statue.

My gut pulls like I've just been punched, and I can't seem to catch my breath. *A baby.* My *baby? With Mae?*

"Don't just fucking stand there and say nothing."

Johnny shoves me against the wall, my head smacking the trim behind me. The pain pulls me into the moment, and I glare at him.

"Back off, Johnny. I didn't know."

His arm keeps me pinned to the wall. "Like hell, you didn't."

I push him off, but Johnny's right back up in my face before I can move away from the wall.

"You son of bitch. You couldn't be satisfied with fucking up your own life? You had to pull Mae into this?"

My blood boils, and the panic flips on its head, turning into a rage that burns so hot, my stomach churns.

I'm done taking this shit.

Shoving Johnny back much harder this time, I pin him to the opposite wall with my forearm.

"I didn't fucking know! You think I wanted to get her pregnant? Of course not! As far as I knew, she was on birth control."

I can feel Johnny gearing up for something just as the sound of steps on the front porch echoes through the house. Mae flings open the door and hurries inside, dripping rain.

Stevie rushes in right behind her and comes around to pull Johnny away from me. I let her, but he's quickly walking back toward me, trying to move her out of the way.

"You're a fucking liar. You just don't give a shit." Johnny struggles to move around Stevie's arm.

"Like I have any reason to fucking lie right now. I told you the fucking truth. So you can screw yourself if you don't believe me!"

Mae steps closer, trying to speak to Johnny, but he doesn't even look at her. Her face is red like she's been crying, and all I can think when I look at her is that she's apparently carrying my child.

Johnny shouts past her, Stevie straining to keep him back. "I told you! I told you what I'd do!"

His girlfriend can barely contain him, and I get ready to catch his punch when he finally breaks free.

The blow is seconds from impact when Mae yells.

"Enough!"

Her scream cuts through the room like a knife, and I dodge out of the way of Johnny's fist, sending him careening off to the side.

As he catches himself and spins to face me, we all stop everything and look at Mae, her anger palpable.

"You ruined everything, Johnathan Marrington! This was my news to deliver, not yours. I was going to tell Reed when I was ready. But no, you just had to butt in, like you always do."

Johnny straightens, moving toward Mae, but she holds up a hand to stop him.

"Don't. Don't you dare come at me with some protective bullshit. This is my life! I should have been the one to tell him, but instead, your fucking pigheadedness stole that from me. You just couldn't let me make my own mistakes. Did you ever think that maybe I was trying to see if this would work out before I dropped the bomb?"

"I—"

"No. It's my turn to give the lecture. I didn't want him to stay only because he felt like he had to. I wanted Reed to choose me because he *wanted* to. I needed to see if the changes Reed said he'd make for Henry actually happened. And he's probably scared out of his mind from all this yelling, by the way."

Mae sighs, her eyes dropping to the floor, and I'm too stunned by her words to speak.

"I didn't plan to get pregnant. But you know what, I guess I have one thing to thank you for. All this shit has made me realize what I've been doing. I wanted to make sure I was bringing the baby into the best situation. That's why I waited. I don't even know who he or she is yet, but I'm already trying to think about what's best for them. And now? Now you've sabotaged that because you're too fucking controlling to let me live my own life. So yeah, Johnny, go screw yourself."

Before any of us can think or react, Mae snags the keys from Stevie's grip and dashes outside. I can hear the rain coming down in sheets, and I immediately sprint after her.

"Mae, wait! Please talk to me!"

Johnny's infuriating face pops up in front of me, and he holds me back with a hand. "We're not done."

The last thing I see is Mae getting in the car and tearing off onto the dangerously slick road. *No, no, no. Please, not again.*

Chapter 31

Mae

Navigating the familiar streets back home is made especially difficult as the rain pours down and my sobbing adds another layer of crappy visibility.

I can't believe what Johnny did.

I was close. I was so damn close to telling Reed, and now everything is a fucking disaster.

Lights reflect off the wet roads, and the red and white blurs as still more tears fill my eyes. I just wanted to do this on my terms, but no.

"Who does this shit? You don't just tear off to your sister's boyfriend's house, all cocked and ready. Argh!"

Johnny couldn't think rationally for even two seconds. I'm so sick of his overprotective nonsense and trying to take control of my life.

He's not Dad, and he needs to stop treating me like I'm not capable of making a decision for myself.

"And they were full-on fighting!"

Images of Reed and Johnny shoving each other, my

brother actually taking a swing at him, spin through my mind. Everything whirls like a washer in the spin cycle.

"What were they going to do? Just punch each other until one of them was knocked out? Yeah, because that would have solved anything."

Sobs rack through me as I ramble to myself. I'm just *so* done with all the drama.

Reed was supposed to start making changes on his own and prove he could do it without the pressure of being a new dad on top of that.

No one wants their partner to stay with them just because they're pregnant. I didn't get to see if he actually cared about me before the baby bombshell was dropped.

The rain pours harder, and my wipers can barely keep up with it.

"Oh, just go away, rain."

At this rate, all I want to do is curl up in a ball when I get home and sulk while watching a cheesy movie. My brother will be lucky if I ever speak to him again.

"And I'm probably going to have to do this on my own now. Thanks a lot, bro!"

Johnny just doesn't see me as a person who can make their own choices, and Reed leapt so fast to anger it's astonishing.

Neither one of them listened to me as I tried to stop them, and it took me entirely breaking down to even get Johnny's attention.

They're, like, fucking cavemen or something.

Sniffling, I wipe under my nose, feeling so damn small. God, Johnny actually found the pregnancy test.

Embarrassment and misplaced shame zip through my nerves even though I know I have nothing to feel bad about.

It's my situation, and like I told Johnny, I didn't plan on getting pregnant.

Who do they even think they are, arguing like that about something that's one hundred percent my decision?

"Hate to break it to you, but this is not, in fact, the nineteenth century!"

The highway is so busy, like everyone is hurrying home to get out of the storm, and I hate how no one ever bothers to drive carefully when it's raining.

"It was my news." My heart aches, a literal pang deep behind my sternum. "I'll never be able to tell him the way I wanted. This is always going to be how Reed found out."

Traffic slows as a bottleneck starts to form near an upcoming exit. I merge into traffic on the left to pass around them, but some people are clearly too impatient tonight.

A car whooshes around the left side, and I have to swerve to avoid getting sideswiped.

I glare out the window at them. "Ah! Asshole!"

But then my tires lose traction, and it's so much worse.

I slide across the road, the car hydroplaning across the wet asphalt. Abruptly, I get traction again, but it's only because the vehicle hits a patch of gravel.

It's too much for the momentum already flinging the car to the side.

Oh my God. Unwelcome certainty grips my chest. *I'm going to flip.*

And I do.

The sedan rolls once, twice, and then I lose track of everything.

Tossed around like a rag doll, my head smashes against the window, and I'm flailing like a crash test dummy. My hands and arms hit various places within the interior.

There's a terrible, weightless feeling that swirls in my

stomach like a roller coaster, and I feel the hair fly up off my neck and tangle around my face.

A horrendous crunch echoes around me as I come to a sudden halt, the car landing on the roof.

Pain roars through me as the world finally stills, and I look around, trying to process what just happened.

I'm upside down, hanging from my seatbelt, and I think I must be in the ditch at the side of the road because I can see dirt and tall grass outside the window.

Unfortunately, I also notice flooding water from the runoff streaming inside.

It starts to fill the car, and panic grips me as I worry it might flood the entire thing, fighting with the buckle to free myself.

More water pours in, but I can finally grab the steering wheel with one hand as I unbuckle the seat belt. It slows my fall to the roof as my hips are released, and I splash down into the cold puddle.

Thankfully, it's stopped streaming in, and I won't be submerged.

Shakes assault my body, making my limbs and head ache all the more, and my gaze snaps to the cracked driver's side window.

I can't stay in this water, and I have to lean back to kick the glass. Shifting onto my elbow, the frigid water soaking new parts of my clothes, I smash my foot into the window.

After a few tries, it breaks, and I do my best to kick away all the little pieces at the edge. Switching to my hands and knees, I crawl out, still managing to cut myself a few times as I do, and fresh pain wells across my skin.

Hands greet me as I struggle to climb out of the ditch, and I see that several other drivers have stopped to help.

Two men have jumped down into the muck with me so I can use their hands to boost me up the side. I reach for a woman's waiting hand, and she pulls me the rest of the way out.

Looking down as I catch my breath, I see how filthy I am, and my arms are bleeding. I reach up for my head.

My scalp burns, and I pull back bloody fingers. I start to notice the warmth sliding down my face, and weirdly, I remember that head wounds have a way of bleeding quite a bit.

The woman standing near me takes my hands, leading me somewhere.

She has a gentle smile, and I realize she's hurrying me over to her car, where she sits me on the tailgate of her SUV. A blanket is wrapped around my shoulders, and she's telling me something about staying calm.

I can't make out her words, the adrenaline of the wreck backing off and being replaced with pain. A lot of pain.

My shaking continues, but at this point, I don't feel the cold. I remember my first aid training mentioning something about shock.

Yeah, that seems right. I'm going into shock.

Staring around the woman's trunk for God only knows what reason, I notice a stroller. A thick black bag is off to the side, too, with a stack of diapers sticking out.

Looking down, I see I'm sitting on a folded-up changing mat, and there's a portable toilet like the one I used for the family that was potty training their son.

Suddenly, nausea pulls at my gut, and my heart rate ticks back up. I feel it pound behind my eyes as fresh tears spill out.

"Hey, now." The woman's hands smooth down my arms. "You're alright. It's okay. You're safe now."

I shake my head.

"Kids. You…" It's all I can get out.

She looks around the trunk, a sympathetic smile on her face. "Yeah. I have kids. A girl and a boy. Just try to breathe for me, okay? Do you have any kids?"

I know she's trying to distract me, but the sobs worsen, ripping through my body.

"I..." My teeth chatter as my whisper barely breaks the air. "I...I'm pregnant."

"What's that, honey?"

My eyes flare wide as a fear I've never felt grips my heart. I turn toward her, reaching out to grab her shirt.

"I'm pregnant!"

The woman's brows raise with understanding, and she sits next to me on the tailgate, smoothing my hands back beneath the blanket.

Her hands keep rubbing up and down my arm, but I can barely feel it.

"Oh, okay, honey. It's alright. I'm sure you're both okay." She lowers her face into my field of vision, holding my gaze. "You're okay. Babies are strong. And we're built to carry them, protect them. You'll be just fine."

"If anything happens..." I cry harder, unable to stop the suffocating sobs from choking out my voice.

"Help is coming. We called 911, and the paramedics will be here soon. You're okay."

But her words fall on deaf ears. I can't hear anything anymore—not her, not the traffic, nothing.

All I can do is think about the life growing inside me and how I've put it in danger. If anything happens, I don't know if I can take it.

Chapter 32

Reed

It's been too long since Mae left, and Stevie's attempts at playing mediator between Johnny and me aren't working. At least she had the presence of mind to get us out onto the porch so we don't wake up Henry.

"How did you not know? How did you not use protection?!"

Johnny's anger still fumes, making him a ticking time bomb, ready to go off again, and I'm right there with him.

"I'm not doing this again! I already told you that Mae said she was taking birth control. I trusted her." I shake my head, huffing out a breath. "And if you really want to know, I pulled out most of the time!"

A wild swing comes my way, and I just manage to duck out of Johnny's range.

"That's my fucking sister!"

I scream at him as Stevie steps between us again. "I'm fucking aware!"

Then my pager goes off out of nowhere, and I grab it

out of my pocket, confused. I almost forgot about the hospital altogether.

Seeing the call for a bad accident, I shake my head. I should have expected it, considering how it's pouring rain.

I start for the door, intent on grabbing my bag and leaving Johnny to sulk like a goddamn five-year-old.

His hard laugh cuts through my attempt to block him out.

"Of course, you're leaving. Choosing work over everything else, yet again!"

Spinning around, I level him with a glare. "You know it's not that fucking simple. I'm on call like every other doctor, and sometimes I have to go help people, you know, not die."

"Whatever. You'll never change."

That bites harder than it should, probably because it's been Mae's big issue since the beginning. I toss the pager on the wicker couch taking up a good chunk of the porch.

"You don't want me to go. Fine. I won't go."

Johnny grins sarcastically. "Well, look at that. Actually sticking around for a whole ass minute. All it took was knocking up Mae to get you to come around."

"Johnny!" Stevie glares at him. "She's my friend, too, and I won't listen to you talk about her like that. I've been struggling with you assholes for way too freaking long now. Work this shit out."

The corners of my mouth turn down as I nod at Stevie. I have to hand it to her, she hasn't quit trying to get us to chill since she arrived.

"What more would you like me to say, Johnny? Because at this point, I'm ready to lay it all out for you again, but I'd rather cut to the chase."

I cross my arms over my chest and hold his stare.

Johnny shakes his head before Stevie elbows him in the ribs.

"Fine." He exhales forcefully through his nose. "You lied. You slept with Mae behind my back, and now she's pregnant. I'm supposed to just be cool with that? You're fucking up her life, and that's exactly what I was worried about. She's a person, not just one of your booty calls, and you've left her broken in your wake, like all the others."

I start to come back at him with another "fuck off" before stopping myself and taking a deep breath.

"Look, I get you're angry. I'm not expecting you to be okay with me betraying or harming Mae, though. I'm expecting you to listen to what I'm saying. I didn't know she was pregnant, clearly. Mae said as much herself. I didn't, don't, want to leave her behind 'in my wake.' I care about her, and frankly, it sucks that you can't see that."

"If you care so much, why didn't you talk to me about it sooner? Why'd you go and get her pregnant? You can't just—"

Johnny's phone rings in his pocket, and the upbeat rock song is so incredibly off base for the situation that I actually laugh.

When he answers, though, I watch Johnny's face go from annoyed to panicked in a flash.

"I'm on my way." He hangs up.

"What was that about?"

My best friend stares at me like he's just been punched in the gut, tears brimming behind his eyes.

"What?!"

The pound of blood in my ears is nearly deafening, and then Johnny blinks, clearing his throat around the lump forming.

"Mae's been in an accident. She's just been brought in to the hospital."

I don't know why, but I rush to my pager and double-check the message.

Car accident. Landed on its hood. Female with head trauma, approximately twenty-five.

Nausea clenches my gut, and I almost throw up.

"Mae." My voice is small and quiet.

"Go. Both of you. I'll stay and watch Henry." Johnny and I look at Stevie in shock. "Go!"

Not bothering with my bag, I rush to my car, Johnny hot on my heels. We slip inside, and in moments, I turn over the ignition, and we're on the road to the hospital.

The interior is silent and I drive as fast as safety allows. My heart rate is too high to even guess, and my chest feels so tight, I can barely breathe.

This can't be happening again. I have to get to her.

The rain coats my windshield, which makes visibility a nightmare, but then I feel something warm on my cheeks. Swiping across one, I realize I'm crying.

Great, just great.

Soon, I'm hyperventilating, and all I can think is that I'm going to someone else because of a car crash. I'm going to lose Mae…

I'm going to lose my child.

Suddenly, I can't breathe at all, and everything goes foggy, my vision tunneling. I quickly pull over to the side of the road and leap out.

Emptying the contents of my stomach into the ditch, my body shakes so hard, I nearly fall over.

"Dude!" Johnny is at my side. "Are you alright?"

"I…I…" Trying to swallow down more rising bile, I shake my head. "I need you to drive."

I don't want to meet his eyes and find that terrible pity everyone always flings at me when I'm gripped by panic.

Still, I have to at least acknowledge he's taken the key because my fingers are numb.

"I got it."

Johnny just nods, opening the door for me without another word, and I remember why I actually like the guy.

He takes over behind the wheel, and we're back on the road to the hospital in seconds. However, the panic doesn't back off, even as I recognize it's there.

My mind just churns like a goddamn blender, and I close my eyes against the swell of nausea rising up again.

I can't lose her. Not like this. I…I…

And then it hits me like a Mack Truck. I love her. I love Mae with everything I have.

I didn't want to admit it. I wanted to protect myself like I always do, but it's clearly too late for that.

I'm already in way too deep, and if I lose her right now, I won't survive it.

"I'll get us there, Reed. I promise."

Looking over at Johnny, I completely abandon any leftover anger toward him. I don't care anymore.

"I know." I nod. "And I'll do everything I can to make sure she's okay, and the baby."

The rest of the drive is a blur, and then we're at the ER entrance. I jump out of the car without a word and run for the doors.

Flashing my ID badge, I get the nurses to let me in, recognizing several but unable to remember their names as terror floods my veins.

It's swamped as hell in here and the ER is backed up. I have some of the available nurses help me suit up.

I've got to find out where she is.

"Mae Marrington? Car accident?" I ask the RN at the nurse's station, realizing it's one of my favorites to work with, Laura.

"Hey, umm." Her sympathetic smile falters as she looks at the charts. "Bed three."

I take off, running down the hall. When I get to the right bed, I skid to a stop as I see Mae sitting on the dim white sheets, just as pale as all the fabric surrounding her.

"Mae!"

Her eyes shoot to mine as she hears my voice, and then Mae bursts into tears. A bandage is wrapped around her head, there are several smaller ones across her arms, and bruising covers nearly every bit of skin I can see.

I'm at her side in a flash, pulling her into my arms and holding her tight against my chest. I have to convince myself she's really here.

"I'm here, Mae." I don't fight the tears, pressing my lips to the top of her head, which is damp and cold. "I've got you, and I'm never letting go. Not for a fucking second."

She turns to look at me, her eyes so red from crying she looks drugged. "There was this car. He flew up along the side of my car."

Mae can barely speak through the sobs.

"I-I had to swerve, but th-then there was all this dirt. I flipped—what about the baby?!"

The stark fear in her eyes is like a dagger to my heart, and I squeeze her tight again.

"They did scans. It's taking forever!"

"Mae!"

Johnny rushes over, coming around on her other side and wrapping her in another hug.

"Johnny!" She cries harder. "Please, Reed—"

Mae looks to me. "Can you check if…"

As the words die in her throat, I nod.

"I'll track down the scans. Johnny—" our eyes meet "—don't leave her for a second."

"Not a chance. Go. Find out what's going on."

I have to practically pry myself away from Mae, but I want answers, too. Running down the hall toward radiology, I hunt for any tech in sight.

I'm getting my hands on those scans if it's the last thing I do.

Chapter 33

Mae

The frenzied spin of the world slows, and the frantic pace that infected everything around me when I was brought to the hospital suddenly flips like a light switch.

Now, time drags on like a snail as I sit here in this stupid bed, listening to the incessant beep of the monitor.

It's been a while since Reed left to find the scans, and I'm going crazy waiting for an update. I'm unsure exactly how long it's been, but obviously long enough that Johnny fell asleep in a chair by the window.

I'm not upset that he did. If dread weren't still keeping my nerves on edge, I'd have passed out from exhaustion long ago.

The doctor who first saw me when I arrived came in a few minutes ago and said I'm being kept overnight for observation. I'll most likely be discharged in the morning.

But I still don't know how the baby is doing.

"Mae."

I snap my attention to the door, and Reed comes in holding a long, skinny printout of something.

"Did you get them?" My heart hammers, and I'm seconds from crying again.

Reed nods. "Yeah."

As he walks over, Reed smiles, and I can tell he's fighting back a swell of emotion.

"I didn't look. I wanted to see the pictures with you, but the tech said everything's fine."

Relief floods through me like a dam breaking, and the crying starts up again.

"I can't seem to stop." Mopping up my face, I feel Reed sit next to me. "Damn hormones."

Reed chuckles softly, holding the images face down. "You ready?"

"Yeah."

As he turns them over, Reed says something about everything being right on track, but I don't hear him, not really.

There's a tiny little bean in front of me that looks like it's wearing a circle on its head. A tearful chuckle escapes, and I squeeze Reed's hand.

"They're just fine, Mae. The baby is safe and healthy and very small. You're not far along. A few weeks."

I'm weeping uncontrollably now as I stare at the pictures of the human growing inside me, and I feel like the Grinch when his heart grows three sizes.

"Why are they wearing a hat?"

Reed laughs. "That's the yolk. It'll disappear. But they're in there. All safe and sound. It's too early to tell a gender or anything, but—"

"They're perfect." I laugh hard through a huge sob, tears streaming down my face. "They're better than perfect."

I look over at Reed, who's all tears and snot, too.

"We made a little person."

He laughs as he wipes his face, pulling my knuckles to his lips and kissing them.

"I was so fucking scared, Mae. I thought I might lose you, both of you. And it nearly destroyed me. It still might if you leave and never come back."

Blinking to clear my eyes, I hold Reed's gaze, letting him say all the things he's been holding on to.

"I haven't been good at this. Relationships are really hard for me, but that's not an excuse. You deserve a lot better than I gave you. You deserve the entire world, Mae."

He shakes his head, glancing at the pictures and then back up at me.

"I want to be the man you deserve. I want to be better. For you. For Henry." He nods down. "For them."

"Reed."

I can't find the words, so I pull him closer, lowering my head to his chest.

"When I lost Clara, I thought I could just fill the hole left behind with work. If I saved everyone who needed me and ensured no one ever died on my watch again, I'd make up for not being there for her. I can't explain how it feels to know I should have been there for her and Henry but wasn't."

He pulls me up to look at him.

"But I know now that saving a life doesn't make up for losing one, especially someone you love. And I know that pushing everyone away, pushing Henry away, was the worst thing I could have done. When I thought I might lose you, I broke. Everything inside me snapped…"

Reed's eyes fall, and I know he can't finish. It's alright, though. He's already said more than enough.

I lift his face, framing it with my hands, and smile. Before he can say anything else, I kiss him.

It's long and slow, both of us just focusing on the feel of the other's skin, and then I look up at him again.

"You didn't lose me. I'm right here, and I promise you, I'm not going anywhere."

With shaky hands, Reed covers mine with his own. "I…"

"It's okay. You don't have to say anything else." I smile softly, exhaustion starting to creep its way through me.

"No. I do." He sucks in a deep breath, then holds my attention, unflinching. "I love you, Mae. I love you more than I ever thought I could love anyone after everything that happened. I love how you call me out on my shit. I love your sense of humor and ability to make everything fun. I love how you are with Henry, how you've made me see how much I was hurting him. I love you. And I never want to be parted from you ever again."

Fresh tears fall, and I laugh as I think about everything that's happened over the past few weeks.

"You know, I just wanted to become a teacher. I mean, I still want that. But I didn't think there would be anything else big happening in my future. I've dated, sure, and I sort of hoped I'd find someone. But I'll admit, my heart wasn't in it. And then all this happened."

I look between Reed and my lower belly.

"I find out you're my nanny gig. The guy I've had a crush on since high school, who has always been off-limits, and suddenly I'm thrust into your life. I never thought this was a possibility, but I never got over you. I think that's why the dating thing never worked. I was holding out for you. And I'm so glad I fell down those stairs and left that job."

Reed and I laugh together this time.

"I love you, Reed. I've loved you since the day I met

you, and I'm sorry that fate took Clara from you, but I am so grateful that we get this chance."

His lips press to mine as Reed's hand finds my stomach. "I won't blame the universe for the accident anymore. Or myself. Bad things happen. But good things happen, too. And this is more good than I ever dared to hope for. I get a chance at a family again, and I am *so* happy it's with you."

"Well, I hope so, because you're officially stuck with me now."

Reed lowers his forehead to mine. "That's fine with me, Lil Bit. That's perfect."

Chapter 34

Reed

The lake smell I'd once known every weekend swirls in my nose, and I can't help but laugh as Henry tries to secure his fishing lure to the pole. It hits me, not for the first time since we got here, that I'm actually fishing at the lake with my son.

I've made a weekend fun for him, and it's not even the first one.

With taking double shifts only out of necessity, I have a lot more time to spend with Henry and of course, with Mae.

It hasn't been long since the accident, only about a month, but it already feels like I've been through a lifetime of changes. And I'll be the first to admit, I didn't know if they were possible.

"Dad!" Henry frowns at me, holding up the fishing rod and lure. "Help."

Chuckling, I take it from him and show Henry how to tie the knot again. "Here you go, kiddo. Try again."

Mae returns from the public restroom at the lake park and sighs as she plops down into her camp chair.

"Still nauseated?" I grin sympathetically at her.

"Yes." She takes a small sip of her water. "I don't know if I can take eight more weeks of this."

"That's just an average. It could go away sooner." Holding Mae's hand as I sit next to her, I give it a squeeze. "Did you try the ginger?"

She makes a face, scowling at the mention of the spice. "Ugh. No. Just the smell was enough to make me gag."

"Well, we'll think of something. I can get some peppermint tea from the store on our way home today."

"It's worth a try." Mae shrugs. "Maybe Dr. Connors will know some trick. Didn't you say she had a baby not too long ago?"

"Yeah. I'll ask her. We've been doing good lately. She'll probably give me a pat on the back for remembering."

"Ha! I know she's a bit of a softy, but I like her. As far as therapists go, you could have wound up with a much worse one."

I nod, knowing how right Mae is. "Very true. Honestly, she's been great, and I'm grateful you helped me find her. I don't think unpacking everything about losing Clara would have gone nearly as well without Dr. Connors's help."

"Trust me," Mae says as she meets my eyes, "I can tell. You've put in so much work with Henry and me. He's so excited for weekends like this. I'm so happy to see you guys connecting."

"Well, I have a lot more work to do, but yeah, it's going great."

We smile at each other, and then I turn back to watch Henry reeling his line in and casting it out again. He's pretty good at that part, and I'm more than grateful I finally got to teach him.

I'm grateful for so many things, actually.

From the baby, to reestablishing my relationship with my son, so much has changed in just a handful of weeks, and it's all thanks to Mae.

She's been an absolute rock, not to mention the best thing that could have ever happened to me. The grace she shows navigating the loss of my first wife while helping me remember the good times has been remarkable.

There are even pictures of Clara in the hall outside Henry's room now. Mae suggested them as a way to remember the good times instead of burying her memory behind sadness.

It was the perfect move. Remembering Clara and allowing myself to be grateful for the time we had has helped me start moving on. And Henry has been able to explore memories of his mother without fear or guilt.

Plus, I've had the added perk of finding Mae standing in front of the pictures on occasion, whispering under her breath. I've caught her thanking Clara and promising to "look after her boys."

If I wasn't already madly in love with her, that would have sealed the deal.

"Oh!" Mae shoots up in her chair, and I can see her immediately regret the sudden movement. "Ugh. Ooh, okay, go away nausea. Anyway, Johnny said yes to dinner tomorrow. I almost forgot to tell you."

"Oh, great. It'll be nice to see them again, and I need to get my leaf blower back."

Mae laughs. I've picked up an affinity for yard work since I've been home more often, and Johnny has used it to his advantage, borrowing all of my tools so he doesn't have to buy any.

I really don't mind. I'll lend Johnny whatever he needs.

I'm just happy I didn't lose my best friend after everything that happened.

Apparently, confessions of love have a way of changing people's minds about you. Yeah, he'd woken up almost immediately after I got to Mae with the scans, and he'd just played possum to give us our space.

Crafty bastard.

Not that I'm actually mad. Hell, I'm thrilled that Johnny was able to see how much I meant what I said.

In his words, *I saw with my own two eyes how much you love my sister*, which had been enough to help him bury the hatchet before Mae was even discharged.

And thank God for that. I don't ever want to fight with him like that again. Johnny is downright scary when he's pissed, and I pity anyone who gets between him and someone he cares about.

"Dad! Dad, I got one!"

Henry calls back over his shoulder, the line jerking, and I run up to help him reel in the catch. It takes a few minutes of tugging; I want Henry to do it mostly by himself, just like my father taught me on this same lake.

With a hearty splash, the fish flies out of the water, and Henry swings his pole over to the shore. The glistening, slippery creature flails around on the lure, and my son smiles bigger than I've ever seen.

"I did it!"

Mae is quickly up and out of her seat, standing next to us as we cheer, and I grab Henry around the shoulder with one arm, giving him a tight hug.

"You did! Your first one!"

"I'm so proud of you, Henry." Mae puts a hand over her mouth. "Oof, okay, sorry, that's grossing me out."

Henry and I laugh as Mae backs away, and I help him get the fish off the hook and back into the water. This is all catch and release, which I'm sure makes Mae happy because bringing home a load of smelly fish in the car would *not* go over well.

"Dad! That was amazing! Did you see how hard it fought?" My son practically jumps up and down as he speaks.

"I did!" I pat him on the shoulder. "Wouldn't you want to fight it if you had a hook in your lip?"

He laughs, and I playfully pretend to hook him, pulling him along after me before mock-throwing him in the lake.

"No! Don't!" He can barely speak through the laughter.

"We should celebrate! What would you like for dinner, kiddo?"

Mae still stands a few feet away, and I shake my head with a smile. We won't be able to disguise her nausea as a virus for much longer.

"Pizza!" Henry claps his hands loudly into a prayer position beneath his chin.

"Pizza it is." I smile. "Let's pack up, and we'll head over to Pizza Luche's."

After driving to our favorite pizza place, our usual server, Dani, finds us a big booth in the back, and we order one large meat supreme, holding the onions on Mae's side.

It's beyond amazing, memories and pepperoni all mixed into the perfect creation, and Mae's actually able to get a slice or two down before her stomach protests.

Poor thing. I really hope her nausea goes away soon. And thank God I'm not the one who has to be pregnant. It does not *look fun.*

I take a swig of my beer and notice Mae eyeing it as she drinks the same thing as Henry—a kid's mocktail.

Leaning forward, I whisper so Henry doesn't hear. "Missing it?"

"Yes. So much. I don't know if you noticed, but I'm

not much of a sweet drink girl, and Sprite with maraschino cherries is literally just sugar with more sugar."

I laugh, but Mae just rolls her eyes.

"It's not forever. How about I promise to have a beer waiting for you after delivery?"

"Can you do that?"

I shrug. "I'll have to sneak it in, but I got you."

"Oh, yes. Please."

"Deal."

She sits back with a smile, and I look over at Henry, who is trying to see if he can fit half the pizza slice in his mouth at once.

"Dude. Buddy. Slow down. I'm not supposed to go to the hospital today, remember?"

Henry looks up at me, a hilarious look of pseudo-guilt on his face. "Okay."

At least, that's what I think he says because it's very muffled by all the pizza.

ONCE WE'VE DEVOURED the entire pizza, and I've thankfully avoided giving my son the Heimlich maneuver, we head back home. It's a later night than usual, and Henry falls asleep in the car.

The street lights and gentle hum of traffic have lulled all of us into a state of supreme relaxation, and I'm half convinced that I'll need to carry Mae into the house after I take Henry in.

"You going to make it?" I whisper to her.

"Yes, yes. It's just dark and warm in here. And I'm always exhausted, okay?"

I chuckle. "I get you. I'm going to carry Henry up. Why don't you put your feet up on the couch, and we'll find something to watch that we've seen a million times. You can pass out whenever you want."

Mae smiles over at me, her eyes half closed. "Sounds perfect."

Pulling into the garage, I'm thoroughly impressed that Henry hasn't woken up from all the noise and that Mae has managed to stay awake long enough to walk inside with me.

She holds the door open as I carry Henry in and then promptly collapses onto the couch.

"I'll be right back, okay?"

"Yup. I'll be here." Mae waves a hand as she lies back on the sofa with her eyes closed.

It's fucking adorable, and I grin as I carry Henry up to his room.

Laying him down in the bed, I switch on the star shaped lights and pull the covers over him. Just as I'm about to leave, I hear him shuffle around.

"Hey, bud. We're home. Go to sleep."

I turn to see Henry sitting up, so I walk over and tuck him in again, his eyes already closing.

"Dad?"

"Yes, buddy?" I smooth my hand through his hair.

"Today was really fun. I'm glad you taught me to fish. Even if it was kind of gross."

I chuckle lightly, trying not to disturb the quiet. "It was fun. I can't wait to teach you more stuff. Maybe even more gross stuff."

Henry laughs, and I gently ruffle his locks before leaning over to give him a huge hug.

"Get some rest."

"Is there water?"

"Yes, buddy. On the nightstand like always."

"Dad?"

I sigh, chuckling once more as Henry stalls. "Yes, bud?"

"I'm excited, too. You're the best."

And just like that, I couldn't care less about Henry's continued efforts to prolong my presence in the room.

"I love you, Henry." I give him another hug. "Now get some sleep, or I'll sell all your toys."

"No, you won't." He giggles with his eyes closed.

"No. I won't."

"High five?"

We've been developing a unique shake, and I hold up his hand so that we can practice and he doesn't have to look.

"High five."

I smack his palm.

"Fist bump."

I tap his knuckles.

"Laser."

I touch the tip of his pointer finger with mine as we make finger guns.

"And shark fin."

I hook my thumb around his as we point our fingers up in a flat shape to look like a fin.

"Good night, Henry. I love you."

"Night, Dad. Love you, too."

As I close the door behind me, I look at all the photos of Henry as a baby, wrapped in Clara's arms and mine. The images of him painting with her at the kitchen table. Newer photos from school where he refused to smile and instead made a face or stuck his tongue out.

"We made a pretty fantastic kid, Clara. I'm sorry I forgot about that."

I step to the edge of the stairs where there's a photo from last weekend that Mae just put up. The three of us are at the arcade holding our mighty horde of tickets after Mae cleaned up in Skee-Ball.

"Thank you for sending her to me. I know you had to have a hand in it. You always knew what this family needed. And this time, it was her."

I start down the stairs with a smile, ready to enjoy a movie with Mae.

Chapter 35

Mae

I startle a bit as Reed comes down the stairs, and he laughs. I sit up, grabbing the remote, before pulling the blanket over me.

"So, what about *Addams Family Values*? We just watched the first one the other night."

Reed is quickly at my side, standing above me as he kisses my head. "Sounds great. Would you like a seltzer?"

"Oh yes, please. It's not wine, but it'll do. Plus, it helps with the stomach stuff."

"Is it still bad?" He furrows his brow.

"No. But I never know how long it'll last."

Reed laughs and pads over to the kitchen to retrieve my most-prized beverage as of late. It hits the spot, settling any of the leftover queasiness, and the movie is just what I want.

When it's finished, and we've thoroughly discussed what *not* to name the baby, Reed flicks off the TV and takes my glass of water from me.

I glower playfully at him. "Hey, mister. I was drinking that."

"I'll grab it in a second. Right now—" Reed bends, scooping me up in his arms, and I wrap my legs around his waist "—I have other plans for you. If you're up for it, of course."

All at once, any lingering tiredness is washed away. All I can think of is having Reed's hands ease away the aches and tenderness of my body and replacing it with pleasure.

"I am most certainly up for it." I rub myself against him. "As are you."

He moans low in my ear as his lips find my neck. Carrying me to the master bedroom, where I've taken to staying on Friday and Saturday evenings, I lean my head back so Reed can work his magic across my throat and chest.

I'll always enjoy how he can easily lift me, dwarfing me with his height. At least while I'm still small enough to do so.

Hanging onto him, Reed uses a hand to get us inside the room and turn on the small lamp by the bed. It fills the room with a warm glow, and he lays me down on the bed.

The comforter is smooth and cool against my skin, and Reed quickly helps me take off my shirt and pants. Shucking his clothes, he joins me on the bed, pushing the cup of my thin bra off my breast and squeezing.

I arch into his palm, reaching around to my back and unfastening the clasp. He pulls the thing off, tossing it to the floor.

His mouth finds my nipple, and they're so incredibly sensitive that just a few swirls of his tongue have me reeling. Low moans rumble out of me, and I tangle my fingers in his hair as Reed lavishes the hard buds with sucks and gentle bites.

"Reed."

The quiet plea fills the space around us, and he pulls me closer, sliding a hand behind my back and pressing me to his mouth. His tongue continues to sweep across my nipple as his other hand reaches my slit, and I buck against him as Reed drags a finger gently across it.

I'm dripping already, my body somehow poised and ready for him even more now that I'm pregnant.

Slowly, torturously, Reed slips his finger between my lips and finds my clit. He rubs in lazy circles as he dips lower toward my entrance and then back up.

The deliberate, agonizing tease sends lightning through my nerves. I can feel every little move and flick and change in pressure as Reed explores my pussy with his deft fingers.

The "come here" motion he uses makes me practically weep with desire, and I hug my legs together around his hand.

Just as he pushes in deep, Reed pulls back, dragging his fingertips across the top of my channel before sliding out and rubbing the fresh arousal across my clit.

My nerves sing as Reed brings me right up to the edge of an orgasm. The sucking and biting he delivers to my nipples goes straight to my core, and I'm grinding myself against his hand without even thinking.

With one last flick of his tongue, Reed releases my breast and works his kisses down my body until his lips hit my pussy. He toys with my clit as his fingers pump inside me, and just when I think I won't be able to stand another second, I climax hard.

My walls clamp around his fingers. Everything is more intense right now, and I thank my lucky stars that I can still enjoy this with him.

Reed moans against me as I flutter, the vibrations dragging out my orgasm. Even as it recedes, Reed licks up my slit, drinking me in like he's dying for the taste.

When he pulls back and looks up at me, the smile shining through him is brighter than the sun, and I grin right back.

"Get inside me, Reed."

"My pleasure, Lil Bit."

Reed stands, ditching his boxers, then sinks between my legs, spreading them wide with his hips. Gripping his shaft, he rubs it against my wet skin, revving me up once more as he teases me.

He swirls the head against my opening, and I rock my hips against him, desperate for him to drive that magnificent cock of his inside me.

"So hungry for it, aren't you?"

"Yes, Reed. Please, I want you inside me. *Now.*"

I scoot down closer to him, forcing the head of his cock in, and I moan as he chuckles, sliding in further, oh so slowly.

He teases, going in halfway and then pulling back, so I hook my legs around his waist and pull him forward. Reed finally fills me up, and I arch as he hits the sensitive spot deep within me.

"Oh fuck, Lil Bit." He rolls his hips, lowering his head to mine. "The way your sweet pussy grips my cock."

Reed's thrusts pick up speed, thank God, and I meet his efforts, rocking myself up and down, using his hips as leverage.

He sinks deep, pressing against my G-spot, and a sharp moan cuts through me as the burn starts in my core again.

I tumble over the edge as he pumps into me in hard, forceful movements, my orgasm cresting like a tsunami and causing me to squeeze my eyes shut.

Reed reaches under my neck and pulls me onto his lap as he leans back. His cock sinks deeper still, and I cry out.

"That's my beautiful girl." He holds the side of my face, and I lean into it.

Our eyes meet as his thrusts slow. I smile as I watch the pleasure on Reed's face, and he wraps his other arm around me.

Pulling my lips to his, he kisses me long and intense, and I swirl my hips in slow circles as I ride him.

"I'm all yours, Dr. Finnigan."

Warmth threads through me, and I fight off tears as Reed holds my gaze.

Intense, heated passion is incredible, and I know we'll have plenty of those nights, too. But this, staring into Reed's eyes as we join in a way that's about more than just our bodies, is truly something else.

I can *feel* the love radiating out of him like the sun, and it makes my heart so full I'm sure it will burst.

We kiss again and again, the desperate joy of wanting each other to know deep down that we're adored, worshipped, and loved beyond anything else.

Our pace picks up again, and Reed holds my hips up slightly so he can piston into me faster. Another release is poised in my core, then Reed uses his grip to place me back onto the bed as he pushes my legs up to rest on his shoulders.

He drives into me, sinking in as far as he can before rolling his hips so his cock rubs against every sensitive nerve inside me.

I moan hard, and Reed finds the perfect leverage to fuck into me with everything he has. His large frame towers over me as he plows into my pussy.

It's more than enough, and I'm coming around his dick

in seconds. And it doesn't stop. His delicious skills keep the orgasm flowing as Reed dominates my body.

"That's it, Lil Bit. Come for me." He moves faster, harder. "Let me feel that pussy beg for my cum."

I clamp down harder, another more intense release shooting through me like a rocket. Joy floods my veins as I lose myself to the sensations.

I'd worried Reed wouldn't want me as much once he knew I was pregnant, but apparently, I had nothing to be concerned with. If anything, he's even hornier.

Reed's delicious dirty talk has only increased, praising the life we've created together. And I adore it.

I internally chuckle. *Who knew I'd have a breeding kink?*

But it's so clear we're both into it. Reed's extraordinary praise turns me on like nothing else as he finds his own release.

"My good girl, taking my cum. Mmm. Fucking hell."

Reed's cock thickens, hardening to its fullest as he fills me up. The warmth of his release seeps into me, and I moan as his dick jerks inside me.

As the world settles around us, Reed slips free, lying beside me as our breaths begin to slow. I look over at him, grinning, and he tucks a hair behind my ear.

"I love you, Mae." Reed kisses me, pulling me against his side. "So damn much."

I giggle, snuggling into him. "I love you, too."

A calm like I never knew before Reed seeps into me, and I sigh. I hug him tight and then push up onto my elbow to look him in the eye.

"What do you think they'll be like?"

"The baby?" He smiles. "I don't know. Henry is like his mom, not resembling me at all. And I'm nothing like my parents. They could be anyone."

"That's exciting." I grin, resting my chin on Reed's chest.

"And a little scary."

"Oh, hush. We'll be fine." I lay my hand across my belly. "They'll have so many people here to look out for them. You, me, my brother, Stevie, Aunty Heather, and, of course, a big brother. Just like me."

I sigh again, my eyes staring off into space.

"What is it?" He lifts my chin toward him.

"Oh, just Henry. I want to tell him. I want to know he'll be okay."

Reed laughs, pulling me into a hug. "I know. And I was actually thinking about that."

I try to peer up at Reed from my position. "Do you know when you want to tell him?"

"Yeah. I was thinking of tomorrow. At dinner."

Excitement blooms in my chest. "Really?"

"Yeah. I think he's ready."

"Oh, Reed. That's amazing! Thank you."

"Nothing to thank me for, love." Reed kisses the top of my head. "I know Henry loves you as much as I do, and he actually used to beg for a sibling when he was younger."

"That's perfect." I smile, my eyes brimming with happy tears. "He's perfect. You're perfect. I love that kid so much. I know he'll be an amazing big brother."

"Me too."

Reed chuckles, squeezing me tight before snagging the covers from under us and pulling them free. "It's all good, Mae. I know I've said it before, but I'm truly excited to see what the future holds. And it's all because of you."

"You're very welcome. Now, please," I say, pulling the blanket up under my arms and closing my eyes, "let the pregnant person sleep."

With a laugh, Reed hugs me one more time. "Sorry,

sorry. Get your rest, Momma. You've got a human to make."

"That I do."

Sleep comes quick and easy after that. And as it gently pulls me into some much-needed rest, all I can think is how incredibly happy I am.

Life couldn't get any better than this.

Chapter 36

Reed

Ringing the bell, Mae, Henry, and I wait for Johnny to open up so we can get this dinner started. I've never been one for family get-togethers, but these nights we have with my best friend and family all in one room are quickly becoming some of my favorites.

Stevie answers the door, smiling wide as she greets us, and Mae hands her the brussels sprouts she roasted.

I can officially say that Mae has not only opened me up to being a more present father and facing my grief, but to vegetables as well. *Brussels sprouts, who knew?*

"Thank you!" Stevie takes a deep inhale of the steaming dish. "Oh, these smell amazing. Did you do something different?"

"I added cranberries." Mae smiles, and we're welcomed inside with hugs for everyone.

Henry quickly dashes to the kitchen, where he knows he'll find Johnny, and we three adults follow behind.

Sure enough, Johnny is working on the meat, placing

the thick roast onto a platter to let it rest. Henry runs up to him, inquiring about the food, and I laugh.

"Hey, bud!" Johnny pats him on the shoulder. "Yeah, this is the roast beef. It'll be delicious. Been cooking all day. What did you guys bring?"

"Brussels sprouts. And they're actually good!"

We all chuckle at that, and Johnny comes around the island to give Mae a big hug. I still wonder how much it would have hurt Mae if Johnny hadn't come around, and there's not a moment that goes by I'm not thrilled he did.

"Hey. How you feeling?"

Mae sighs, putting a hand to her belly and frowning. "I'm very ready for the first trimester to be over. Nausea and exhaustion are not exactly what I'd call fun."

Johnny raises a brow as Mae doesn't sensor her words and glances over at me.

With a nod, I turn to Henry. "Hey, kiddo. Do you want to tell them what you learned today?"

My son nods vigorously, yelling out through the kitchen, "I'm going to be a big brother!"

Stevie and Johnny smile at Henry, who is lit up like a Christmas tree, and I get that warm feeling in my chest that threatens to have me tearing up.

"Congrats, bud! You're going to do a great job, I'm sure." Stevie ruffles Henry's hair before walking to Johnny and wrapping her arm around him.

"I can't wait to meet my new baby brother or sister. I hope it's a sister." Henry looks to Johnny. "So I can be like you and Mae."

Emotions flood Johnny's expression, and I walk over, clapping a hand on his shoulder. "He certainly loves his Uncle Johnny."

Johnny grins at Henry, who's still beaming and nods at him. "And I love my favorite nephew!"

Henry runs back over to Mae, pulling her down to meet his eyes. "Maybe it's twins in there, and I can have two siblings! That would be so cool!"

"Oof, I hope not, buddy. I don't think I can handle making two babies at once." Mae frowns playfully. "Maybe you'll have a cousin someday."

She looks over at Stevie, her brows up to her hairline. Stevie smiles with a noticeable bit of a blush before sharing a look with Johnny.

I furrow my brow. "Wait. Are you—"

Stevie shakes her head with a smile. "Way to ruin the surprise, Mae!"

Mae rushes over, squeezing her in a hug. "I knew it! Mimosa Queen didn't even have one at brunch the other day."

My heart hammers with excitement, but I'm completely speechless. Then Henry tugs on my sleeve.

"I don't get it. What's happening?"

Johnny puts a hand on Stevie's belly, and together they answer him. "We're pregnant! We're having a baby just like Mae."

"Oh!"

Henry grins wildly with excitement, and the room erupts into hoots and joyful screams. I can't believe my ears, and with all the noise, poor Henry just stares at the adults like we've lost our minds.

After a moment of dumbstruck awe, I mentally shake it off and hurry to Johnny to pull him into a wholly unmanly hug.

"Hot damn, buddy!" I pound his back happily, and Johnny smiles like a loon.

"You really thought you could put this past me. You devil!" Mae hugs Stevie, then pulls her brother in. "And you, do I need to sit you down and talk about responsibilities and financial burden?"

Johnny rolls his eyes. "Ha ha, very funny. I'm sorry for the thousandth time!"

Mae eyes Stevie's stomach. "So, how far along are you?"

"I'm two weeks behind you. We'll have our babies in the same month, maybe even on the same day, if one of us is late and one of us is early."

With a chuckle, I walk behind Mae, putting my hand on the small of her back. "That's actually quite possible. Most babies aren't born on their due date, and first-timers can often be late. I think I waited an extra two weeks. My mother said she was about to be induced."

"Oh, no thank you. I don't want to be pregnant a moment longer than I have to."

Stevie shrugs. "It's not that bad."

"Um, morning sickness, thy name is Mae." She points to herself.

"Sorry." Stevie hides behind a guilty smile. "Mine hasn't been bad at all."

"Oh, you suck!"

We all laugh at poor Mae's terrible luck. Stevie gives her a hug, coming back to glance at her with a smirk.

"I hear having sex can help." Stevie winks at me.

"That can be true, hon." I smile, but Mae just narrows her eyes at me. "It *can* help you go into labor, actually."

Johnny eyes me. "Really? Shit. Well, I'll keep that in mind. I'm studying up to be the absolute best birth partner."

"He's been reading more books than me!" Stevie exclaims.

"Oh, well, maybe I can borrow them? Do you have any

on home birth?" Mae steps toward Johnny, raising her brows.

Stevie is quick to step in. "Nope. No, we do not. I'm a total wimp and not dealing with pain. But that's on you, boo. I'm just surprised Dr. Finnigan here is ready to let you do that."

Mae eyes me. "It's been quite the challenge, actually, but—"

I hold up my hands. "It's not my body. We'll take all the necessary precautions, and that's all I can do."

Mae points at me. "That's right."

With not a little embarrassment, I add, "I think it's all the perineal massage and meditation that'll be the hardest for me. I'm still not great at 'clearing my mind.'"

"Like I told you before, you just help me be that clear, and we're golden."

"Whatever you say, boss."

Johnny steals Stevie for a kiss. "See, babe. We got this. I'm going to be a dad expert."

"I don't know, Johnny. You think you can handle having a baby girl? You're not going to go all super-protective papa, are you?" I raise my brows at him.

"Oh, that is definitely a possibility."

"Well—" I walk over to the fridge, snagging beers for Johnny and me while doling out some sparkling grape juice to the mommas and Henry "—I think that calls for a toast!"

"Here's to our family growing even bigger and stronger!" Mae calls out, raising her glass.

"Here's to designated drivers for nine months!" Johnny returns, and both the women nail him with a glare.

"Yeah, that joke is done now." Mae eyes him, Stevie elbowing him lightly in the ribs. "And it's actually ten months. Forty weeks, dude."

I nod as Johnny looks over for confirmation, and he holds his hands up in surrender. "I'll never mention it again. You're both doing way more work than we have to. We just supply the genetic material."

Henry glances at me, confused.

"I'll explain when you're older."

My son just shrugs and continues to chug his juice as giddy chatter echoes throughout the kitchen.

AS WE SIT down at the table, everyone helps pass out all the food, huge helpings piled high on each of our plates.

They've truly outdone themselves. Between Mae's fabulous side dish, Stevie's incredible homemade bread and delicious dessert, and Johnny's perfectly cooked roast, I've been close to drooling since we arrived.

The entire house smells fantastic, like celebrations from childhood, and memories of a lifetime of joy ripple through my mind like a movie reel.

I smile as I watch my family enjoy a delicious meal together.

My family. Because that's what they are.

Filled to the brim, my heart swells, and I sniff to fight back the sting of tears. I will *not* cry at dinner.

Still, as the warmth of the food and the love of the people who cooked it fill me, I can't help but be profoundly grateful.

This wasn't supposed to happen; I had my chance at happiness, and it was taken away. Yet here I am.

Surrounded by my absolute favorite people in the world, I'm just so damn thankful for this second chance. And it's all thanks to Mae.

While I wouldn't have guessed I'd meet the woman I'd

fall in love with when she walked up to my front door to be the nanny, I can't say I mind.

Our relationship will be quite the story to explain to Henry when he gets older, and I'm sure as he makes friends, they'll wonder at my much younger partner.

But the heart wants what it wants, and mine wants Mae with every beat.

I'll never stop regretting how I didn't get in the car with Clara that day or stop missing her, but every day hurts a little less.

My every waking minute is no longer consumed with a guilt I'm all too sure could've kill me, and I don't hide away from my own son because I can't face how like his mother he is.

I'm happy, Henry is happy, and I know deep in my bones that Clara would be happy for us.

Our son is thriving, excited to have a baby brother or sister, and loved so completely by Mae, you'd never believe she didn't birth him herself.

I have a family again. The thing I wanted for so long, and I can see clearly how much I've become a better man because of it.

While the trauma still lingers, I haven't had a panic attack in weeks, and even when I can tell something is about to set one off, I've actually been able to use the tools Dr. Connors taught me.

And boy, are my coworkers happy about that. Sure, they sometimes miss the guy who took every double shift, but I've realized plenty of other people will step up and be there when the hospital calls.

It doesn't always have to be me. I'm allowed to take a break.

Therapy has clearly been helping. There's peace in understanding and accepting.

I take a bite of the delicious brussels sprouts, squeezing Henry's hand as he sits between me and Mae. She quickly notices me staring at him and looks at me with a worried smile.

Shaking my head, I grin. I whisper, "I'm good. Happy."

Mae holds my gaze in that knowing way, and it's a few seconds before we both return to eating. I can see my future as I look into her eyes, how she'll grow and carry my child.

I'll do anything to keep her with us, keep her safe, and our little baby is already so incredibly loved. I know my heart will grow to hold all the love for them when they actually arrive.

I reach for my beer again, holding it up as I meet everyone's eyes.

"Here's to new beginnings."

We drink up, and I get back to the food, enjoying the mouthwatering roast beef and veggies that would give any five-star restaurant a run for its money.

Epilogue

Mae

A moment of pure bliss radiates through me, blocking out every sound in existence until I hear the brand-new cry of my baby. With a final push, Baby Finnigan comes out into the world.

Relief and exhaustion wash over me after eighteen hours of labor, and I look down at this little bundle lying on my chest, beyond excited to meet them.

"What is it?" Reed's excited, overwhelmed voice is right at my side.

I reach down, inspecting the squirming baby. "It's a girl."

"A girl!" Reed can't contain the joy, and tears spill from his eyes, quickly followed by my own. "Hello there, Grace."

We'd talked about names for months and finally settled on Grace Clara Finnigan. It's perfect.

She's in my arms. I'm holding her. She's real.

"Hi, baby girl." I look down at her and still can't believe I did it. "I'm your momma. Happy birthday."

"You did so great, babe. I'm so proud of you." Reed kisses the top of my head and then showers attention on Grace.

"I'm a rockstar." My head falls back, my eyes closing as the adrenaline subsides.

"That you are. Congrats, you guys. You've got a beautiful baby girl. When you're ready, we'll get you all set up in your bed." My midwife smiles, and I honestly cannot find the words to thank her for how much she's helped me.

"We have a baby girl, Reed. Just like Henry wanted."

"I..." Reed shakes his head with a laugh. "I'm a dad again. And she's so perfect."

I sing "Happy Birthday to You" to our newborn daughter, and Reed can't stop staring at her. She's only a minute old, and she's already got him wrapped around her little finger.

It's just tears of joy then, filling the quiet after what was the hardest thing I've ever done in my life. And I wouldn't change it for anything.

ONCE I'M all cleaned up, Reed had his moment to cut the umbilical cord, and Grace is all warm and cozy against my chest as we're wrapped in a blanket, we have the midwife get Henry.

He's been waiting in the living room with Stevie and Johnny, and as he walks in, I can't help but notice the nervousness on his face.

"It's okay, bud. I'm sure I got a little loud at the end, but everything is great. Would you like to meet your baby sister?"

He lights up and hurries over to the bed, where Reed

and I lie against the headboard. Climbing up gently, he crawls over between us and takes his first look at Grace.

Just like his father, Henry positively swoons when he sees her, and my heart feels like it'll burst from all this happiness. He kisses the top of her head so gently, and I can't help but chuckle.

He's already being so careful with Grace. Henry was a sweetheart with me when I was too pregnant to do anything. He really is going to be the best big brother. *Well, tied with Johnny for first place.*

"So, it's Grace, right?" Henry's voice is just above a whisper.

"Yes, bud. Grace Clara Finnigan." I tip my shoulder so he can see more of her face. "Grace, this is your big brother, Henry."

"I'll look after you always." His little eyes fill with tears as he looks up at me. "I love her so much."

"I love you, Henry." I kiss his cheek. "I love her, and I love you and your Dad so very much."

Reed, who's been happily watching, tears brimming in his eyes more than he'd like to admit, wraps his arm around Henry, squeezing us all into a hug.

A gentle knock on the door grabs my attention, and I call out, "Come in."

Stevie comes waddling in, still looking like she could pop at any moment, and Johnny quickly follows.

"Oh my God, Mae." Stevie sniffles as she takes in baby Grace. "She's so beautiful."

Sobs pour out of her, and we all laugh as Johnny rubs her back.

"Oh, shush. You all know it's those damn pregnancy hormones." Stevie wipes under her eyes and sits down on the rocking chair nearby.

"Well, here's hoping that little one takes the hint and

decides to come join us." I nod at her belly.

We chat for a few moments, and Grace finishes her first meal before gently snoring as she falls asleep. I sigh, looking up at Johnny.

"Would you like to hold her?"

His eyes well up, and all he can do is nod.

Reed helps bring Grace to him, giving her a quick kiss before handing her over. Johnny is so careful and looks to Stevie with a smile when Grace is settled.

Stevie starts crying again, and I demand she come over and give me a hug immediately.

"Hi there, Grace." Johnny rocks her slowly. "I'm Johnny. I'm going to be the best uncle ever. I'll spoil you rotten, just like I do Henry."

My brother looks over at him, and Henry smiles ridiculously big.

"Between the two of you," I say, nodding at Reed as Stevie sits with me on the bed, "Grace isn't going to want for anything."

"Nope." They say in unison, and Stevie and I smile.

Johnny's going to be a dad in no time, and I know he'll be amazing. Our growing family is so very lucky.

"Are Mom and Dad here?"

I stretch on the bed gingerly. Everything feels weird and sore in a way I just can't describe.

"They were on their way, last I checked. Should be here any minute."

After all their travels, taking the extended anniversary trip they've always dreamed of, they're coming home to become first-time grandparents.

I can't wait to actually see them. Delivering the news on the phone just wasn't the same.

Cassie, my midwife, checks to make sure I'm doing

okay, giving me the rundown of what I can and shouldn't do, now that I've given birth.

And as promised, Reed gets me my first beer in months, and the taste nearly makes me cry again.

"It'll help your milk come in," Cassie adds, and we all chuckle. "Alright, little girl. Time to do the checkup."

Just as she's setting up all the items to run her first list of checks, I hear a commotion in the hallway.

"We're here!"

My mom nearly sprints through the door, carrying a massive bundle of baby supplies stuffed in a basket and a giant stuffed bear.

"Mom!" I smile as she rushes to my side, squeezing me in a hug, and then she turns to see Grace.

"Oh, baby. She's so beautiful. You did it." Tears stream from her face. "My baby had a baby!"

"Oh, Mom."

I shake my head, and my dad comes in, dipping low to hug me, then moving to Reed.

"Well done, Mae." He shakes hands with Reed. "I still can't believe you two are together."

"Dad!" Johnny and I object.

"I didn't say it was bad. I'm just still surprised, is all. You're dating your brother's best friend."

I can't help but laugh. Dad always did have a way of being incredibly blunt.

"Actually, about that." Reed steps back from my dad and comes around to the side of the bed.

Helping Stevie to stand, he kneels on the floor next to me, reaching underneath.

"What are you doing?" I furrow my brow.

Reed pulls out a small black ring box, and the tears immediately start back up.

"You've had that under there the whole time?" I giggle.

"Yes. You were too pregnant to look." He smirks. "Henry, come here. It's time."

I look over at him, and my heart pounds so hard I imagine everyone in the room can hear it.

"Mae, we have a question." Reed looks to his son.

Henry clears his throat and takes my hand, just like Reed. "Mae—I don't want to call you that anymore."

My cheeks hurt from smiling.

"I think what he means is that he'd like to call you something else. And I would, too."

"Oh yeah, that's it."

Reed smiles at me, tears brimming. "I love you, Mae Elizabeth Marrington. I love you more than I can put into words. And I'm so grateful for everything you've done for me and Henry."

"I love you, too, Mae. I don't ever want you and Grace to leave."

I sob, barely able to keep it together and let them finish.

"I want you to be a part of my life always. I want to stand by your side through thick and thin, rain or shine. I want to be there while you grow into an incredible mother, and I want to make this little family of ours official."

Reed can barely speak around the lump in his throat and he turns to Henry.

"Mae," Henry says, trying his best to sound serious, "would you be my mom?"

I can stop the heavy flow of tears that stream down my face.

"Mae," Reed speaks next, "will you marry me?"

Nodding frantically, I pull them both into my arms, kissing their heads and crying like a fool.

"Yes! A hundred times, yes!"

They each offer me a grin, and I don't think I can feel

any happier or more complete. Johnny walks over with Grace in his arms and gives her to Reed.

The three of us create a little bubble around her, and I whisper, "Yes. So much, yes."

"I promise to be there for you, Mae. When you're up for it, and she's a bit older, go back to school. Get your teaching degree."

"What?" My eyes go wide. *Can this be real?*

"I'm serious. It means so much to you. Get your degree. I'll do all the double shifts of diaper duty to help you get through it."

"I'll help, too!" Henry nods.

"You boys…you are my favorite people in the universe. And now we've added a little girl to the mix. My family—" I look at everyone gathered around me "—is the best in the world."

We look down at Grace. I take Reed's face in my hands, meeting his teary eyes with mine.

"Here's to beginnings."

Extended Epilogue

Mae

Twelve months later

Warm sun shines on my face as I lie back in my chair. The light breeze is a welcome respite from the heat, and it's all made that much better because I can hear the delighted squeals of Grace playing with Sophie.

"You going to fall asleep over there?" Stevie's teasing voice cuts through my near dozing off, and I can't help but chuckle.

"Bit of a rough night with this one. She woke up so many times last night."

I smile over at my little piggy playing in the grass with Stevie's little girl. They're so close in age but couldn't be more different.

"Oh, Gracie, give your momma a break. Think she's going through a growth spurt?"

Straightening in my chair so I don't fall asleep, I consider that and nod thoughtfully.

"Very possibly. Twelve months was a big milestone, right?"

Stevie takes a sip of her beer, nodding in agreement, while I'm rocking a mimosa.

"Oh yeah. Lots of big things going on in their little brains and bodies." She sighs. "But I feel you. Sophie has never been a good sleeper. I swear, I might have to go off to college with her."

I laugh, but it's damn near possible from what I've heard. Poor Stevie can barely get a moment to herself because her tiny munchkin enjoys taking naps only on her chest or near her.

With a sympathetic frown, I pat her shoulder. Sometimes I wonder if it's karma since her pregnancy was so easy.

As we relax into easy conversation again, the girls play with a turtle toy they're obsessed with, chasing it around the playpen by using a hilarious combination of crawling and wiggling.

"I just hope all this work we've been doing to get her more used to her crib pays off." Stevie sounds as exhausted as me, and I remind myself she's been dealing with rough nights from the beginning.

"Good luck, babe. Hang in there. I keep telling myself, they're only this little for so long."

"That's a good reminder. Thanks."

We offer each other that insider's smile of mothers understanding one another's plight, then return our attention to the babies.

They're so very cute, and they seem to get along well, which, of course, was not a guarantee.

And we were worried at first. Sophie is a shy baby and doesn't trust strangers right away. Grace is the complete opposite, always waving and smiling at every new face she sees.

Thankfully, Gracie seems to help Sophie out of her shell, and they've become quite the pair.

"Score! You both lose!"

Henry's voice booms from across the yard, and Stevie and I look over at him doing the goofiest touchdown dance as he spikes the ball to the ground.

Reed and Johnny are both totally out of breath, and we can't help but laugh as Henry literally runs circles around them.

"You're much younger than us, buddy! And you're not the one who's been up with Gracie half the night."

He stops and considers, then Henry tosses the ball to Reed, grinning wickedly at his dad.

"Is that why you had, like, a million cups of coffee this morning?"

"Why yes, it is." Reed huffs in a breath, walking toward Stevie and me. "Alright, time for a break."

Johnny comes up behind Henry, ruffling his hair as they all come over. Henry immediately plops down next to the girls, helping them reach the rings and pushing all the buttons on the turtle at once.

The toy blares loudly, and I'm seriously considering taking the batteries out of it, but then Grace laughs, and I positively melt.

"How'd the match go, dear?" I look at my exhausted partner, and Reed smiles through his heavy breaths.

"Henry is way too fast. I'm not made for this anymore."

Reed walks over, leaning down to plant a warm kiss on

my lips, and I giggle through it as he lingers just a moment longer than expected.

"I think you're doing quite well, Dr. Finnigan. And isn't physical exercise good for you?" I cock a brow at him, teasing.

"It is when I'm running on a full night's sleep. That rocking chair does not a long-term sleeping position make."

"Ha! I know, babe. Thank you for getting up with her so I could sleep." I hold Reed's face in my hands, peppering him with more kisses.

"You're very welcome, love. But now—" he looks over at Henry, who's entertaining himself with the babies "—it's time to relax."

"Oh, that looks heavenly. Are there more?" Johnny eyes Stevie's beer, coming up to her after tossing the football back in the storage bin, kissing her on the top of her head.

"I believe so." She reaches up to take his hand. "Just remember, one of us has to drive home tonight, and it's not *my* turn."

"Of course, babe. You definitely deserve this one." Johnny only nods his head as Stevie eyes him, and it's yet another moment that convinces me these two are meant to be together.

As Johnny starts for the door, Grace begins fussing and whining, and I glance over to see Henry looking to me as Grace holds his fingers.

"She's sucking on my fingers." Henry laughs, and I stand to go pick her up.

"That means this little one is hungry. Come here, you." I lift her into my arms, soaking up that delightful baby smell, and follow Johnny into the house to make a bottle.

"Wait up, would you?" Johnny stops, holding the door open for me as I bring Grace inside. He kisses her sweet red-haired head as I walk past.

"Hungry little devil." My brother walks with me to the kitchen. "Though, I have a feeling that means Sophie isn't far behind."

He reaches into the fridge to pull out a beer, taking one of Grace's bottles and one of Sophie's out to get warmed up.

"So, how's it going? I know Stevie is stressed. How are you holding up?" I take the bottle, giving it a shake before putting it in the bottle warmer.

"It's…" Johnny cracks open the beer and takes a swig. "It's a lot, sis. Sophie is my whole damn world, but this lack of sleep is tough. Stevie needed this day so much. I just wish I could help more."

"This *is* helping. She did need today, and she needs to remember that she's not just a mom. She's still Stevie." I sigh, knowing it's always easier said than done. "We both do. Man, I remember how excited I was to finally sleep on my stomach. Now, I'd kill not to have bottles and diapers taking up my entire life."

"Oh, Mae. Well, it's not your whole life. You also have to study for class."

I chuckle as the warmer signals, pulling out the bottle and shaking it up again to make sure it's all heated evenly. Grace holds her tiny hands out for it, and when she's got her "baba," she settles immediately.

"Well, the hard studying is over. I just took finals. Now, there's just worrying if I was able to pass. Studying and early motherhood are hard to juggle."

"Speaking of."

Reed enters through the back door, the entire troupe

behind him. Henry runs up and stands over Grace as I feed her, always loving watching her like this.

"Did you want to open it now?"

"Open what?" Stevie looks between Reed and me, taking the newly warmed bottle from Johnny.

I look at Reed, rolling my eyes a bit. I should have known he'd pull a dirty trick like this because he knows I've been too nervous to open it.

Handing Grace to Reed, I walk to the counter, going to the catchall where we keep the mail. I pull out the letter and go over toward Stevie.

"I got my grades. This right here says if I've passed the first semester. Brings me one step closer to being a teacher."

"She's been too scared to open it, but I thought maybe —" he switches Grace to his other side so he can wrap an arm around me "—you'd feel more ready with your family around."

Stevie jostles Sophie to keep her eating and awake, then lays a hand on my shoulder.

"I'm sure you have nothing to be worried about. You worked so hard. Open it!"

Johnny comes closer as well, and soon, I'm surrounded by my family, the most important people in my life, and my brother nods before speaking.

"Go for it, sis."

A nervous chuckle slips through, and I take the letter opener off the top of the fridge, sliding it through the seal to pull out the document. My heart is in my throat, my fingers shaking, and I scan the list of classes, each with their appropriate grade listed to the side.

After those, right at the bottom of the page, is the overall GPA. I got a 3.37.

"I passed."

The room hangs in suspension and I take a deep breath before the outburst.

"I passed!"

Everyone erupts with happy cheers, careful not to scare the babies too much, but I can feel the electricity buzz through us as we all celebrate the win.

"I knew you would, babe." Reed kisses me deeply, Grace reaching out her little hands to come to Momma. "I'm so proud of you. Next semester, here we come!"

Taking Grace, I lean into another kiss from Reed, and then Stevie and Johnny hug me with everything they have.

Henry slips under everyone, hugging my waist, and I look down at him, ruffling his hair. "Hey, buddy. Thanks for being such a good big brother. Your help made such a difference."

"I'm really good at giving her cereal!" He smiles, the grin fully stretching from ear to ear.

"You are, honey. Thank you so much."

"I think this calls for champagne!" Stevie calls out. "Please tell me you have some."

"I'm not sure. I mean, it wasn't like I—"

"We do, in fact." Reed steps to the fridge, moving aside a few jugs of almond milk and sliding out a thick glass bottle.

"How…" But I stop myself before I finish. "You planned this, you sneaky devil."

"I may have hoped it would be easy to convince you during Grace's play date." Reed opens the champagne, pouring it into four glasses. "Here's to next chapters!"

I smile, the sting of tears not strong enough to keep me from holding them back.

"You're so sentimental."

We all clink glasses, Henry lifting up his Gatorade as well, and we toast. My heart continues to stretch to accommodate all this love, and Reed pulls my face to his again, kissing my cheek before whispering in my ear.

"I can't wait till this evening when we can properly celebrate."

Even after the months have settled our lives into a routine and the intrigue of our slightly off-limits romance is gone, it only takes a few words from Reed, and I'm ready and raring to go.

Johnny takes Grace and motions for Henry to follow him and Stevie into the living room. He knows I need just one moment alone with Reed.

When the room is empty, his arms come around my waist, and he pulls me close. The kiss we share is hot and heavy, alluding to so much more to come when it's evening and we're alone in our bedroom.

"Thank you for making this possible, Reed. Without your help, it would have been nearly impossible."

"Anything for you, Lil Bit. And besides," he says, his hands taking my ass in two firm grips, "I know the perfect way to show me just how grateful you are."

"You really sure you're still interested?" I raise my brows. "I've seen plenty of nurses and young doctors checking you out at work."

"They're nothing compared to you, Mae."

"Even after all the baby weight and stretch marks and leaky—"

His finger comes to cover my mouth, silencing me. "Yes. It'll always be yes, Mae. You've never been more beautiful to me after carrying our daughter. I watched that from the front row, and it's damn impressive."

"*You're* impressive, Dr. Finnigan. And I love you more and more every day."

"I love you, too, Lil Bit. So—" he squeezes my ass cheeks one more time before gesturing for the living room "—do me a favor, and let's make sure we seize the opportunity once Henry and Grace are down for the night. Grace had you all day. Tonight, it's my turn."

Reed winks, and I can't hold back the giggle as I follow him to the other room. Sometimes, life really is incredible.

THE END

Did you like *Nanny for the Doctor*? Then you'll LOVE *Nanny for the Grump: An Off-Limits Age Gap Romance.*

* * *

It doesn't get any more off-limits than your dad's billionaire best friend who also happens to be your new boss.
But I've never been one to follow the rules.

I never imagined spilling a cold brew all over him in the interview would turn into passion hotter than the sun.

Noah, with his guarded glances and silent battles.
Those late-night paperwork sessions…
Spreadsheets turn into me spread on his desk.
My brattiness turns him into the dominant alpha he always was inside, and it's…scorching.

Beneath those designer suits and hard exterior, there's a storm brewing.
His ex-wife is a tempest ready to take him down.
His son is a ray of sunshine whom I adore.

And me? I'm caught in the middle, trying to break down his walls.

Now, there's a new forecast showing up in the form of two pink lines on a stick…

* * *

Start reading Nanny for the Grump NOW!

Nanny for the Grump Sneak Peek

Olivia

Interviews are the worst, and I'm late for this one. Because I got lost. Inside the building. *Ugh.*

Jogging down the maze of hallways, dread creeps through my veins as I imagine selling myself to a stranger, sweaty and out of breath.

Even worse, I'm meeting my dad's best friend. I'll be some kid to him, barely worth his time. He's doing this as a favor, after all. So why am I bothering?

New York City rent rates pop into my mind. *Oh, yeah, that's why.*

I scan the placards on the doors until I finally reach one with Noah Steele plastered across it. I knock lightly and enter, but it's empty.

I didn't get lost again, did I? I saw his name, for heaven's sake. Is there another door?

"Mr. Steele? It's John's daughter, Olivia. Hello?"

No one answers, so I sprint back toward the entrance, searching for a door I could have missed.

"Mr. Ste—"

Turning the corner, I run full speed into a man's firm chest. With a surprised shriek, my plastic cup of cold brew is smashed between our bodies, launching the frigid liquid onto the both of us. As the mess drips down my chest, I see it's landed all over his face and is spilling down his pristine white shirt. *Oh, shit.*

"Well, excuse me."

The man's deep voice is as smooth as whiskey, and underneath the coffee he's now wearing, he's absolutely gorgeous—and really pissed.

"Oh, God. I'm so sorry. I wasn't watching where I was going. Crap."

I scramble in my purse for a few spare napkins and frantically wipe at the growing stains on his shirt.

"Clearly. Please, just stop. I don't—"

His hands reach for mine, holding them in place as he glares at me. Times slows, and I'm locked in his mesmerizing gaze as his grip on my hands tightens ever so slightly.

"I'm terribly sorry. I…"

A chill runs through me as coffee drips under my shirt, but my cheeks burn. The guy is about my dad's age, with stormy green eyes flecked with gold that I can only see because I'm mere inches from his face.

Laughter cuts through the tense silence.

Startled, I look just behind the older man to see a young boy who's the spitting image of the one I'm entangled with. I quickly drop my hands and step back.

Tears prick the corner of the boy's eyes as he continues to laugh so hard I'm afraid he might fall over.

It's completely infectious, and I break into my own giggles that have me fighting for breath.

"Ha! Look at your shirt, Dad! Didn't you, like, just buy that one?"

Looking back at the tall, physically fit gentlemen to whom I've given an impromptu makeover, my eyes widen, and my heart drops again.

"Oh, really? I'm… wow, I can only say I'm sorry so many times, but I really am. I'm late for this nanny interview." *Wait.*

My ears ring as my pulse skyrockets. *Little boy. Older guy. Oh, fuck, seriously?*

"You're Mr. Steele, aren't you?"

He wipes a hand across his face, clenching his jaw.

"Yes. You must be Olivia." His glare is all daggers and ice.

"Is it too late to say no?" I can feel the heat rush to my face as I let out a nervous laugh. "Unfortunately, that's me. Great first impression, huh? Bet the other nannies didn't do that."

"They did not."

He scrutinizes me for a long moment as his son continues to chuckle, doing a poor job of hiding his amusement. That's when the kid steps forward. I instinctively bend lower to match his height.

"Hey, buddy. Don't happen to have any napkins in that backpack of yours, do you?"

He smiles, shaking his head.

"Nope. But Dad has a bathroom inside with paper towels."

"Good thinking. What's your name?"

"Elijah." He grins even wider.

"Well, hello, Elijah. I'm Olivia, but you can call me Liv." I shake his tiny hand, coated in a typical child stickiness. "As much as I'd like the towels, though, I'm not sure if your dad still wants to talk with me."

I crinkle my nose at him, and Elijah snorts a laugh before pulling on his dad's sleeve to get his attention.

"But Dad. She's actually nice. And way prettier than that Beverly lady. And not a hundred years old."

Hiding a smile behind my hands, I chance a look at Mr. Steele, the name incredibly accurate at the moment.

He looks at his son, held there by the boy's pleading eyes. A long sigh escapes him, and Mr. Steele rolls his eyes before looking back at me.

"All right, all right. I'll meet with her. But no promises, young man."

A flicker of a grin hides behind Mr. Steele's cleanly styled beard and my heartbeat stumbles.

"I'm very grateful for the opportunity. I don't usually get lost before an interview. The hallways were confusing, to say the least."

He steps to the side, gesturing back to his office. "Well, allow me to guide you to the correct door this time."

I chuckle half-heartedly, wiping some of the coffee off my shoulder. Mr. Steele opens his arm for me to walk in first, placing a hand on the small of my back while he opens the door for me.

The heat of his palm melts through the thin material of my dress, and I can hear my pulse in my ears.

"Thank you."

The words come out on a shaky breath.

My potential boss turns back to his son, sinking onto one knee.

"Elijah, go ahead and get the snack you wanted from Marnie. She'll be watching the front desk for a little while longer. I'll come down as soon as we're finished."

"Okay, fine. But be nice! I like her."

Elijah grins at me and scampers off down the hall, obviously much more familiar with the place than I am. Mr. Steele follows me inside his office, pointing out the chair in front of his desk.

"Have a seat. I'll just be a moment."

I struggle to breathe evenly as Mr. Steele exits, leaving me waiting in his uncomfortable chair. When he returns, he's wearing a clean shirt and holding a handful of neatly folded brown paper towels. He hands me the stack, and our fingers brush again, making gooseflesh break out on my arm.

What is wrong with you? You're acting like a schoolgirl with a crush. This is your dad's best friend and your potential boss. Get it together!

"Thanks. I do hope I didn't ruin your shirt."

Mr. Steele takes his place behind his desk, his fresh shirt pristine and crisp.

"I have more. Those are for you to clean yourself up." He nods at the towels in my hands. "So, you're Olivia. John's daughter, correct?"

"Yes, that's me. And you're Mr. Steele. You need a nanny, correct?" I sit straighter in my chair, tucking soggy hair behind my ear.

"You can call me Noah. And yes, I need help running the house. Did John tell you anything about what to expect?"

Cool intensity fills his eyes as he crosses his arms and leans back.

"A little. My dad said you're going through a divorce and need help with Elijah because your business demands a lot of attention. Dad's job is similar, so I have a basic understanding of what you'll probably need."

Noah's jaw clenches when I mention the divorce, and he furrows his brows.

"Leave it to John to be blunt." He reaches into his desk and pulls out what looks like a list. "This is a basic rundown of what I need help with and what I expect to be done at the house while I'm working."

He hands it to me, and while it's long and pretty strict, it's not anything I haven't seen before from the other families I've worked with.

"All right. This looks doable. Many of the other families I worked with while abroad had similar requirements. I should let you know that I like to squeeze in some time for fun, too. Elijah was so sweet. I'd love to show him that we can have a good time and still get things done."

Noah adjusts in his chair, narrowing his eyes at me. There's scrutiny in that green stare, and my cheeks heat once more.

"Look, Ms. Francis, I—"

"Please, call me Liv." I smile.

"Liv."

Noah clears his throat and circles his desk to sit on the edge closest to me. As he leans against it, he crosses one ankle over the other.

His leg brushes mine, but he doesn't pull back. *Did someone bump up the thermostat when we walked in?*

"I run a tight ship. My job is…demanding. And there are several things I need to juggle. I need to know you can handle what I'm asking for."

Meeting his gaze, I raise an eyebrow and smile.

"Trust me, Noah. I can rise to any challenge you throw at me. I'm here to provide balance and assistance. You shouldn't have to stress over basic day-to-day stuff with so much going on. That's where I come in."

"Good to know."

Noah stands, offering me a hand to do the same.

"I'll call tonight with my decision. Same number you provided on your resume?"

"Yes."

Our hands are still joined, and Noah stands just inches

from me. My gaze flicks to his lips before I quickly meet his eyes again. *Oh, Olivia! Come on!*

But then I notice Mr. Steele's eyes tracing a line from my neck to the top of my dress. *Oh, this is bad.*

"Good. I'll reach out tonight, then."

"I look forward to hearing from you."

Noah clears his throat, shaking his head, and stepping back. I finally blink and do the same, heading for his door.

"It's a left at the end of the hall for the elevators. Can you find your way this time?"

"Ha!" I look at the floor. "I think I'll manage. Thank you."

When I glance back up, Noah is in front of me, opening his door wide.

"Talk to you soon—" he pauses "—Olivia."

MY HEART IS STILL RACING when I arrive back at my dad's and make a beeline for my room. Sitting on the bed, I eye my cell on the nightstand.

He's supposed to call.

The green of Noah's eyes haunts my mind, and I remember the feel of his hands on mine.

Maybe I missed it ringing?

I know I haven't. I'm just being impatient. What a turn of events. I was dreading this interview, and now I'm chomping at the bit for a response.

That man, though. Noah's commanding presence was like being in the room with royalty or something. He owned the whole place, and you could tell by just looking at him.

Sure, I'm no stranger to well-off parents, but Mr. Steele is something else. *Mr. Steele…Noah.*

"Yeah, I'm going to need to cool down if I'm going to be able to look my dad in the eye at dinner."

I peel off my coffee-stained dress and turn on the shower in the large guest bath. Ditching my bra and panties, I step inside and enjoy the way the water slides down my skin.

I think back to the way Noah looked at me, the feel of his hand at the small of my back.

It's completely ridiculous. I can't be feeling this way about a guy I just met, let alone my dad's best friend and someone I'm supposed to nanny for.

But…

Electricity dances in my veins as I picture Noah sitting on his desk so close to me. I imagine the chiseled physique he's hiding under his button-down.

My fingers roam my body, but I stop.

It's not going to happen. Noah is totally off-limits, and landing a steady paycheck is way more important than whatever *this* is.

Then I hear my phone ring from the other room, and I dash out of the shower to answer it, dipping water all over the floor.

"Hello."

"Ms. Francis. This is Noah Steele."

Holy shit. It's him. I guess I didn't think he'd really call. I mean, I spilled coffee all over his expensive shirt, for Christ's sake.

"I've reviewed your resume, and I'd like to invite you to nanny for me. Your past experiences are impressive, and —" he pauses "—Elijah really likes you. You can start tomorrow. What do you say?"

Start reading Nanny for the Grump NOW!

Printed in Great Britain
by Amazon

37539577R00159